"HOW DO YOU DO THIS TO ME?"

Roarke's tone held a bit of wonder. "You're back for one day, and I've already spilled my secrets."

Wren inhaled sharply. "If we're sharing confessions, then you should know I care, too. I've cared ever since the day you walked into my house, all pissed off and angry at the world."

"I should regret telling you this, but I don't." He swallowed, and his voice dropped to a whisper. "I think my biggest regret would be walking out of here without knowing how you taste."

The desire for his kiss had been constant since last night. Her lips were moving before her brain gave a command. "Then find out."

"This is a bad idea," he whispered.

"Good ideas are never fun," she whispered back.

ZERO HOUR

ZERO HOUR

MEGAN ERICKSON

FOREVER

NEW YORK BOSTON

This book is a work of fiction. Names, characters, places, and incidents are the product of the author's imagination or are used fictitiously. Any resemblance to actual events, locales, or persons, living or dead, is coincidental.

Cover design by Elizabeth Turner
Cover illustration by Patrick Kang

Forever
Hachette Book Group
1290 Avenue of the Americas
New York, NY 10104
hachettebookgroup.com
twitter.com/foreverromance

First Edition: January 2018

Forever is an imprint of Grand Central Publishing.
The Forever name and logo are trademarks of Hachette Book Group, Inc.

ISBN 978-1-5387-4388-1 (mass market edition)
ISBN 978-1-5387-4389-8 (ebook edition)

Printed in the United States of America

OPM

10 9 8 7 6 5 4 3 2 1

To Neal: I've loved you since the first IM.

ZERO HOUR

CHAPTER ONE

ROARKE Brennan's answer was a metallic crunch as he crushed the Diet Coke can with a clench of his tattooed fingers. He tossed it to the side in the dark alley and took a deep breath to prevent blowing this whole mission with a full-scale meltdown. He glared at his best friend.

Erick sighed heavily but didn't back down. "Come on—"

"No." The crisp word sliced like a knife through the cold night air. "End of discussion."

Erick's lips thinned. "You don't get to decide when this discussion is over. You need to remember this mission isn't personal for just you. All of us want revenge for Flynn."

Roarke stuffed his hands in the pockets of his leather jacket and tightened his jaw. Maybe when he'd made the person responsible for his brother's death pay and this was all over, then he could hear his brother's name without it feeling like a stab in the gut. He tried to keep his voice as even as possible. "We're not involving your sister. This'll all be over her head."

Erick's face darkened, a rare look for him. "You're being a total asshole about this. You have no idea what she's capable of. You haven't seen her for over a decade."

True, he hadn't seen Wren since she graduated high school—when she'd been homecoming queen, prom queen, every other queen that signified she was beautiful and charming and full of life. She wasn't a keyboard warrior like them, living on the fringe of society. To him, Wren would always be fresh-faced, eighteen, happy...and unattainable. Ten years later, he preferred to remember her that way.

"Okay, I'll admit it," he muttered, kicking aside some trash with the toe of his black combat boots. "I don't know what she's capable of, but that doesn't change the fact that I don't want her involved." He looked up at Erick, blinking away the hair that had fallen into his eyes. "How come you're not on my side about this? Aren't you worried about her safety?"

Erick shot out a lanky arm and shoved Roarke's shoulder. He bristled at the contact, but Erick was one of the lucky few who could touch Roarke without his permission, which was the only reason he didn't sock him in the mouth.

Erick rolled his eyes. "Of course I do, dipshit. But I don't control her life." He paused and turned his head away to murmur something that Roarke couldn't catch. "Look, she asked to be involved because she said she could help. Told her I had to run it by you."

Oh. "And you did, and I said no. So that's the end of it."

Erick turned away with a heavy sigh and mumbled something again.

"What was that?"

Erick slowly met his gaze, and a familiar spark of humor flashed across his face. Roarke didn't like that, because it usually meant bad things for him. Erick shrugged. "I said, you don't always get what you want."

Roarke put a hand up because he knew what was coming. "Don't—"

"I said you can't always get..." Erick threw back his head and proceeded to sing "You Can't Always Get What You Want" by the Rolling Stones.

Roarke groaned and leaned his head back against the brick wall as Erick mimicked Mick Jagger complete with lip pout and a hip shimmy of his tall, wiry body. This was typical. They were in a dirty, trash-covered alley next to a dumpster. He could've sworn he'd seen a rat the size of a cat earlier. The only light was a yellow bulb hanging off the side of the building by a frayed wire. It was close to midnight, and they were about to head inside a seedy off-track betting place to convince a morally ambiguous man to join their team. And Erick was dancing and crooning and...oh great, he'd moved on to simulated sex with pelvic thrusts and tit squeezing.

Totally fucking typical.

The first time Roarke talked to Erick was behind a maintenance shed at their middle school in Erie, Pennsylvania. He'd skipped gym, because no way was he about to run a goddamn mile. Erick had a similar aversion to PE and had hid behind the same brick building. When Erick had pulled out a hand-held Game Boy from his pocket with a sly grin—he'd smuggled it in his gym shorts—Roarke had known this kid was special. They'd been tight ever since. And they both still hated to run.

Roarke rubbed his temples because he'd had enough of Erick's crooning. He grabbed him, and they tussled until Roarke managed to get him into a headlock. Of course Erick wasn't scared. He was laughing. "Fine, I tap out," he wheezed.

Roarke shoved him away. "You should be frightened right now. I could snap your neck if I wanted."

Erick stumbled back, laughing as he pushed his black

hair out of his eyes. "Sure, whatever, buddy." He grinned. "You'd never hurt my pretty face."

"Ugh, you're irritating."

"My ability to irritate is why you keep me around."

Roarke laughed at that. It was the fucking truth. Erick's specialty as a hacker involved anything that was irritating as fuck. A virus. A prank. Basically, Erick was amazing at making people want to smack him in the face.

Most people didn't though. A, because he managed to be charming at the same time. And B, because they often weren't on the same continent when he pressed a couple of keys with glee. Freelance hacking jobs didn't exactly bring them into contact with lots of people. At least not in person.

Roarke glanced down the alley at the door to the off-track betting facility. They'd driven from DC to Maryland to track down Dade Kelly. If he wasn't inside like he was supposed to be, Roarke was going to punch something. Hopefully not Erick.

He gestured to the door with a jerk of his chin. "Ready?"

Erick rubbed his hands together with glee. "Yeah, man."

Roarke's boots crunched on broken glass as they made their way toward the door, each step closer to the man he hadn't wanted to see again, and certainly not with a plea for help. He turned up the collar of his jacket to hide the distinctive tattoos that crept up his neck and took his ball cap out of his back pocket and placed it on his head. Pulling the brim low, he swung open the door. Erick walked in first, tugging up his hood to cover his black hair.

Dade would know both of them on sight. The element of surprise was important, because Dade was sketchy and skittish as fuck, as well as loyal to no one but himself. If Dade spotted them first, he'd ghost. Roarke would have sent someone else if he could have, but he didn't trust anyone else to convince Dade to help them.

He hated the fucking games and hated Dade even more, but he needed the guy's skills. Dade broke just about every hacker ethics code, but his intelligence was unparalleled. And if Roarke was being honest, the main reason he wanted him so badly was because of his loose morals. Flynn's death had a way of rearranging his priorities and forcing him to swallow his pride.

So here Roarke was, breathing in stale cigarette smoke and body odor, leaning against a wall peeling with what was probably lead-based paint and about to scrape to a guy he didn't even like.

He'd met Dade in Denmark, where they'd been hired, along with Flynn and Erick, for a freelance computer security job. One look at Dade's sneer and he'd known it wasn't going to end well. He should have followed his instincts. Because instead of turning over the programming information to their employer, Dade had stolen it. Probably sold it. The last time he'd seen Dade, they'd fought with words, then with fists, and walked away with matching bruises. Dade refused to say what he did with the information. So yeah, Roarke hated him. Sneering motherfucker.

Roarke pulled his cap lower and crossed his arms over his chest. Beside him, Erick rocked on his heels, glancing around like he planned to make himself at home.

"Your cheeriness is pissing me off," Roarke grumbled.

Erick beamed even brighter and stuck a strip of gum in his mouth. "I know."

Roarke sank farther back against the wall. "Jock ready?"

Erick glanced at his phone. "Yup. Waiting for my text."

Roarke nodded, his mood lifting slightly. Plans running well was like sandpaper soothing his hard edges. He hoped this kept up. Every member of his team was unpredictable. But they were the best he knew, so their inability to be controlled was a side effect he had to put up with.

A man emerged from the bathroom, and Roarke tensed. Dade Kelly was a chameleon who could disguise himself to fit into every situation, but he had a presence about him that he couldn't hide, a presence Roarke could recognize anywhere.

Today, Dade wore a pair of cargo pants, boots, and a flannel shirt. His hair was short now and light brown. Roarke wasn't sure of the man's natural hair color, but based on his pale skin, he guessed it was blond.

Dade took a seat at a table in the corner, which had a view of the door and the dozen TVs along the far wall that displayed various horse races. A group of men on stools along the bar hooted and hollered as they cheered on their bets.

Dade's light eyes began to scan the bar, and a grin tugged at the corner of Roarke's mouth. The last piece to complete his team and get revenge for Flynn was here. Actually here. Now all Roarke had to do was convince the bastard.

"Now," he said out of the corner of his mouth. "Before he sees us."

"On it." Erick's head was bent, typing on his phone. He turned it off and shoved it in his pocket. "Ten seconds."

Roarke split his gaze between Dade and the TVs, counting down in his head. His stomach rolled, and he cracked his knuckles one by one, ready to run in case Dade took off.

"Five," Erick whispered, the glee in his voice evident. "Four…three…two…"

"One," Roarke finished.

The TVs went black. The inebriated men at the bar threw

up their hands. An employee frowned and strode off to a back room, probably to check on the feed. He could try, but Jock Bosh was back at the warehouse, probably staring stone-faced at his monitor while he hacked into Paradise Valley Off-Track Betting's feed.

Dade hadn't moved. The men at the bar were still grumbling and pointing at the black TVs. Roarke had sworn Dade would bolt, but instead he looked at the screens casually.

White words rolled across the screens quickly. "Your mom says hi."

The screens went black one more time before the feed restored to the races. That hack wasn't that difficult, but it had Erick's signature all over it. Roarke should have known that was what he'd do.

He kept one eye on Dade and sighed. "Your mom?"

"What?" Erick shrugged. "Your mom jokes are classic."

Roarke smacked him in the back of the head. "Dade never knew his mom. He's an orphan. Grew up in a Russian orphanage."

Erick pursed his lips together. "Oh. Oops."

Roarke pointed a finger at him. "Don't expect me to step in if he beats your ass."

With a smirk, Erick cracked his knuckles. "I don't need you to defend me."

True, Erick was a scrappy fighter, cunning and quick. Roarke was just all flailing punches and brute strength. Sure, they mostly hid behind computers, but the stuff they did behind computers could get them beat up. Hence the self-defense skills.

Dade hadn't moved, his gaze still on the screens. Then slowly his head swiveled until he met Roarke's gaze across the room. Roarke hadn't seen Dade for more than five years, but Dade would recognize him. Roarke hadn't changed much. Some more tattoos maybe.

He might have been imagining it, but he swore Dade's lips twitched into something like a smile. Then he bolted, his body a blur as he darted back down a hallway.

"Motherfucker!" Erick shouted, but Roarke was already in pursuit, pumping his arms as he took off after Dade. That goddamn sneer on Dade's face. He was going to do his very best to wipe it off when he caught up to him.

At the end of the hallway, a door closed with a harsh bang. Roarke swung it open and tumbled out into another alley, Erick on his heels.

A flash of something caught his eye in the dark, and he raced after it, boots splashing through unknown liquid. "I fucking hate running," Erick panted behind him.

"I'm going to kill him," Roarke promised through clenched teeth.

The metal clang of something solid echoed along the brick walls on either side of them. Roarke's eyes finally adjusted in time to see a lean body scurrying up an iron fence. Unable to stop himself, he slammed into it and reached out in time to close his fingers around Dade's ankle.

Dade grunted and pulled his knee up, trying to dislodge him, but Roarke held on. Dade brought his heel down, and Roarke swerved to avoid getting his eye socket crushed but the man still managed to crack down on his ear.

The pain only fueled Roarke, and as he saw Erick's hand close around Dade's other ankle, he knew they had him. "Pull!" he hollered.

The two of them yanked hard on his limbs and Dade's body crashed down on top of them. Roarke landed on his back, a two-hundred-pound body of pissed-off hacker on top of him and a sharp object digging into his spine.

For about thirty seconds, there was only pain and limbs and punches and kicks. Grunts and curses. Roarke flailed, not knowing if he was punching Erick or Dade and not really caring because, at this point, he was reaching homicidal levels of rage.

A fist glanced off his cheekbone, and he saw red, either from fury or from the blood spilling from his split skin.

He managed to grab Dade—brown hair signaling he had the right guy—and slammed him chest first onto the concrete. He climbed on his back, got an arm around his throat, and squeezed. Dade clawed at his arm, gasping and choking, while Erick lay on his back in front of them, chest rising and falling, blood trickling from his nose. Dade bucked, trying to dislodge Roarke, but he gripped tighter with his thighs.

"I'll let up," Roarke gritted into his ear, "if you stop fucking struggling."

"Fuck you, Brennan," Dade spat.

Roarke squeezed harder. "There are two of us, and one of you. You're a crafty shit, but you're not that good."

Dade's nostrils flared, and he stopped struggling. Roarke kept his arm where it was but let up the pressure. While Dade sucked in oxygen, Roarke let his forehead fall forward as he sought to catch his breath. His cheek hurt like a motherfucker.

Finally, he rolled off, hoping Erick would pick up the slack if Dade bolted again. He fell onto his back and turned his head to see Dade rising slowly onto his knees, rubbing his neck. Roarke tensed as his hand reached into his back pocket. Dade met his eyes, his movements slow, before he pulled out a pack of cigarettes. Roarke relaxed while Dade stuck a cigarette in his mouth and leaned against the fence with a lighter in hand.

The flame illuminated his face in orange, revealing a five-o'clock shadow, a cut lip, and a bruised eye. Except the bruise didn't look fresh. Christ, did Dade make it a point to get in fistfights on the regular? Truthfully, Roarke didn't know much about Dade, and he doubted that was even his real name. He knew about the orphanage but wasn't sure if the guy was actually Russian. Dade had an accent that sounded somewhere between Russell Crowe in *Gladiator* and Colin Farrell in *Phone Booth*. Roarke assumed he spoke that way on purpose, to hide who he really was.

Erick rose to his feet with a groan, wiping at his nose.

"You all right?" Roarke stood up, brushing off his jacket.

"Yeah. You?"

"I'm fine."

Dade exhaled a ring of smoke. "I'm just peachy, too, guys. Thanks for asking."

Roarke ignored the snark and gestured to Dade's eye. "What happened?"

Dade took a drag and exhaled slowly. His gaze drifted to Erick. "Your mom."

Erick pulled back his hoodie and laughed nervously. "Uh, yeah, so . . . about that . . ."

Dade stood up and waved his hand, sending ashes scattering. "Forget it, Lee. Shitty jokes are your hallmark."

Erick's shoulders went back, and Roarke groaned. They did not need another fistfight in this filthy alley. He held out a hand, stopping Erick from advancing on Dade to defend his goddamn jokes. "All right, simmer down."

"Wasn't necessary anyway," Dade said. "Saw you two the minute you walked in."

"You weren't even in the room when we walked in," Erick said.

Dade cocked his head with a curl of his lip. "You sure about that?"

Cocky motherfucker. Damn, Roarke hated this guy.

Dade blew out another column of smoke. "So I let you do your thing in there, and now I'm allowing this fucking get-together out here, so I better get something good out of this, yeah?" He winked at Erick. "How's your sister?"

This time, Roarke wasn't holding back his friend because Roarke himself was going for the jugular. Erick was right there with him ready to strangle the guy. Of course Dade, being Dade, was like the smoke drifting from his cigarette, because he easily evaded both of them.

When Roarke's angry haze cleared, he found himself staring at a fence, Erick breathing hard next to him. He whirled around to see Dade walking backward down the alley, hands up, laughing like a psycho. "Ah, now I know what buttons to push. So we're even, huh?"

Dade's gaze settled on them as he came to a stop about ten feet away. "Interesting you both have the same reaction to an innocent question about Wren, huh?"

"Can you shut your fucking mouth?" Roarke said.

Dade flicked his cigarette on the street and ground the butt with his boot. "How about you talk about why you tracked me down."

Right, Flynn. Revenge. Destruction of Arden Saltner. Roarke took a deep breath and focused on what Dade could do. "Flynn's dead."

Dade's body immediately stiffened. He stared at Roarke with thinned lips and a full minute passed before he spoke again, hoarsely. "What?"

Erick shifted next to them, his shoulders up around his ears. Flynn and Erick had been best friends. Inseparable.

After Roarke, Erick had taken Flynn's death the hardest. But they weren't the only ones mourning. Flynn had been well liked by everyone who met him—he had been funny and good-looking and charming.

"He's dead. Ruled suicide, but it wasn't a fucking suicide. He was about to blow the whistle on his boss, but before he could, he was found with a bullet in his head."

Dade took a step closer to them, his bruise more livid as he stepped into a small circle of light. "Is there a crew?"

Roarke nodded.

Dade blew out a breath. That'd always been the problem with Dade. He didn't like working with people. He didn't trust anyone but himself, and he had his own agenda. Finally Dade pointed at Erick. "I don't like you." He shifted his gaze to Roarke. "And I actively hate you. But I liked Flynn, and you caught me on some downtime when I'm bored. So fine. I'm in."

Wow, Roarke had thought it was going to be much harder than that to convince him. "Is there some catch? Why're you agreeing so easily?"

Dade was quiet for a moment, and he took a step closer. Roarke could see there was also a fading bruise on his jaw. "If I do this? You owe me."

Ah, there it was. Nothing in life was free. He clenched his teeth. "Owe you? Do I get to declare some boundaries on that?"

Dade shook his head. "If it's within your abilities, I expect you to do it."

Roarke swallowed. With Dade that could mean… fucking anything. The guy didn't operate within the bounds of the law or hacker ethics or even decent morality.

But this was about Flynn, so he manned up. "Deal."

Dade grinned. It was an evil grin, but at least Roarke

was going to benefit from his brand of evil. He hoped. Dade stuck out his hand. Roarke shook it, and when he pulled his hand back, a business card was in his palm. When he looked up, Dade was walking away. He called over his shoulder. "Text me time and place."

"I will," he said.

"And get that cheekbone checked. Looks like you might need stitches," Dade said right before he opened the door to the betting place and disappeared inside. The slam of the door closing made Roarke flinch.

"I really hate that guy," he muttered.

Erick snatched the card out of his hand and flipped it over. "Just a number."

"Probably a burner."

"Dade Kelly is one shady motherfucker, man."

Roarke took the card back. "I know, but I'm not sure we can do this without him."

"I know, whatever. Fuck. I hate that we can't do this ourselves. I'm so antsy to erase Saltner from the earth."

Roarke swiped his hat off the ground and tugged it back on. He nudged Erick with his elbow to encourage him to walk down the alley. "Me too."

Erick wrinkled his nose. "This place makes me want to shower."

"Yeah, those designer jeans of yours probably have puke on them. Or syphilis. Whatever was on the ground of that alley."

Erick shuddered. "Fuck you, don't remind me."

Roarke plucked at Erick's racing jacket. "You got a hole in the arm here now."

Erick craned his neck to look at the elbow of his sleeve. "Goddamn it! That bastard ruined my brand-new jacket."

Roarke laughed, which only made Erick madder. "Hey,"

Erick said. "Remember that you have a hole in your jacket, too. Also courtesy of Dade Fucking Kelly."

"I got this jacket in Denmark. I'm not giving it up just because he was pissed and tried to burn me with a cigarette."

Erick shook his head as they reached the end of the alley and entered the parking lot. "I hope this isn't a mistake, asking for his help."

That sobered Roarke quickly. His cheekbone hurt like hell, and he wiped his face with the back of his hand. When he checked it, the black-and-white skull tattooed there was now colored red. He and Erick both looked like delinquents, which meant they probably fit in in this part of town.

Roarke glanced up, trying to get his bearings so they could find the car and get the hell out of there. The small parking lot was deserted, and he thought they were the only two around until he heard footsteps. He went on high alert, scanning their surroundings for an escape route. There was a streetlamp in the far corner, and a figure slowly stepped into the light.

Roarke stopped walking. He blinked a couple of times because his eyes had to be playing tricks on him. Did Dade drug him and he didn't notice? Because the woman standing in the parking lot had Wren's face, for sure, but she couldn't be Erick's sister. Her hair—normally a straight, shiny black inherited from their South Korean parents—was dyed a silvery light lavender. She wore thick-soled black boots, fishnet stockings, and a short black skirt. Her leather jacket was pushed up to her elbows, revealing colorful tattoo sleeves and a dozen metal bracelets that jangled when she moved.

Last time he'd laid eyes on her, she'd been wearing a

floral sundress and flip-flops, with a clean face and hair still damp from her shower. Over the years, he'd tracked her the only way he knew how—from behind a monitor. But what he couldn't know, and hadn't thought about, was how she'd changed. The innocent smile he'd vowed to protect was now replaced with a defiant smirk that turned him on.

Her makeup was heavy, her lips a bright red. And she was looking right at him with a glint in her eye that was completely foreign in her gorgeous face.

"Oh shit," Erick muttered from beside him.

Roarke rubbed his eyes and opened them. Nope, she was still there.

Finally, Wren parted those sinful lips on a grin. "Hey brother dearest. Hey Roarke. Heard you're starting a crew."

That was when he found his voice. "No way in fucking hell."

CHAPTER TWO

HE was still a fine, fine man.

His chest had filled out some since Wren had last seen him, and his posture was more confident. Standing there in a ball cap, torn jeans, bloody shirt, and a scowl, Roarke Brennan was a dream.

Well, if a girl's dream was a tattooed tech-head who was now glaring at her like he wanted her to disappear.

Okay, so the dream needed work.

Erick had told her Roarke wouldn't want her involved, but she'd managed to tease it out of her brother that they'd be here tonight. So here she was, ready to convince the man she'd carried a torch for since high school that she could help him in the most important mission of his life.

Because she had a card to play, and it was the ace Roarke needed. He just didn't know it yet.

She wondered if he still saw her as the innocent teenage Wren who loved books and crushed on boys. He might not see her as she was now, a woman ten years older who'd been through hell and back.

She straightened her spine, wishing now she'd worn heels because Roarke always towered over her petite frame. She clutched the edges of her jacket. "Let's try this again. I say, 'Hey Roarke,' and you say something back like, 'Hey' or 'Hello.' I'll even accept a grunt, which is better than a 'No way in fucking hell.'" She tilted her head. "So. Hey Roarke."

If he glared any harder, he was going to pop a blood vessel in his tattooed neck until the inked rose bled. He whipped his head to Erick. "Why is she here? What does she know about a crew?"

Erick's face was bright red, and if Roarke didn't kill her first, Erick would do the job. His eyes bored into hers, promising retribution. *Oops.* "Dude, she fucking played me."

"She played you." Roarke's voice was deceptively calm. Since it wasn't directed at her, she hid a smile behind a cough. "We've single-handedly brought down multimillion-dollar businesses, rerouted an oil tanker in Alaska, and exposed that shady prince in Morocco, and you can't keep a secret from your fucking sister?"

Erick shifted his weight, alternating his glare between her and his best friend. "I was pissed about Flynn, okay? So I told her."

"And how is she here?"

"Um—"

"He told me about that, too," Wren piped up, probably at her own peril. But if Roarke stayed angry at Erick, it took less heat off her. "Because I asked if the crew was complete. He said you were coming here for Kelly." She pointed at the cut on his cheek. "That from him?"

Roarke gritted out one word. "Yes."

She raised her eyebrows. "Should I make a joke about the other guy, or..."

"It took some convincing, but he's in," Erick said.

"Great!" She smiled brightly on purpose. "And now you have me, so we're all good."

Roarke was shaking his head before she finished speaking. "You're not on the crew."

She'd told herself on the ride there to keep her cool, knowing Roarke could be cautious. Where Flynn had used charm and positivity to cover his pain growing up, Roarke let it all play out on his face in the form of a near-constant glare. He kept everyone at arm's length except for his brother and Erick. Every once in a while, that glare would drop, and she could see the depth in those hazel eyes of his. She knew she'd barely seen the tip of the iceberg.

All she'd ever wanted in high school was to be in that inner circle, for Roarke to treat her like she was more than just Erick's annoying little sister. Sometimes she swore he'd let his gaze linger on her just a second too long, but then the next day, he'd pretend she didn't exist. So she'd poured herself into her studies and meeting her parents' expectations, and that had crashed and burned epically.

She'd pulled herself out of the ashes, put her energy into doing what she'd always loved, and now she was here, hoping to use those skills to help Roarke and to avenge Flynn. And that other little revenge of her own, but that would be dealt with later. Right now, convincing Roarke was the priority.

She tossed her hair. "What, you think a girl isn't capable of being on the team?"

"Nice try, but we got Marisol. This ain't about you having a fucking vagina, Wren."

Ugh, why was he still hot while sneering at her? "Okay, then what's it about?"

His mouth moved with no sound, like he wasn't sure what to say until he blurted it out. "It's about the fact that it's *you.*"

His open and honest rejection stung. She reared back,

and a flash of regret crossed over Roarke's face. "The answer is no, and that's final." He speared Erick with a glare. "Deal with her. I'm out."

He turned on a heel and strode toward his car. She glanced at Erick, hoping he would come through for her, but he was staring after Roarke and biting his lip.

Fine, fuck it. She'd show her ace. She cracked her knuckles, bracelets jingling, and called to Roarke's back. "Darren Saltner wants me."

Roarke stopped so fast that dust swirled up at his booted feet. He didn't move, and she stared at his shoulders, waiting to see what would win out—his desire for revenge or his apparent distaste for her.

He turned slowly, and the brim of his cap shaded the top half of his face so all that was visible were the tense lines of his mouth. Finally, his lips parted, and his voice was eerily calm. "What did you say?"

Erick straightened slowly, his eyes cutting to Roarke, and she should have listened to the warning bells in her head. Spoiler: she didn't.

"Darren Saltner has been trying to tap my ass since he saw me shake it at Alpha." She didn't add that it had been her plan all along because she'd wanted to get Darren's attention. "So if you want information on Arden, what better way to get it than through his son?" She pointed at herself with both thumbs. "I can be your valentine."

"Oh motherfucking Christ, Wren." Erick leaned forward and braced his hands on his knees. He shook his head while moaning, "No, no, no."

Roarke moved fast, faster than she thought he was capable. In two strides, he was in front of her, the heat of his body slamming into her. His hat was off, dark hair hanging in sweaty strands across his forehead. She held her ground even though his sudden proximity sent her into vertigo.

Through gritted teeth, he hissed, "Stay away from Darren Saltner."

Oh hell no. How dare he get in her face and tell her what to do? "Excuse me?"

"Wren"—he exhaled roughly and dragged a hand through his hair, his gaze drifting away before snapping back to her—"this isn't a game."

"I don't think—"

"I can't get into what's at stake, but trust me when I say that Arden will not hesitate to take out anyone who messes with him." His voice dropped. "He killed Flynn, and over my dead body will you be next."

She wasn't sure if he cared about her or didn't want a murdered woman on his conscience. "If anyone else came to you and said they had an in with Saltner, would you take them up on it?"

He didn't hesitate. "Yes."

She counted to ten, not wanting to respond in a way that would put him on the defense. She placed a hand on his solid chest, curling her fingers against the soft cotton of his T-shirt. His light hazel eyes shone brightly in the harsh streetlamp, and as she tilted her head back, his gaze roamed her face. "So what's wrong with me?"

A muscle in his jaw clenched, and his chest beneath her palm tensed. He didn't speak for a long moment, until finally his hand lifted slowly, tattooed fingers curling around her wrist. He lowered his head as he plucked her hand off his chest and rotated her wrist. His thumb rubbed over the pink rose of Sharon inked there, the point of contact spreading heat up her arm and through her chest. When he dropped her arm back at her side, he sighed. "There's nothing wrong with you, Wren. That's my point."

A lump rose unbidden in her throat. Oh shit, she hadn't cried for years. Of course Roarke would be the one to break her literal dry spell. "It's been ten years, Roarke. I wasn't perfect then, and I'm not perfect now."

He leaned down, so close that she could feel his breath on her face. "Didn't say you were perfect. Just said nothing was wrong with you." Before she could respond, he was backing away. "Fly home back to the nest now, little bird."

He spun on his heel, and words failed her, the old nickname he'd given her when she was a teenager ringing in her head. His back was to her now, long strides widening the distance between them. She tried to plead with her eyes to Erick, but he was following his friend to the car. The two men slid into an old Mustang, and the harsh sounds of the closing car doors were what finally shocked her out of her stupor.

She retreated to her Ducati Diavel and shoved her purple-and-silver helmet on her head while Roarke's words rattled between her ears. She straddled her bike, revved the engine a couple of times, and peeled out of the parking lot.

At first, she hadn't known what to feel, but as she sped down the highway back to DC, the fire burning in her chest was clearly anger.

Anger over Roarke's dismissal, his apparent need to still treat her like she was fragile. *Little bird.* Ten years ago, she'd loved the nickname, happy that she ranked anywhere in Roarke's life to deserve a nickname. And while some residual feelings of affection hung on those words, she couldn't help but think that they also represented what he still thought of her. That she was the same hapless teenager.

She'd thought she was over her high school crush, but

clearly not. Why why *why* did she want what she couldn't have?

She was only a year younger than Erick, and the first time she met Roarke Brennan, he was a gangly middle-schooler. Even then, he seemed so much older. He had to be a parent to Flynn after their parents were killed, because they lived with an uncle who neither wanted them nor even seemed to like them.

Wren was fascinated by Roarke. The more walls he threw up, the more she wanted to tear them down. She'd never been successful though. No matter how often she'd tried to tag along with Erick and Roarke and Flynn, no matter how many questions she asked, eager to talk tech with them, they never welcomed her into their inner circle.

Why had she let herself believe Roarke would treat her any differently than he had in the past? She'd changed, but he didn't know that. The vision in her head of Roarke's face lighting up—*did Roarke's face even move like that?*—was such a dumb fantasy.

She passed a slow-moving minivan and kicked up the speed on the open highway. Her hair whipped around her neck from under her helmet. She squeezed her thighs around the bike, loving the feel of the machine under her.

She was angry at herself for getting hung up on this. She wasn't back in DC to connect with Roarke; she'd returned for the mission. Her own personal one of revenge, and one for Flynn. Every time she thought about the younger Brennan, her heart broke all over again. She wasn't sure there was a person on the planet who hadn't liked him. Where Roarke dealt with their difficult home life by retreating inward, Flynn sought attention elsewhere. When Flynn died, Erick had been devastated. She'd never seen him so distraught. After she found out who was responsible, she knew it was time to make her move. For Flynn—and for her friend Fiona, who'd also suffered at the hands of the Saltner family.

By the time Wren was speeding down I-270 into the city, it was closing on 1:00 a.m., and she was too amped for sleep. Roarke didn't think she could hack it? That she needed to be preserved like a fucking artifact? She'd show him.

She managed to find a street parking space outside Alpha and parked her bike. She didn't have time to slather herself in makeup cover-up so she left her jacket on but unzipped it. Underneath, she wore a tight tank top, and she adjusted herself so the girls looked extra perky. She peered into the side mirror to add another coat of red lipstick and headed to the front entrance of the club.

She'd been back in DC for a week, and she'd spent much of that time digging up info on Darren Saltner. He owned Alpha—a dance club in the U Street Corridor—and was often seen there, as well as in the local gossip rags. What Erick and Roarke didn't know was that Wren had her own reasons for investigating the younger Saltner. One night in college, Wren had gone out to a party with her roommate, Fiona. Back then, Fiona had been sweet and shy, her long hair always pulled into a knot on her head, held up with chewed pencils. But what happened to them that night had changed both of their lives, Fiona's even more than Wren's. It'd taken Wren years, but she'd followed the digital trail as far as she could, seeking those responsible for preying on young women like them. And that trail led Wren to Darren Saltner.

Wren and Fiona had spent every day since that night looking over their shoulders, and it was about time Wren put an end to that. She felt responsible for that night, and despite her mission, she knew nothing—even revenge—would ease the guilt. She'd learned to live with it.

Wren looked different now than she had back in college, especially with her hair. To Darren, she was just another Asian girl. She'd caught his eye on her second night in Alpha and played hard to get. She hadn't intended for him to notice her that fast. Now was the time to take this to another level.

She smiled at the bouncer and flashed her ID. He gave her a look like he recognized her, but she was pretty sure they were all told to look bored and scary, so he didn't say anything and waved her inside.

As soon as she opened the door, the bass vibrated her bones while the humid heat of a couple hundred bodies writhing on the dance floor nearly suffocated her. She scanned the floor and the upper balcony and sure enough, there was Darren, leaning over the railing, his eyes on the women in skintight clothes below. He wore his typical uniform of dark slacks and a black button-down dress shirt with slicked-back blond hair. He got his style from the House of Patrick Bateman. She hoped he didn't have a chainsaw in his penthouse, too.

Rolling her shoulders to loosen up, she made her way onto the dance floor. The good thing about her hair was that it caught the lights from the DJ booth as they panned over the crowd. All she needed was for Darren to notice her, and she knew he'd ask her to come up to see him.

She liked the song that was playing, some Rihanna remix, so she threw her hands in the air and wriggled her ass against some bro with a thick chain around his neck and a goatee. He was into it, and his breath smelled like whiskey, so she kept her inhales to a minimum until she was lightheaded.

It wasn't long before a hand wrapped around her waist, and she was drawn into a wall of human flesh. A deep voice said in her ear, "Saltner would like to buy you a drink on the VIP floor."

Bingo. She knew Darren's ego would want a second chance to impress her. She peered up at the bouncer and batted her lashes. "Oh, really? I was about to go home, I think. I'm not sure..." She let her voice trail off as she nibbled her lip.

The man's eyes dropped to her mouth. "Just for a half hour."

She made a big show of thinking it over and even glanced up to see Darren watching them. Finally she sighed and wrung her hands. "Um, okay. I guess so."

The bouncer was probably three hundred pounds, so they cut through the crowd with ease and made their way over to the wide staircase that led to the second floor. Another bouncer unhooked a rope blocking their way to let them through. With each footstep, the dread in her stomach grew. She had to keep her wits about her, so she decided two things. No drinking. No moving to a second location.

Fuck, she sounded like she was preventing a kidnapping.

She took a deep breath and straightened her back. She could do this. Darren Saltner was just a club owner who was involved in an underground sex ring along with his dad, Arden, who committed hush-hush murder.

No biggie.

The music wasn't as loud on the second floor. The bodyguard led her over to a couch in the shape of a crescent, occupied by about half a dozen people, and flanked by two guys who looked way more important than just bouncers. They wore suits, and she would have bet a hundred bucks they had concealed guns. Bodyguards, maybe? That was a red fucking flag. What club owner needed bodyguards? Darren sat in the middle of the couch watching her approach. He patted the empty space next to him, which would sandwich her between him and a woman who was half sitting in the lap of a man wearing jeans and a visible gun holster.

Stupendous.

"Lacy, right?" Darren asked, smiling his perfectly straight, white smile.

Lacy Kim was an alias she'd had for years. On paper, Lacy was a single woman who came into money after her wealthy grandparents died. She'd recently moved to DC and had a nice apartment on U Street. Wren, however, had an apartment in Northwest DC.

She nodded as she slid into the seat next to him. He handed her a highball glass with a clear liquid inside with a lime. "Mojito?"

Yeah, sure, whatever. She placed her lips on the small black straw and pretended to drink. When she leaned forward to place the glass down on the table in front of them, her hair brushed his arm. He lifted a hand, running the ends between two fingers. "I thought this was a wig when I first saw you, but it's real, isn't it?"

Why were they talking about her hair? "It's real. Just dyed."

He smiled again, and her skin crawled. "I've been looking for you since last time you were here, when we got cut short."

She'd made an excuse that she had to leave, and he'd bought it. So now he was letting her off the hook for that excuse and was giving her a second chance not to bail. "Yeah, sorry. I've been busy." She swallowed because the next words were not easily forthcoming. "I'm so glad you sent your man down for me. I was hoping I'd see you again."

His hand dropped from her hair to rest on her knee. The heat seared through her fishnets to settle on her skin like a brand. He squeezed, and she forced down the bile.

"Is that right?" he asked.

She blinked, working hard to play the ingenue. "Of course. Me catching the eye of the owner of this awesome club? I'm honored."

He studied her. "You didn't seem all that flattered last time."

Shit, shit. "I know, I'm sorry. I was having a bad night. Remember? My cat wasn't feeling well." Honestly, she'd blamed her mood on a nonexistent cat. She was an awful person.

"Oh, that's right. How is she?"

Wren's heart was pounding so loud that she was surprised he couldn't hear it. "*He.*" She smiled, knowing he was trying to catch her in a lie. "My cat is a he, remember?"

His smile grew bigger, and he laughed. "Right! *He.* How could I forget?"

She shrugged and pretended to take another sip of her drink as his hand slid higher up her leg.

She had to ball her fists so she didn't shove his hands off her. She looked away, pretending to get caught up in the music. A woman was sitting at the end of the couch watching her carefully, and Wren smiled at her. She returned it tightly. Okay then, guess Wren wasn't making best friends here.

The two beside her were going to town on each other. The man's hand was up the brunette's skirt, and based on the sounds coming out of her mouth, Wren was pretty sure he wasn't just grabbing a nice handful of ass.

She eyed Darren's hand on her leg and hoped it didn't go much higher. He was talking to a man beside him now, and she shimmied a little dance to get closer to hear what they were saying.

"—taken care of," the other man said.

"I'm not interested in getting involved in his business," Darren said, flicking his wrist out to check the time on his gold wristwatch. "I only care about him fucking up and me getting blowback."

"There'll be none, sir."

Darren nodded, and he changed the subject to something boring about the club's upcoming renovations. She didn't give a fuck about the renovations, but she could have used a little more of that previous conversation. What was taken care of?

She wished she could drink, but no way in hell did she trust Darren not to slip something in it. As Darren's hand on her thigh grew heavier, and his one finger slipped under her skirt, the first niggle of fear began to seep into her brain. She had a couple of exit strategies, but all would involve potentially damaging her reputation with Darren. That wasn't something she wanted to risk. Not when she was pretty damn sure that previous conversation was about Flynn and Darren's father's business.

Darren turned to her, his grin taking on a predatory leer. His hand slid under her skirt, and she sucked in a breath. He tugged slightly, urging her to spread her legs, and she counted to ten before glancing around and giving off a nervous laugh. "Darren, not here."

He tilted his head. "Ah, so you want privacy then?"

Wait, no. That was not her intended consequence. "I'm not sure about tonight."

He raised his eyebrows. "Oh? Why's that?"

She pursed her lips. "I require a little wining and dining."

Darren threw back his head and laughed. His hand left her thigh, and she breathed a sigh of relief until his arm snaked around her waist, and he tugged her to his chest. She braced herself with her hands on his shoulders and looked into his eyes, her skin crawling, her heart pounding, as she lay sprawled over him. "What makes you think you're so special that I'll take that much time on you?"

She licked her lips, and his gaze dropped. "I don't know. You're the one who called me up here and haven't stopped touching me the entire time."

His breath coasted over her face. He smelled like whiskey and cologne, and she was going to have to take five showers to get the scent of him out of her hair after this. His hand slipped under her skirt and cupped one cheek of her ass. He squeezed, his lips tilting into a smirk. Ugh, she was going to throw up.

Remember Flynn and Fiona. Remember revenge.

"Mr. Saltner." One of the bodyguard-looking men on the edge of the couch interrupted them. "So sorry, but we seem to have a security issue we need you to take a look at."

Darren didn't take his eyes off her the whole time the man was speaking. He heaved a sigh and gently placed her back on the couch. He reached into his pocket and pulled out a card. "Call me about that wining and dining," he said. "Or I'll find you."

She plucked the card from his fingers, feeling like she'd dodged a bullet. "Okay."

He nodded. "Have a good night, Lacy."

"You too."

He stood up and followed the man in the suit off the floor and down a hallway, to what she assumed was an office.

She slipped the card into her pocket, then got the hell out of there as fast as she could.

She burst through the front doors and walked to her bike with her head down, eager to get home and wash off this entire day. She hopped on her bike and was at her apartment complex in fifteen minutes—Wren's apartment. Her alias Lacy had an apartment as well. She'd set up the second apartment shortly after moving to town, knowing she'd need to be prepared once she made contact with Darren.

Wren parked and grabbed her helmet, then retrieved her Sig Sauer P220 from the pocket on her bike. She holstered it at her back and rummaged in her jacket pocket for her keys as she made her way to the sidewalk.

A sound echoed off the brick building and shoved all her instincts into overdrive. She darted to the side, withdrawing her gun in a quick motion and leveling it on the source of the sound. The figure leaned forward, and she froze when she met the gaze of Roarke Brennan.

He stood with his arms crossed over his chest. And he didn't look happy. At all. "Put the gun down, little bird."

Well, now she was just embarrassed. With a frustrated grunt, she shoved the gun into her waistband and tried to act like nothing had happened. She cocked out a hip and waved. "Hey Roarke."

He didn't speak for a long moment. "Darren Saltner is the thirty-five-year-old owner of Alpha who is just as bad as his father and is less good at hiding it."

She swallowed.

Roarke wasn't finished. "He's been known to funnel drug sales through his club, and several women have brought sexual assault charges against him, only to drop them. And that's just the tip of the shit sandwich of things he's involved in."

She knew all of this. “Look—”

“And after I told you to stay out of it, you drive back down here and go right to his club and cozy up to him? Seriously, Wren?”

“Were you following me?”

“Yes, I sure the hell was!”

She scowled. “That’s rude.”

“I don’t give a fuck,” he shot back. “I *am* rude. And I can’t believe you put yourself in that situation—”

“I didn’t take the drink he offered me.”

Roarke threw up his hands and turned his back on her, walking a few steps away before stopping abruptly and turning. “You didn’t take a drink from him. God, Wren, I—”

“I got out of there fine!”

Roarke stared at her incredulously. “Sure you did, because I raised an alarm on their security system so you could escape.”

She forced down the growl that was roaring up her throat. Of course he interfered. “I’m not an idiot, Roarke!” She surged toward him. “I researched him, I know what he does and who he is. Tonight he mentioned something to his bodyguards that made me think he knows what his father is doing. And I intend to find out more.”

“I can’t let you do this,” he gritted out. “You’re not prepared for this kind of work.”

“What do you think I’ve been doing for the last ten years?”

For the first time, uncertainty crossed his face. “You went to college, then you traveled.”

“I traveled,” she said slowly. “I sure did.” She took another step closer, even though she knew what she said next was going to piss him the hell off. “I traveled all over as a for-hire hacker. And everything I know, I learned from Dade Kelly."

Roarke didn't move, didn't blink. He went full wax sculpture on her for about ten seconds before his lips parted. "What? Erick said you were writing freelance for magazines and other publications. I saw the articles."

"Yep, I did do that, but that wasn't all I was doing." She spent her college years doing what she was told, becoming editor in chief of the school newspaper and everything. In her spare time, she was with a group of amateur hackers on campus, learning everything she could after what happened to her and Fiona. When she graduated, she tracked down Erick, Roarke, and Flynn, only to have Dade make her an offer she couldn't refuse.

Roarke didn't seem to know what to do with this information. "Jesus Christ."

She pulled Darren's card out of her pocket. "So anyway, I got his number, and I'm supposed to call him for a date. With your approval or not, I'm doing it."

"What if Darren knows nothing?"

"I think he knows a lot. But even if he doesn't, what's the harm?"

"What's the harm? You wrapped up in that parasite!"

"I can disappear," she said quickly. "I've done it before, and I'll do it again."

Roarke rubbed his hand over the back of his neck, his mouth twisted into a grimace. "Fuck."

She took a step toward him, softening her voice. She didn't want to argue with him. She was on his side. "I'm doing this for Flynn." He didn't need to know about her other plan yet. He'd be even less likely to say yes if he knew.

At the sound of his brother's name, Roarke's shoulders

slumped, and he squeezed his eyes shut as he ran a palm over his face. "I don't like this."

"I don't like any of this either."

Roarke studied her for a long time. "I guess I don't really know you, do I?"

She shrugged. "You knew me at one time, I guess. And I'm still Wren. I'm just…grown up."

She didn't miss the way his gaze coasted down her body. His hazel eyes bored into her as he took a step closer. The air between them was charged, and a bead of sweat trickled down her back.

"Did he touch you, Wren?" His voice was low, barely above a whisper. "Did he put his hands on you?"

"It was nothing I couldn't—"

"Answer me."

"Yes." Heat pooled in her stomach as his eyes blazed, and she couldn't stop the tremble in her voice. "Why're you looking at me like that?"

He placed a fist in his other palm and cracked his knuckles, an agitated tell he'd had since she'd known him. "Because Wren…fuck." The curse was a growl. "The thought of him touching you, thinking he can, thinking he has a right"—his hand sliced the air—"it's driving me crazy."

Her throat went dry and words failed her. This was a side of Roarke she'd never seen, never thought possible. He rarely deviated from his aloof scowl, and this possessive side—over her—was kind of turning her on.

She wasn't sure if that was healthy, but fuck it, she wasn't going to lie to herself. "Look, I know you feel obligated to protect me because I'm Erick's little sister—"

He turned away with a bitter laugh, flattening his hands on top of his head.

She stamped her foot. "Will you quit interrupting me?"

He whirled around and advanced on her so quickly, she retreated until her back hit the wall. Then he was in her space, all up in it, their chests brushing, his thighs touching hers. He braced a hand on the wall beside her head. "You think this is about you being Erick's little sister?"

Her head was spinning. She didn't know what was what anymore. "Roarke, I don't understand."

His jaw was so tight that she swore a light tap would shatter it. He was so close now that she inhaled the scent of his leather jacket with every breath. The tension in his body was a tight coil that seemed about to unleash any second. A large vein in his neck cut through the inked rose, and without thinking, she ran a finger down it. His entire body shuddered.

"Where?" he asked.

"Where what?"

A pause. "Where'd he touch you?"

Oh. She fluttered her hand at her side. "My leg."

"Where on your leg?"

She couldn't look away from his eyes, and she had to tilt her head back to hold his gaze. His lips were parted, eyes shining in the dim outside lights of her apartment building. "Roarke, it doesn't matter—"

"Tell me," he said, and this time, his tone held a hint of a plea.

"My inner thigh."

He exhaled roughly. "Did you want him to?"

She swallowed. "Of course not. He grosses me out."

He gave a small lip twitch and then something brushed the front of her thigh. She startled and glanced down to see his fingers grazing her skin. She didn't move but kept her eyes on that tattooed hand as it flattened on her thigh. "Is this okay?"

Her head jerked up. Roarke's eyes were wide, pupils blown. She swore she could feel the pulse of his heart in the pads of his fingers where they rested on her skin. What was going on? Whatever tentative relationship they'd had was shifting beneath her, and she couldn't get her bearings. All she knew was that her entire body was on fire, and it was taking every bit of self-control not to climb that big body and finally see what those full lips felt like on hers.

Get a grip.

She still hadn't answered his question so she licked her lips, tasting the last of her lipstick on her tongue. "Yes."

His hand shifted, and four fingers ran up the inside of her leg, dangerously close to where she ached for him to touch. He curled his fingers around her inner thigh so one rested on the seam of her panty line. She balled her hands into fists because it was the only way to prevent herself from reaching for him. "Roarke," she croaked.

"I don't want him touching you if you don't want it, do you understand?" he said, his voice ragged.

"I—"

"This is going to be a fucking disaster," he muttered almost to himself, as his gaze began to roam. Down her neck, across her chest, which heaved with deep breaths, and then down to where his hand was tucked between her legs. "He's going to make one wrong move, and I'm going to fuck up the whole thing by blowing his brains out."

"Roarke—"

"I didn't want you in because I can't be objective with you," he interrupted, his gaze once again cutting to her. "Do you understand what I'm saying?"

Not really, but when his thumb brushed ever so lightly over her underwear, she sucked in a breath and nodded.

"But you already made contact with Darren, so there's nothing I can do now."

"Guess not," she whispered.

He dipped his head for just a second, and she thought he was going to kiss her, but then he took a step back. She almost reached for him but stopped herself.

He shoved his hands in his pockets and began to walk past her, as if he hadn't just rocked her world with a touch. "Better get some rest. We're meeting at eight a.m. sharp."

She glanced at her watch. That was in five hours. Shit. "Uh..."

He was already in the parking lot. "I'll have Erick text you the address," he called over his shoulder.

"Okay!" she yelled back.

She waited until his car pulled out of the parking lot before sagging against the wall, a hand on her chest as she sought to calm her racing heart.

In one night, she'd placed her safety in the hands of a very dangerous man and allowed another equally dangerous but also sexy man to touch her.

She hoped like hell she wasn't in over her head.

CHAPTER THREE

ROARKE stared at his orange juice, wishing there was vodka in it. Anything to calm his trembling hands. He'd slept like shit last night and was paying for it this morning with frayed nerves.

His apartment in Northeast DC was his safe haven. One thirty-foot room on the first floor of an old warehouse with a kitchen on one side, a sitting area in the middle, his bedroom at the far end, and his bathroom with a shower stall behind a curtain. Normally he came here to clear his head, to forget about the last mission he'd completed before he had to focus on the next one. But now everything about this place made him think of his brother. So he wanted to burn it all to the ground.

Flynn's laptop sat on the scarred wooden table. On the lid was a peeling Green Day sticker and a scratch along the side where he'd dropped it on the sidewalk outside his apartment. Roarke remembered that day because he'd been juggling his Italian sub along with Flynn's pastrami on rye while Flynn fretted over his laptop.

Growing up, they'd always had each other's backs. Their parents died in a car accident when they were kids, and so their legal guardian was Uncle Frank, their mother's brother, who worked at a local factory. Frank made it clear from the first curl of his lip while he blew cigarette smoke in their faces that their presence wasn't wanted in his home, but he was happy to *hold on* to the money left to Roarke and Erick by their parents.

It was a mindfuck to go through the formative years of your life feeling like a burden. Flynn had been so young, and while he understood more than Frank probably thought he did, Roarke made it his life mission to be his brother's shield. All of Frank's hissed words, his derision, his utter contempt at having to provide their basic needs—Roarke stayed on the front lines of it all. He'd covered the inner scars with the ink on his outer skin, but it hadn't helped much.

When Roarke was old enough, he'd thrown himself into the Web—fandoms, chat rooms, any place where he could feel like he fit in. When he found a coding tutorial, he felt like he'd found a home. Within a year, he was doing minor hacks for pranks. As a teen, he did everything from hack into radio show phone lines to ensure he was the fifth caller for Pearl Jam tickets to writing open source code for other hackers to use. Of course, he'd gone too far once, and ever since he'd done his best to stay within the law.

He'd been so proud when he'd shown Flynn some basic programming skills and Flynn showed natural talent. It gave them something to bond over, something that shut out the outside world. Roarke had scored a pair of old laptops for cheap when his school sold them because they'd upgraded the staff's equipment. So he and Flynn sat huddled in the bedroom they shared, threadbare carpet beneath their toes and paint peeling around their heads. And they'd learned how to be a couple of the most elite hackers on the eastern seaboard. They'd been just kids, and it'd all been fun and games at the time, until it wasn't.

Roarke downed the rest of his orange juice and juggled the glass between his palms. Flynn's face flashed in front of his eyes, and Roarke swore he could feel the heat of Flynn's arms as he gave him one of his famous Flynn hugs.

He cocked his hand and threw his glass at the brick wall opposite him.

The crash and subsequent rain of glass shattered the silence. Juice and pulp dripped from the bricks as Roarke stood there, clenching and unclenching his fists as the anger burned through him, hot, bright, and sharp.

Roarke was a fixer. Flynn had called him that. If there was a problem, he fixed it. He wasn't about empty promises or platitudes. But he couldn't fix Flynn. He couldn't bring him back, and the helplessness was nearly crippling. Flynn, his little brother, with his big, white grin and lanky limbs and infectious laugh, was dead. He'd failed to protect him, and the way to get revenge was to place in danger another person he cared about—Wren.

He closed his eyes and pictured how she looked last night, lavender hair framing her face, those bright red lips, that fucking body he couldn't help but touch.

He'd crushed on her as a teen, but as an adult, he fucking *wanted* her, like he'd never wanted anyone before, and wasn't sure he'd ever want anyone else in his life. When all he'd had of her was links and lines of code, he could handle it, but now that she was back, in the flesh, all rules he'd set for himself regarding her were breaking apart.

Roarke had seen Darren Saltner a couple of times. He was a smarmy bastard. His touching her, flirting with her, thinking he was worthy of her attention was like a vice in Roarke's chest. He'd wanted that to be his touch, his hands between her legs.

Fuck, he was an asshole.

As a teenager, he'd tried to ignore the gorgeous, charming younger sister of his best friend. He'd practiced his scowling in the mirror, as if it would ward off everything he was feeling for her, but it never worked. She'd tagged along with him and Erick, asking questions about programming. She smiled and laughed and always smelled like a dream—*how did women always smell so good?*

So he did what a fuckhead teenage techie who was crushing hard on a girl did. He hacked into her online journal. Total dick move. He squirmed every time he thought about it.

He didn't know what he was looking for, maybe a poem where she professed her love for him? He sure as fuck didn't find that. He found a whole manifesto about what she wanted for her future—a husband and three kids and a happy domestic life with a house in the suburbs and a dogwood in the front yard.

That wasn't him. Even at sixteen, he knew that was never going to be him. Erick and their parents placed her on a pedestal, and he didn't want to be the person who dragged her off it.

So he'd turned off the part of him that wanted Wren. That hadn't stopped him from tracking her life as best as he could from behind a monitor. So maybe he'd done a little puppet mastering behind the scenes and made sure Wren never saw the strings. Watching her life for ten years through a web of links was not satisfying, but it'd been all he had.

Which was why it burned him that he hadn't known what she'd been up to with Dade. Dade Fucking Kelly.

With a frustrated growl, he turned away from the mess he'd made and sagged against the wall until his jean-clad ass touched the floor. He stared at his bare feet, a roaring lion inked on the top of one and a sleeping lion on the other.

So Wren was back, and she'd changed, but he hadn't. He'd known since he was thirteen that he'd never have a normal life with a nine-to-five job. He'd always wanted to travel and play a little fast and loose with his profession. Hell, he paid taxes on only about a third of his income. The government thought he was a landlord. They had no idea his main source of income was from hacking. *Hacktivism* was the term he preferred, or white hat hacking. He wasn't a criminal. He maybe did criminal *things*, but it was all in an effort to defeat the real bad motherfuckers.

Flynn had been his sidekick, along with Erick, since they were teenagers. A couple of years ago, Flynn had said he wanted to get straight, have a family, and be an active member of society. So he got a job at Saltner Defense—a computer security software company—where he'd planned to work and pay taxes and fit into the general population.

Until he uncovered something he wasn't supposed to and paid for it with his life.

Roarke stared at his hands, where GAME OVER was tattooed on his knuckles. He cracked them, deep breathing to get himself under control before the hot rush of anger took over and he *did* actually burn his apartment down.

After glancing at his watch, he rose to his feet. He had a half hour to cross town to where his team was meeting in the basement of a warehouse he owned.

He finished getting ready, grabbed a can of his ever-present addiction, Diet Coke, for the road, and was in his vintage Mustang within five minutes.

Roarke owned an old warehouse in Southeast near the Anacostia waterfront. When he arrived, he tossed his empty soda can into the dumpster and entered the code to the door. The keypad beeped, and he opened the heavy metal door. It latched shut behind him as he descended the stairs that would lead him underground. After another code and another door, he entered the room where the team was gathering. There he found Jock, their best programmer, hunched over his computer at the single conference-style table in the corner of the room.

Jock glanced up, his blue eyes taking in Roarke's appearance before he nodded and resumed whatever he was working on. The man had earned the name Jock long before Roarke met him; it was a hacking term that meant using brute force tactics. One look at the six-four, two-hundred-fifty-pound Jock and anyone could see the name fit.

Roarke met Jock—real name Jamison Bosh—on a job a couple of years ago when they were hired to hack into a terrorist cell's network. Jock was a silent mastermind, stoically dismantling the cell's communications until the leader lost contact with his team. It wasn't until later that Roarke learned Jock's brother—while on deployment—had been killed by the cell. He'd shown zero emotion, and when the task was done, he'd walked away.

He knew Jock would understand why this was so important, to avenge the loss of his brother just like Jock had done. When Roarke asked the man to participate, he hadn't hesitated.

Marisol Rosa was the next to show up, the buckles on her black boots rattling as she stomped her way across the concrete floor. She blew a bubble of pink gum and popped it with a click of her teeth as she tilted her head. Her purple hair was shaved on one side and long on the other, so it draped over an eye as she took him in with purple contact-colored eyes. "What's good, Brennan?"

He could never figure out if she was coming on to him or

punking him. Gender didn't matter to Marisol when it came to loving and fucking, so it was anyone's guess. "Pissed off."

She grinned at him. "Wouldn't want you any other way." After winking, she sauntered over to where Jock sat. She hopped onto the desk beside his computer, where she perched with her legs swinging. "Can I touch your beard?"

He didn't acknowledge her presence. She shrugged and smacked her gum. "Guess that's a no."

Marisol was a little unpredictable, but she was loyal and crafty. She grew up in the Bronx surrounded by her Puerto Rican family, who had no idea they had a social-engineering mastermind in their midst. Marisol had an uncanny ability to ferret out information from anyone and could change her appearance and personality easily to slip into situations. Hacking wasn't just coding, it involved using people skills. The greatest security threat was human stupidity, and Marisol had a lock on finding the weakest links. That wasn't even getting into her coding skills, for which she'd served three years in the New Jersey prison system. She operated legally now, mostly, and Roarke had worked with her recently on a server's security breach. She'd outsmarted every offense the hackers had thrown at her, smiling the whole time. It was all a game to her. But it was a game she played to win.

Voices drew Roarke's attention, and he turned to see Erick trudge inside, dark circles under his eyes. He glanced at Roarke and jerked a thumb behind him. "So she wore you down, huh?"

Roarke shifted his gaze to the door as Wren walked inside. This morning, he'd wondered if he'd imagined the whole thing, the heat of her soft skin on his palm, the sound of her breath catching in her throat, the rise and fall of her chest.

This was going to be a fucking disaster. He wasn't impartial with Wren. She was a wild card he couldn't control, and he couldn't keep a handle on the emotions surging through his blood.

And of course, she was looking as hot as ever. She wore tight jeans, a blue shirt that hugged her curves, and heeled brown boots. Her hair was pulled up onto the top of her head, and her nails were tipped with hot pink polish.

Her eyes didn't leave his as she made her way to where he was standing. Roarke had to force himself not to look at her breasts, which were close to spilling out of her shirt. He swallowed and looked at a random point over her shoulder.

A wolf whistle sounded in the cavernous space, and he whipped his head around to see Marisol wiggling her eyebrows. "No one told me there'd be pretty eye candy on the team," she said.

There was a beat of silence before Wren started giggling. He narrowed his eyes at Marisol. "No fraternizing with other members of the team."

She rolled her eyes at the empty threat. "You're a buzzkill." She beckoned to Wren. "Come on over, sweet cheeks. I don't bite, and I'm really good with my hands."

Roarke dropped his chin to his chest. "Fuck me."

Wren's hand brushed his arm as she passed. When he glanced up at her, he saw the old Wren for a moment. The one with the innocent smile, who saw *him* and noticed his inner turmoil when no one else did. Then, in a moment, it was gone, lost beneath the click of her boots as she made her way over to Marisol.

He thought belatedly he should have complimented Wren. Told her she looked nice. Smelled nice. Did something new with her hair. Wasn't that how to treat women? He'd never been good at it. Lately, he relied on his tattoos and moderately attractive face to get women into bed. Wooing one? Fuck if he knew how to do that.

Wait, there'd be no wooing. None at all. He shook his head. Enough with the distractions. It was time to rally the troops.

He walked over to the table and stood at the end, drawing his laptop from his bag and placing it gently in front of him. Everyone took a seat except for Marisol, who still sat on the table, watching him.

He took a deep breath. "So—"

A door banged open, the sound like a shot, and every person in the room flinched. Roarke's heart leaped into his throat as he whirled around to see Dade swagger into the room.

Roarke's shoulders dropped in relief. It was just this fucker. He resisted punching Dade in his perfect face. "Nice of you to join us."

Dade shrugged, and as he drew closer, Roarke spotted another cut on his eyebrow. What the fuck was this guy doing? He gestured to Dade's face. "Is whatever you're doing that's making you bleed going to interfere with this mission?"

Dade leaned against the wall beside the table, purposefully not taking a seat. "Nope." His eyes scanned the table before landing on Wren, and then his lips split into a grin. "Hey there, Wren."

Marisol straightened. "Roarke said no frater—"

"Everyone just shut up, for fuck's sake," Roarke growled. "Swear to God, this is like herding cats."

"Well," Erick pointed out, "we're your cats. That you handpicked from the shelter. So that's on you. I prefer wet food by the way."

"My catnip is for medicinal purposes," Marisol piped up.

Roarke breathed in through his nose and out through his mouth before he committed multiple homicide. "All right, enough. I gotta go over why I got you all together. Some of you know the basics, and some of you know next to nothing." He glanced at Dade, who stared back impassively. "So listen the fuck up, okay?"

Roarke knew talking about this was going to be like ripping off a Band-Aid, one that took skin with it. He opened the laptop in front of him and tapped some buttons. An image projected onto the far wall. He ignored the *ooh*s and *ahh*s as he focused on a picture of the graying, skinny, sallow-skinned motherfucker who killed Flynn.

"This is Arden Saltner, owner of the computer security software company Saltner Defense. Two years ago, my brother, Flynn Brennan, decided he wanted out of hacking and was hired at SD in their research department."

He flashed the company logo. "His job was to analyze possible viruses and malware so SD could protect their clients from those threats. Everything was fine until he discovered a previously unknown zero-day vulnerability in the latest release of the QuartzSoft Operating System."

He glanced around and found most people nodding, but he needed to explain everything so there were no team members left behind. "A zero-day is a weakness that is unknown until after a product launches, which gives developers zero days to fix it." He tapped another button. "Some companies, like the developer of the operating system Flynn found, offer bounties for a zero-day. Flynn took his findings to Saltner—as he was supposed to do based on the rules in his department—who said he'd take care of it and notify QuartzSoft. This was important because this vulnerability allowed a hacker to access personal information from OS users, like credit card numbers."

He took a deep breath. "All of this we know because Flynn told Erick. The rest of what we know is based on what I pulled from Flynn's hard drive after he died." He tapped away again, pulling up several screenshots. "Flynn inquired about the result of his zero-day findings with Saltner in an e-mail dated December 18, two months before his death. The response was from Saltner himself, who said QS had been notified. A month went by, and Flynn did some checking on his own, discovering the vulnerability hadn't been fixed. He contacted a friend, Matthew Dominguez, who is an employee at QS, and he informed Flynn that QS was never told about this vulnerability. They dug deeper and found that the zero-day was being sold on the black market for three million dollars."

The room filled with whispered curses. Even Dade winced and rubbed his face with his hand. The black market for hackers was infamous. Anything and everything was up for sale—credit card information, IDs, and zero-day vulnerabilities that even a low-level hacker could exploit for financial gain.

Jock spoke up, his voice gruff. "So Saltner put the zero-day up for sale rather than taking it to QuartzSoft and collecting their paltry bounty."

"QS offers like...maybe five figures for their zero-days," Erick said.

He pulled up a picture of a young man with glasses. "That's Matthew Dominguez. During his last conversation with Flynn, my brother informed him that the seller was Saltner. Their code name for Saltner was Evelyn, after the Angelina Jolie character in *Salt*."

Roarke pressed another button, swallowing around the lump in his throat and breathing through the tightness in his chest. The images on the wall went dark. "That was the last communication from either of them. Three hours later, Matthew was killed in a single-car crash. And approximately six hours after that, Flynn was found with a bullet in his head."

Marisol shook her head while Dade stared at the blank wall. Wren was crying silently, her shoulders shaking. Erick stood behind her, biting his lip while rubbing her shoulder. And Jock looked... Well, his face never really changed, but there was something like anger simmering beneath his tanned complexion.

Roarke wanted to take his computer and throw it against the wall. Instead he quickly deleted the files permanently from his hard drive.

He took a minute to get himself under control while his team processed this information. Then he raised his head and spoke around gritted teeth. "I brought you all together because you are the most talented hackers I know. Whether I trust you with my life"—he glanced at Dade, who kicked up his lips into a smirk—"is another story, but it doesn't matter, because I trust you with code. When I recruited you to this team, you all agreed you wanted revenge for Flynn, and that's what we're doing.

"The mission is twofold. First, we need to find out if the zero-day sold, because if it has, we have a lot of vulnerable people. Then we get dirt on Saltner and take him down." Just saying the guy's name tightened Roarke's chest. "This is dangerous, possibly deadly, and I understand if you want to walk out that door right now. This is your chance, no judgment, to back out and go on with your life."

He closed his eyes slowly and opened them to level a look at Wren. Part of him wanted her to stand up and walk out. She didn't have to get in deeper with Darren. This could all go away for her. She could be safe.

But the other part of him, the part he wished he could delete off his hard drive, was the bit of him that wanted her to stay because, now that she was back in his life, he didn't want to let her go.

She met his gaze steadily, and he wondered if she could see his emotions swirling in his head like a two-toned tornado. Her eyes were dry now, staring back at him with that same defiance she'd shown in the parking lot. She stood up, jerked her chin into the air, and mashed a fist into the table. "I'm in for Flynn."

His emotions warred in his heart—having Wren stand up for Flynn was a beautiful thing to see, but knowing this would put her at risk made him want to slam his head into a brick wall. Instead, he nodded at her, and she nodded back, flashing him a brief smile.

One by one, the rest of the team stood up, echoing her and saying, "I'm in for Flynn."

Dade hadn't moved from where he stood, still staring at that spot on the wall where Roarke had projected images to plead his case.

As his team waited silently in the underground room, their fists on the table and their words reverberating off the bare walls, Dade strode over to the table. He licked his lips and brought his fist onto the table with a crash. "In for Flynn, too. So when can we get this motherfucker?"

Roarke smiled.

* * *

Gathering the team was the easy part. Formulating a plan? Not easy.

It really was like herding cats. Roarke hadn't chosen the team members for their cooperation skills. Hackers were notoriously solitary, egotistical, and resistant to authority. He quickly reworked his leadership strategy because lording over them like a master coder was only going to piss them all off.

He had a tentative plan to reach Saltner, but the inclusion of Wren made their job easier, as much as he didn't want to admit it.

"So lemme get this straight," Marisol said, tapping her long nails on the table where they all sat. "Pretty bird here is our foot soldier. She's gonna peddle her ass to Darren—"

"There'll be no ass peddling," Roarke growled.

Marisol lifted her eyebrows but kept talking. "And get dirt to use against Saltner."

Erick cleared his throat. "We want to ruin the fucker. Wren getting in with the family will give us access to information we can't get remotely."

Roarke watched Wren carefully, scanning her body for any sign of nerves. When he saw her fingers shake a little before she clasped them and shoved them into her lap, he was relieved. Nerves were good; it meant she understood what this meant, that it wasn't some game.

It still didn't ease his conscience over her being involved though.

Dade leaned back in his chair and laced his hands behind his head. "Is the ultimate goal to make Saltner disappear or to turn him over to the police?"

"Police," Roarke said quickly. "As much as I want to tie cement blocks around his ankles and throw him in the middle of the fucking Atlantic, I care more about watching him go down for a computer crime or homicide."

"So we're going to gather information on him, showing he committed a crime, and hand it over to the police?"

"That's the plan." Dade knew of Roarke's refusal to kill anyone. Roarke had been close once, so close to doing it, and he wondered all the time whether he would have regretted it if Mother Nature hadn't take care of it for him first.

Dade narrowed his eyes. "You're willing to trust the justice system to get revenge for your brother?"

Roarke clenched his teeth. After what he'd done in his teens, he'd vowed to be as lawful as possible. Killing Saltner was pretty far off that vow. "I have to. I just have to."

Dade was silent for a long moment. "And what if we can't pin anything on him?"

Roarke rapped his knuckles on the table. He'd deal with his morals if that was the only way they could take Saltner. "Then we figure something else out."

Dade smiled, his evil grin sending chills down Roarke's spine.

Marisol was watching Dade with raised eyebrows. "Well, aren't you a scary mofo."

Dade blew her a kiss, and Marisol ran her tongue over her lip seductively.

"Christ," Roarke said. "You all need to get laid, then come back. The hormones in here are making me antsy."

"You're just mad Korean Princess over there has a date with your sworn enemy." Marisol looked at her nails, refusing to make eye contact.

"Okaaaay," Erick interrupted, which was good, because Roarke wanted to throttle Marisol with his bare hands. "Let's all go home, get some rest, and come back tomorrow same time."

Jock was the first to get up, probably over the shit show that was forcing him to be around people. Marisol shrugged and hopped off the table, linking arms with Wren as they walked to the door. Wren glanced back at Roarke, but he couldn't read her face, and within seconds she was out the door.

He blew out a breath and tugged on his hair. Across the table, Dade was watching him intently. "This could be bigger than Saltner, you know."

Roarke nodded. "I realize that."

Dade opened his mouth like he was going to say more but then closed it. "All right then."

"I don't have the answers. And I don't even have a solid plan," Roarke said. "I know that's fucked up, but Flynn is dead, I have a trail, and I'm going to fucking follow it until I can't anymore."

Dade chewed his lip before standing. "I understand. See you tomorrow." He nodded at Erick before opening the door and letting it slam shut behind him.

Roarke steepled his fingers and squinted at his best friend. "Why do I have this sinking feeling in my stomach?"

Erick kicked a chair leg in front of him. "Because this is a clusterfuck."

"You were supposed to say, 'Gee, Roarke, this is all going according to plan.'"

Erick snorted and glanced up, blinking through his bangs. "You know I'm not happy about this Wren thing either, right?"

"I know."

"But this is her choice."

"I know that, too."

Erick was quiet for a moment. "We can protect her. But I think…she's gotta do this. For herself. No matter the outcome."

Nothing made Roarke as bitter as when he wasn't in the

know. “What exactly has happened with Wren the past ten years?”

Erick eyed him. “Man, that’s her business.”

Right, and so it wasn’t Roarke’s.

“Look, we have a good team.” Erick said the words like he was trying to convince both of them. “A team and an underground bunker. What else do we need, really?”

Roarke leveled Erick with a glare. “A well-developed plan would be nice.”

Erick’s lips shifted to the side. “Oh yeah, well, that.”

CHAPTER FOUR

WREN didn't have a chance to call Darren.

He called her first.

She didn't ask how he got her number, but any decent hacker could have found a cell for Lacy. The apartment bills were all in her alias's name. Still, it creeped her out.

Darren's voice was slick as oil, and just as greasy, dirty, and stained with blood. "We were interrupted last night."

"That was your fault, not mine." Coy was not her default, and just playing the part made her a little nauseous.

"I'm sorry about that, Angel."

Oh fuck, he had a pet name for her. Bile rose in her throat. "It's okay. I'm sure you'll make up for it." Ugh, she was baiting him now. She needed to make sure she kept her wits about her when she was with him. She had a job to do. She wasn't a distraction, she was an information extractor.

He laughed. "Oh, I will. We have reservations at Belview for Saturday."

Belview was a fine-dining restaurant his father owned. Interesting… "That sounds lovely."

"I'll pick you up at eight."

"I'll be ready."

"Oh, and Angel?"

"Yes."

"I like you in red." Then he hung up.

She gagged and clutched the phone until the edges dug into her palms. Catching the eye of Darren Saltner was both the best and worst thing that had ever happened to her.

She'd have to think of a way to keep Darren's hands off her. She'd do her job, but she sure as hell didn't want to sleep with Darren. If it came down to that...she shuddered. She'd deal with it when the time came. That was just another reason to stay away from Roarke. This job could potentially ruin them before they ever began.

Wren inhaled deeply. She could deal with Darren. Dade had trained her and trained her well. He'd also never once hit on her, so it was clear his flirty greeting was just to rile Roarke. She'd have to talk to Dade about that, because he actually listened to her. Sometimes. Maybe because she knew more about him than most people.

Even when she thought ahead, trying to picture how this would all shake out on the other side, there were too many variables, too many things that could go wrong or be altered permanently. So she couldn't console herself with promising to pursue anything with Roarke when this mission was over. Depending on how deep this went, this mission might never be over.

She had to deal with a slimeball, yet it was the one thing that finally forced Roarke to notice her.

Her leg still tingled from Roarke's touch.

But dwelling on the way her body responded to Roarke's proximity was not something she had time for as she sat in a secluded corner of a coffee shop. She eyed her lukewarm chai latte on the table in front of her and considered asking the barista to warm it up for the third time. But it was nearly closing time so she decided against it. She settled back into the frayed recliner, laptop on her crossed legs.

After the meeting that morning, she'd returned to her apartment in Mount Pleasant to get out of the clothes she'd worn earlier. The clothes she'd slipped into while thinking of Roarke—she smiled remembering the way his eyes had dipped to her cleavage before darting away—but now she pulled her hair into a knot on the top of her head and changed into a pair of high-top sneakers, gray sweatpants, and a white tank top.

She'd thought about going to her brother's place, because he'd always been a source of comfort to her. But all these years of keeping secrets—while he lived as a hacking consultant—had strained their relationship.

Their parents were loving but often stifling, as first-generation Korean Americans often were. They still lived in Pennsylvania, where they'd all grown up. Her parents had been ecstatic when she graduated college and began to travel the world. They proudly displayed all her magazine articles and told their friends her byline proved she was famous. They had no idea she had an alter ego named Seocheon and that she could write code disabling their house alarm in under an hour. Or what had happened to her and Fiona. The only reason she'd been able to finish college was because on paper, as Wren Lee, she wanted everyone to think she was moving on with her life. But she hadn't done that at all.

Her parents were still pushing her to get married, to settle down with a nice man and have a family. At one time, she'd wanted that. Roarke had been a teen crush she'd been determined to get over. Her plan was to find a great guy on the debate team or something in college. Then shit went south and that dream went out the window. Now she didn't even want a nice boy. She wanted a man with an edge, with tattooed fingers and a scowl. And there she went again, pining for goddamn Roarke Brennan. She wished she could want it, that she could settle down near her parents and be the good Korean daughter. But she didn't want that and her parents were impressed enough with her successful fake career to support her and not nag about settling down. Still, she missed them so much, and if she could ever put all this behind her, she'd return to be the daughter they'd always wanted. They'd liked Roarke as Erick's friend. They'd invited him into their home, fed him, treated him like family. But if she announced she was actually dating Roarke? Hoo boy.

She focused back on her laptop in front of her. For the last couple of hours, she'd been trolling a secret forum for DC clubs, where posters talked about everything from where to buy drugs and sex to which bouncers allowed underage patrons—mostly girls. Her skin crawled, but with a few choice questions, she'd learned all about the rumors surrounding Alpha. Except there was one password-protected subforum she couldn't get into. She had bided her time because she hadn't wanted to draw attention to herself and after a while had messaged the admins, who hadn't responded. She'd found no vulnerabilities to break into the subforum and was frustrated as hell. She suspected that was where she'd learn more about Darren's involvement in Fiona's situation.

A private message flashed on her screen from user yoman, and she clicked to read it.

new here?

For real? Like she had time to flirt. If he sent her a dick pic, she was going to blow up his hard drive with the worst virus she could find.

Nah, she typed back. He could see she'd joined a couple of months ago.

What you looking for

That's my business

Ah but, my business is your business, little bird.

She jerked her head up, glancing around the coffee shop, looking for a tattooed man with a deep scowl. And yep, there Roarke was, leaning against the wall near the door, the light from his phone illuminating his light hazel eyes.

"Motherfucker," she whispered to herself.

She signed out of the forum and slammed her laptop shut. Her latte was cold now, but she took a sip anyway so she could glare at him over the cardboard rim. The only other people in the coffee shop were the barista and a teenage couple.

He strode toward her, lips pulled down in a disapproving frown. She wondered how he didn't attract attention wherever he went. He didn't—he had a way of blending in—and it baffled her. She could never take her eyes off him. Even when she was irritated. Like now.

She kept her face fixed in a glare. "Do you have a fucking tracker on me?"

He clenched his jaw, his nostrils flaring as he muttered seemingly to himself. "I normally have perfectly healthy blood pressure."

She had no idea what that had to do with anything. "Well, good freaking for you. That doesn't answer why you're following me."

"I'm not following you—" His words cut out with a frustrated growl. He sank down onto the couch across from her and ran his hands through his hair. The dark strands were a mess, like he'd been doing that all night. Then his eyes pierced hers. "I've been watching the Saltners since Flynn was hired. Nothing happens in that forum without me noticing. And I noticed you."

His confidence was arousing and infuriating at the same time. She could play dumb like she didn't know what he was talking about, but that was a waste of time. "Is this where you lecture me? Tell me I gave myself away? I'd love to hear your wisdom, Mr. Brennan."

His lips stretched into something like a smile. "I recognize that as sarcasm."

"You're astute."

"But I'm going to give you advice anyway."

"Of course you are."

He gave her an actual smile then, and she swore his eyes sparked with amusement, an emotion she didn't think Roarke was capable of having, at least not in her presence. "Your character was good. You came in as an interested rich boy socialite, but your questions were a little too smart. Should have talked about yourself more. Been a bit more narcissistic."

She pressed her lips shut because that was good advice.

"Your brother and Marisol are the best social engineers on the team although, I have to admit, you're better than I thought you'd be."

"That's called a backhanded compliment, Roarke."

He laughed, a nice sound. A rare sound. Especially after the day they'd had.

"I thought you were at Erick's?" she asked.

"I was. Left after I got a notification you were active in the forum."

"How'd you know it was me?"

"I'd been watching the account. Didn't make the connection until tonight." He shrugged. "Hunch. Intuition. Whatever."

"Have you made it into that private room yet?"

He shook his head. "Been working on it."

"I can try, too—"

"You have a big enough job already." His expression darkened.

"Yeah...about that." She cleared her throat. "I have a date."

He flinched, and his eyes hardened. "When?"

"He didn't waste time. Called me tonight. Dinner at Belview on Saturday at eight."

Roarke snatched her latte and took a big gulp. He grimaced as he set it down. "What the fuck is that?"

"A chai latte that was hot about an hour ago."

"Tastes like Christmas and grass. And I fucking hate Christmas." He wiped his mouth with the back of his hand. "Anyway, a date on Saturday gives us a week to prepare."

"You don't—"

"If you think I'm just sending you off with that body in a tight dress and no protection, then you're fucking dreaming."

There he went again with his *this is how it's gonna be* tone. He was getting on her last nerve. Had he always been like that? "Fine."

"Fine," he spat back.

She rose from her seat and stomped toward the bathroom. Her heart was fluttering in her chest, a warning drumbeat of anxiety. After she did her business and washed her hands, she tried to fix her messy hair in the mirror. She agreed she needed protection, but around alpha Roarke, she could barely get a word in. Didn't he understand she was a member of this team, too? If she was putting her neck on the line, she wanted a say in the plans.

When she returned from the bathroom, Roarke had two

cups sitting on the table between them, steam rising from the top. He gestured to the one in front of her as she sat down, his expression slightly contrite. "Got you a new shy thing."

"Chai."

"Yeah, that."

She picked it up, accepting it as the peace offering it was. "Thank you." While she took a sip of the hot brew, her anger still lingered below the surface. She refused to make eye contact with him until she was sure she could keep from snapping at him.

Finally he reached out and lightly fingered an errant strand of hair that had escaped from her messy bun. "I like the hair," he murmured softly.

She closed her eyes for a moment, remembering how sick she felt when Darren touched her hair, compared to how soothing Roarke's touch was. She slowly lifted her gaze to his. "Thanks."

"The color is pretty." It was obvious he didn't compliment people much, because his voice balanced precariously along the words like they were wire thin. "And the sleeves." He pointed to her arms. "Looks good on you."

She shifted her biceps, and a riot of color rippled over her skin. "I worked at a tattoo parlor for a while. You know how addictive they can be."

He laughed softly. "Ink gets in the blood." He set his coffee down in front of him and rubbed his hands together between his knees. "Look, I know I'm not adjusting well, and I'm sorry for that."

Shocked by his admission, she took a minute to consider how to answer. She didn't want him to get defensive or lash out. "It's not about that. You interrupt me whenever I'm trying to talk. This is a team, and I know you're the leader, but hear me out sometimes. I know how to handle shit or I never would have stepped foot in Alpha."

He was watching her, those unusual hazel eyes thoughtful. "You're right."

She wanted to cheer because he admitted it, but she played it cool. "I know I forced my way into this. But I want to help, and I'm capable. I'm not a teenager anymore."

He nodded, his gaze dropping, and picked up his coffee again, draining it. "Things were a little simpler when I last saw you."

"When my parents tried to force-feed you kimchi?"

Roarke huffed a laugh. "Can't eat it anywhere else. Nowhere compares to the Lee house in Erie."

She grinned. "You're right about that."

His tattooed fingers clenched where they rested on his thigh while he held his empty coffee cup with his other hand. From her view, all she could read was ME OVER. She knew what they said though; he'd had those tattooed the day he graduated high school. "High school seems forever ago."

"It seems like a *lifetime* ago."

"Yeah, back when I dated dumb boys who were cheating jerks. I still can't believe Brandon got caught looking at porn in school. What a moron."

Roarke avoided her eyes with an odd smirk on his face.

She squinted at him. "What's that look for?"

He snorted and glanced down at his knuckles. "Nothing."

In high school, she would have let him fall silent. But not anymore. She slid off her chair and kneeled on the couch next to him. He stared straight ahead. With careful hands, she cupped his chin and turned his head to face her. His eyes went wide for a split second, and she thought belatedly that this was one of the few times she'd ever touched him. “Tell me why you have that look on your face.” As soon as the words were out of her mouth, a thought hit her. She flexed her fingers against his stubbled jaw. “Wait, did you...? Roarke, did you have something to do with that?”

He parted his full lips and tried to duck his head, but she held on and pressed closer until his biceps nudged her breasts through her thin tank top. “Roarke—”

“I planted ’em.” His voice was low and quiet, and for a moment, she thought he was angry. She dropped her hand from his chin as his mouth stretched into an evil grin. “Motherfucker cheated on you. Wren Lee. Hottest girl in school and too damn good for him. Brandon knew it, too, fake-ass lowlife.” Roarke shrugged. “I know it was a shit thing to do to him, but I was eighteen and pissed.”

Her mind whirled as she tried to process this information. Roarke had defended her honor in the modern era—with hacking rather than a duel. He was not a fighter, or a talker. But he could do some serious damage with a keyboard. Her heart kicked up a faster beat in her chest as she thought about what this meant. “You did that. For me.”

Roarke didn’t look away this time. He held her gaze. “Yeah. I did. He hurt you. That wasn’t okay with me. He had to pay for it.”

“But I thought...” She chewed the inside of her cheek as she mulled her words. “I thought you didn’t really notice me then. Or care.”

There was a pause, a beat of frozen time between them, during which Roarke seemed to weigh his next move. Then he surged toward her, his arms caging her in. His body loomed closer, and she had to lean back on her heels to prevent their faces from crashing. He wasn’t aloof now, not this Roarke. This one was in her face and meant business. It might have been because of the adrenaline of their mission or because he was no longer a kid. Either way, she didn't care, because every word coming out of his mouth was a shock to her system.

"I cared, Wren. Every day, all the time. I *still* fucking care. I told myself I wouldn't..." He blew out a harsh breath, pupils dilating. "Fuck it. This is why it kills me to see you involved in this, because all I wanna do is see you safe. I cared back then when you were young, and I still care now that you're back, all woman and hot as fuck and still so goddamn untouchable."

Her entire body awoke from a ten-year slumber at his words, arousal pooling in her gut, heat spreading to every limb. How long had he kept this to himself? Had he told anyone? Her mind was spinning, and she wondered if she should be angry that he'd waited this long to tell her. And how was she *untouchable*? He'd touched her last night. "Roarke," she rasped.

"How do you do this to me?" His tone held a bit of wonder. "You're back for one day, and I've already spilled my secrets."

She inhaled sharply. "If we're sharing confessions, then you should know I care, too. I've cared ever since the day you walked into my house, all pissed off and angry at the world."

"I should regret telling you this, but I don't." He swallowed, and his voice dropped to a whisper. "I think my biggest regret would be walking out of here without knowing how you taste."

The desire for his kiss had been constant since last night. Her lips were moving before her brain gave a command. "Then find out."

His nose brushed hers, and she gripped his face, her fingers sliding into the thick hair at his temples. There was a brief pause as his eyes locked on hers and he was moving closer. Her tongue snaked out, wetting her lips, wanting his kiss so badly that she thought she'd combust.

"This is a bad idea," he whispered.

"Good ideas are never fun," she whispered back.

She let her eyes fall shut as they both closed the distance.

"Closing in five minutes, kids!" the barista called out.

Wren's eyes snapped open. Roarke was on his feet so fast that she pitched forward and had to catch herself with her hands in front of her. She scrambled off the couch as Roarke stood with his back to her, hands gripping his hair.

The teenage couple in the corner were gathering their things, and the barista was chatting with them. Wren blinked, trying to come back to earth, because holy hell, she'd been in the clouds with Roarke's big body on top of her.

The barista turned to them, and Roarke cleared his throat. "Sorry, just leaving."

"No problem! I'll close up after you." The barista was being friendly, but she clearly wanted them to get the hell out.

Roarke did, too, apparently. He was backing away from her toward the door. The distance grew between them, like every one of his steps was a mile long. "Didn't realize the time."

Wren busied herself putting her laptop away in her bag. "Me either."

"Do you need a ride?"

"I have my bike." His reaction was pissing her off, like they were high schoolers caught dancing too close at homecoming.

He nodded, and with a jerk of his head and a short "See you soon," he was out the door.

Yeah, her feelings were hurt. They'd just had a goddamn moment when real shit had been shared, and now he acted like she was fucking poisonous. What was he afraid of?

When she strode to her bike, a movement by a nearby building caught her eye. The sound of a Mustang engine roaring to life as she reached her bike assured her that Roarke had been watching. The sentiment was nice, as was the chai latte and the unsolicited advice. But it didn't make up for the almost-kiss and run.

As she gunned her bike out of the parking lot, she vowed never to put herself in that position with Roarke Brennan again. No matter how much her heart wanted to. Too bad she couldn't recode that soft thing.

* * *

Roarke turned the radio louder and gripped the steering wheel tighter as he sped away from the coffee shop. If he kept doing this hot and cold cycle with Wren, it would only make everything worse when this whole mission ended and they inevitably crashed and burned. After Flynn died, he wasn't sure he'd be okay. At all. Every loss in Roarke's life took a chunk out of him that didn't regrow. Right now, he was fueled by revenge, but when this was over and all he had was his memories of Flynn and the faded recollections of his parents... Well, he wasn't sure what kind of man he'd be. He wouldn't be the kind of guy who had any business being with Wren. How could he give her the love she deserved when he wasn't sure he had any of those... loving parts of him left?

He knew this wasn't fair, but part of him was angry at Wren. Why hadn't she slapped him? Told him to fuck off? She had no problem telling him where his leadership skills were lacking so why was she letting him be an asshole personally? She'd treated him well when they were kids, but he'd never thought it was anything beyond admiration. There was nothing admiring and innocent in the way she looked at him now. The way the blush rose up her chest as he drew close, proving to him this attraction was a two-way street.

And there was Erick to think about. The man had always been protective of his sister, but he also respected her decisions. And while Erick was his best friend, he didn't quite know everything about Roarke, about the yawning nothingness he'd felt since Flynn died. It wasn't Erick's approval that was holding Roarke back from Wren. He was holding himself back.

He couldn't dwell on this though, not while Arden Saltner was still free to do what he wanted with Flynn's blood on his hands. Roarke had poured over Arden's credit card receipts, and he knew he'd be at the country club tonight, enjoying a gin and tonic, red-faced and jolly in a pair of pleated khakis and a pastel polo.

He hated that old fuck.

Getting close to his targets was not something Roarke did—he was a hacker for a reason. He didn't brawl, and while he owned some guns for protection, he preferred not to use them. This job was personal though, and he didn't hate the idea of looking Arden in the eye when he took him down.

Roarke parked his car in his garage and unlocked the door to his apartment. Once inside, he went right to his work station, which was tucked into the corner near the bed. His desk was six feet long, topped with three keyboards, four monitors, and two laptops. Underneath hummed four towers.

He didn't actually work at his desk though—it was

mostly for storage. In the corner, he had an orange beanbag chair. It was dingy from traveling with him since high school, and he'd patched the thing about five times. Even now, there was a small rip in one corner and a couple of white beads littered the floor. But it was where he did his best work. Erick laughed at him, said he looked like a tattooed kid as he sat on it and typed away. Whatever, man. Some artists painted naked. Roarke's art was done in his beanbag chair.

After stripping off his shirt, he sank down onto the beanbag chair with his primary laptop. After he opened it, he went right to his music, where he scrolled through a series of movie soundtracks. He needed background noise when he worked, and the flowing instrumentals worked perfectly. Once he had the *Inception* soundtrack going, he was in the zone. He pulled up the file he had on Darren and squinted at it. If Wren was going to put herself on the line with him, he wanted to make sure it would be worth it.

Publicly, Arden was squeaky clean. And so was Darren, even though rumors had been floating around for years. If Arden had wanted to get rid of someone, Roarke was pretty sure he'd call in his baby boy to help.

Darren's payroll was what interested Roarke the most. He'd hacked into his bookkeeper records weeks ago and now pulled up the file to look through again. Darren employed an exorbitant number of bouncers. Roarke had studied their shifts, and there were names on the payroll that were never actually on the bouncer rotation.

Roarke hadn't gone into the club, worried his Brennan features would be recognizable. He could ask Wren if she'd noticed anything unusual about the bouncers. His suspicion was that these guys did much more than a typical club bouncer did.

Bodyguards? Shakedown guys? Drug dealers? Worst of all…hit men? He didn't know what Arden was involved in that he needed to kill Flynn to keep quiet, but he imagined it was pretty big.

There had to be a connection. And if Wren could get Darren talking, then they'd know.

Roarke's stomach churned. He set his laptop on the floor and rubbed his eyes. He rose to his feet, stretched, and grabbed a Diet Coke out of his fridge. This carbonated shit was going to kill him if he didn't kill himself first, but he was addicted. Erick said he could have worse addictions.

After chugging the entire can, crushing it, and tossing it in the bin with an embarrassing amount of identical cans, he stripped off the rest of his clothes on the way to the bathroom.

He didn't bother looking at himself in the mirror as he walked past, because he probably looked like shit—bloodshot eyes, permanent scowl lines, and hair grooved from running his fingers through it. He turned the water to a scalding level and stepped inside his shower.

For a long while, he stood with his hand braced on the wall, letting the water pelt his head and upper back. The heat slowly loosened the tension in his back. After he washed his hair, he closed his eyes, needing to forget about this mission, about Flynn, about everything really. But he couldn't let his mind go blank. When he tried, he saw Wren.

The teenage crush was nothing compared to how badly he desired her now. Then, he'd wanted to hold her hand, kiss her, talk to her. He wanted to do all those things now, but he also wanted to press her up against the wall with her legs clamped around his waist. He wanted to hear her moans when he licked down her neck, and he wanted to know what color her nipples were after he finished sucking on them.

He wanted her to say his name when he was inside her.

Roarke trailed a hand down his chest, over his abs, until he reached his groin. He was hard just from imagining an orgasming Wren in his brain. He could still feel the heat of her on his hand when he had it tucked between her thighs. Her lips had been parted, watching him with those big, dark, liquid eyes.

He closed his fist around his dick and stroked, a moan escaping his lips as he grew harder. He braced his legs. If he finished this now, let this fantasy go, then maybe once his balls were empty his mind would be, too. He felt dirty as fuck, but he let the image play out in his head. Wren in the backseat of his car, her dress hiked up to her waist while he buried his head between her legs. Wren on all fours in his bed, watching him over her shoulder with a wicked grin while he closed his hands over her hips.

He stroked himself harder, twisting his hand at the top, his legs trembling as he panted his way toward release.

Wren sitting on his computer desk, her head thrown back in laughter, as he entered her. Imagining her tightness around his dick was all he needed to shoot all over the wall of his shower with a hoarse cry.

He thunked his head on the wall as he rode it out, until his brain was fuzzed, until the water ran cold. With a slam of his palm, he turned the shower off. He'd effectively cleared his head because the only thing he had the energy to do was dry off haphazardly with a towel and crawl under his covers.

Work started tomorrow. He had a crew to manage, a woman to protect, and a man to ruin.

CHAPTER FIVE

SPRING had settled in DC, which meant the weather waffled between rainy and sunny days. Roarke drove with the windows down in his Mustang, large sunglasses shielding his eyes from the setting sun. It was the first time he'd been outside all day, and his aching back was proof he'd been leaning over his computer for far too long. The only reason he was leaving was because Erick had called him and told him to get his ass over to Erick's apartment.

Roarke hadn't wanted to see his friend until he had his head straight about Wren, but he decided he'd never have his head straight about her. If this was going to work, he needed to keep his mind focused on the mission. No more staring at Wren's lips or admiring the swing of her hips when she walked. No more trying to catch a glimpse of her smile.

He parked and took the steps two at a time to Erick's third-story apartment.

The door opened before he could knock, and Erick ushered him. "Hey man."

Roarke shut the door behind him and tossed his coat on top of a pile of papers on Erick's kitchen table. "Hey, how's it going?"

Erick was already back on the couch, his laptop open in front of him. "I ordered some sushi."

"There a reason you needed me here?"

Erick shrugged. "I wanted some company."

"You acted like I needed to be here for some reason."

Erick grinned. "Me wanting a dining companion wasn't a good reason?"

Roarke groaned and sank down onto a recliner.

"Also," Erick added, "I know you were in deep and hadn't eaten all day except for a six-pack of Diet Cokes."

Roarke didn't answer. Erick was right.

"You probably worked out, too. Sustained by Diet Coke."

He was right about that, too. Roarke had a weight bench in the corner of his apartment, and it was the greatest source of his stress relief.

"And your silence is acquiescence, so good thing you have friends like me who make you eat actual food."

Roarke grunted.

Erick smirked and went back to typing. Roarke's laptop was in his book bag at his feet, but he didn't take it out.

He'd avoided thinking about Wren most of the day, since he'd been knee deep in Darren's life, but he knew that Wren and Marisol were off dress shopping for Wren's date. The thought of her in danger made his fingers curl into fists. He had to remind himself that, if she had learned from Dade, she'd learned from the best.

"Did you know she's been working with Dade?" Roarke was putting Erick on the spot, but he didn't give a fuck. Wren had been back in town for two days, and he was already consumed with her whereabouts and past.

Erick's head was bent as he tapped away at his keyboard. He shot a quick look of disinterest at Roarke before focusing again on his task. The zero-day was no longer for sale, but they didn't know if Saltner pulled it or it sold. They'd been spending every spare minute digging up information and getting in touch with their contacts. No one was talking. It was like the zero-day had never been on the market in the first place. Last night, Roarke had sacrificed sleep for work and had finally given up only to get about two hours of restless shut-eye.

So now he was here, sneering and cranky while his friend was trying to work. He was a horrible person.

"I learned when you did," Erick said without looking at him.

Roarke waited, but Erick apparently didn't plan to elaborate. "And do you have a reaction to that?" he asked.

Erick shrugged. Roarke seethed. Rather than sitting on Erick's couch and stewing over shit he couldn't control, he pulled his laptop out of his bag and opened it up. He was about to resume his research on Saltner when there was a knock at Erick's door, followed by Jock's deep voice. "It's me."

Erick was deep in concentration, so Roarke let the big guy inside. Jock strode in wearing a pair of camo pants, boots, and a tight T-shirt, which seriously tested the elasticity of Hanes black cotton. In his massive hand, he held a bright pink shopping bag by its black strings. The outside said Fetterman's Jewelers in a script font.

Roarke raised an eyebrow at him. "The bag kinda defeats the purpose of wearing camo."

Jock didn't even bother to reply. He shoved aside the black tissue paper inside and pulled out a long box. "Wanted to get your approval of my work."

Roarke took the black box from him with a grin. "Aw, for me?"

"Just open it," Jock growled. Erick joined Roarke's side, his eyes on the box and his hands on his hips.

Roarke pulled the top off to reveal five tiny strings of diamonds, all connected into a solid band. It looked too long to be a bracelet. He touched it, and the stones sparkled from the overhead light in Erick's foyer.

Jock pointed at it with a thick finger. "It's a ch…" His brow furrowed, and he rubbed his forehead. "Shit, it's a type of necklace, and now I can't fucking remember what Marisol called it."

"Choker?" Erick offered.

Jock snapped his fingers. "That's it. Fucking odd name for a necklace. Anyway, I installed the camera for Wren's date. Wanted to see what you thought."

Roarke had known the women were to meet up with Jock after shopping to discuss where to hide a camera. Holding the necklace in his hand made his heart thump loudly in his chest. This was actually happening—they were sending Wren to the wolves in only a dress and a choker.

He unclipped the necklace from one side of the box and wiggled his fingers so the light caught on the stones. It was heavier than he thought it'd be, and his breath caught, imagining how beautiful it would look on Wren's tawny skin, the way the stones and metal would warm with her body heat, and the way it would shift when she turned her head.

But she'd be wearing this while dining with another man. He clenched his jaw at the thought and flipped over the necklace to reveal the back. The only indication it had been altered was a very small square of black metal hiding the circuitry on the back.

Jock cleared his throat. "The camera is positioned between the diamonds. I clipped it around my wrist, and it was undetectable."

Roarke wanted to see for himself. “Marisol gave this to you?”

Jock nodded. “They went shopping today. Got Wren stuff for her date, then they dropped this off for me.”

“They paid for this with the money I gave to Marisol, right?” Roarke inquired.

“Assume so, didn’t ask.”

“I’ll check,” Erick said, pulling out his phone.

Roarke wrapped the necklace around his wrist and held it up, rotating it this way and that, but sure enough, the circuitry at the back of the necklace wasn’t visible, and neither was the camera.

He placed it back in the box and put the lid on. “That’s great work, Jock. Impressive.”

He thought the man would preen, but instead, he only nodded and dropped the box back inside the bag. His gaze drifted to the coffee table, where their laptops sat open. “Need some help?”

“I think we’re about to take a break,” Erick said. “I ordered enough sushi for an army, and it’ll be here soon if you want to stay.”

Jock dropped the bag by the door and made himself at home on the couch. “Sure.”

While they waited for the food to arrive, Erick tapped away at his phone. “Wren said they used the money you gave them. And she said thank you.”

Roarke was spending a lot of money to fund this entire operation, and for the first time, he was a little bitter about it. The dress Wren bought had been demanded of her by another man. The Wren who was quick to point out to him that this was her life, and he couldn’t control her.

Now that another man was stifling her independence, that wasn’t okay with Roarke. Nope, not at all. His Wren was a free bird, and it was going to kill him to see her bow to appease Darren. He still didn't know how she felt about being told what to do, but this only made Roarke more determined to keep her as safe as possible while still respecting her privacy. And he hoped like hell he didn't have to make a decision that made him choose between the two.

When the sushi arrived, Erick immediately shoveled shrimp tempura into his mouth and spoke around it. "I got the van. It's registered with an alias."

One of Erick's tasks had been to get a van that couldn't be traced to any of them. "Awesome. So by Saturday, we have to gut the back and get it wired to monitor the date."

"I researched the area around Belview. Found a spot we can park and not be bothered," Jock said.

Roarke was still uncomfortable as hell with the whole thing, but he was fully prepared for at least one of them to blow their covers if Wren needed help. Probably Marisol or Dade.

"What do you think she'll be able to get?" Jock said. "Like, is this going to be a thing? She gonna keep seeing this fucker until we can get intel out of him?"

Roarke didn't want to think that far ahead, but he had to. "I'm not sure. I'm willing to let Wren make that call, based on his behavior on this date. He gets too handsy and she wants to bail, then we go back to our original plan, which didn't involve Darren." But the more digging he did on the guy, the more he suspected he was involved. Wren getting in with the guy could very well be how they succeeded.

Jock's gaze shifted between Erick and Roarke as Jock chewed slowly. He shook his head as Jock dipped his fork into a hunk of wasabi, and shoved it in his mouth. He swallowed without a wince.

"Seriously?" Erick said. "I'm like, biologically predisposed to like spicy food, and your white ass just downed that wasabi like it was mayo. What the fuck is your esophagus lined with?"

Jock's answer was to pick up the rest of the wasabi, plus some pickled ginger, and shove it all into his mouth while watching Erick. Roarke held in a chuckle as he gulped down a tuna roll.

"Gah," Erick said, mock gagging, but Jock remained unaffected.

Jock swallowed and stuck his tongue out. "I like it. Clears out my sinuses."

"Surprised you even have sinuses," Erick muttered and went back to dipping his rolls in soy sauce. He stuck one in his mouth. "So"—he pointed his fork at Jock—"what's your stake in this? Roarke vouched for you because of a job you two did together, but I don't know you. And Flynn was my buddy, too."

Roarke was a little taken aback at Erick's tone, but then Flynn's death had affected all of them in different ways. Flynn and Erick had grown closer in the last couple of years, and Erick had a sense of possessiveness about Flynn similar to Roarke's.

"I was between jobs," Jock said. "Worked with Roarke before and I liked him. Met Flynn, too, and he was a good guy. So when Roarke asked me to help, I said sure." He dropped his fork on his empty plate. "To be clear, I know loss." His gaze flicked to Roarke, a question in the quirk of his brow, and Roarke shook his head. It wasn't his place to tell anyone about Jock's past. Jock had confided in him only after the job had been done, and they'd both been drunk as hell at the time.

Jock nodded once. "Not telling the story, so don't ask, but I lost my brother, too. So I kinda have a thing for revenge, especially when it involves family." He lifted his gaze to Erick. "That a good enough explanation for you?"

Erick didn't say anything for a moment, and Roarke was unsure if he'd take Jock's last question as a challenge. Erick swallowed his sushi roll and took a swig of his water before extending his hand. "Looking forward to taking out this murdering fuck with you, man."

Roarke breathed a sigh of relief as Jock flashed a small smile before shaking Erick's hand. "Same to you."

Roarke leaned back on the couch. "We all good now?"

"Yeah," Erick said. "I just wanted to have a word with the guy who's working to keep my sister alive."

"Hey," Roarke said, knocking his knee, "we're all working to do that."

"I know." Erick wouldn't look at him. "I know."

Erick was quiet for the rest of the night, and after Jock left, Roarke finally confronted him. "You okay? What's going on in that head of yours?"

Erick had started drinking right after they ate, and now he was on his third beer, face flushed. "I'm thinking about Wren, of course."

"Of course," Roarke said, wishing he could say he wasn't thinking of her.

"I don't know how we're going to get her out of this without the wrong people suspicious of her. She's going to have to disappear probably, for a couple of years, until some of this blows over."

Erick was right, and the possibility had been in the back of Roarke's mind. It reminded him why touching Wren—hell, why being in her presence—was bad for both of them.

Erick was clueless about Roarke's inner turmoil, and he hoped to keep it that way. "It's like, I finally got her back, and now she's going to have to vanish again. We can't risk her being tied to us."

Roarke needed to shore up his backbone and have some self-control around Wren. There was no other choice. "I know. And I don't like it any more than you do."

"We need to make sure she's thought this through. There's still time to bail—"

"She has," Roarke said with a firm voice. "I think Wren knows every consequence and is willing to risk it. For Flynn and for us."

"Can you call her?" Erick asked. "If I do it, she'll see an overprotective big brother. With you, she'll listen to reason. I'm not saying I don't support her anymore. I only want to make sure she knows what the aftermath is going to look like. And that we're okay if she decides it isn't worth it."

If only Erick knew how much Roarke had already tried to make Wren listen. This was a disaster waiting to happen. Roarke hadn't even spoken to her since last night, and he doubted she was happy with him. But now her brother was in front of him, pleading for him to talk to her, and at the same time solidifying the reasons they couldn't be together. Having any sort of future with her would jeopardize their lives. His life could fuck off, but he gave a shit about hers.

So he looked his best friend in the eye, and he said, "Yeah, I'll talk to her. Make sure she knows the consequences."

For the first time in the last couple of hours, Erick smiled. "Thanks, man."

Roarke slung back his beer, intent on getting blitzed before he had to face Wren again. He had to set a tone for how the rest of this mission went, and come hell or high water, it'd be platonic. That's what he told himself on beer five, but by his seventh, he wasn't sure of his plan at all.

CHAPTER SIX

WHEN Roarke woke up, it took him a solid ten minutes to realize the pounding in his ears was not loud bass from a car outside. He regretted drinking himself into a stupor. After he'd left Erick's place, he'd come home and drank more. This was becoming a habit and a seriously shitty way of dealing with his issues.

Now he was sitting at his kitchen counter in his boxers with a bottle of Advil, a glass of water, and his cell phone sitting in front of him. He gave himself a minute to drink his water and let the Advil work because he needed his wits about him when he called Wren. He feared it was already too late to pull her out of this mission, but the date with Darren would clinch it. After this mission was over, even the most basic research would put a spotlight on Wren as something new in Darren's life before everything went to shit.

His phone sat there silently taunting him. Why had he agreed to do this? Why was this up to him and not her brother? "Just get it the fuck over with, Roarke," he said to himself before he snatched up the phone and called her. The line rang five times before she answered. "Hello?"

Her voice sounded soft, without the hard edge she'd added to it since she'd burst back into his life.

"Hey." He rubbed his forehead and jiggled his leg, the pounding returning along with cold sweats. Great. "How are you?"

"I'm okay." Something about her quiet voice on the other line felt intimate. He should probably clear the air about what happened at the coffee shop, but what the hell did he say? Shit, he hadn't prepared to talk about that, but now that he heard the vulnerability and a bit of hurt in Wren's voice, he knew it had to be addressed.

He cleared his throat. "Wondering if you have a minute so I can talk to you about something."

"Sure, just doing my research on Darren. He's had hair transplant surgery because he was self-conscious about his receding hairline. He's also had laser hair removal on his back."

He blinked. "Wren, are you hacking his medical records?"

"I figured why not," she mumbled. "Anyway, sounds like he has a complex about hair, huh?"

In spite of how serious all this was, he had to smile. "His hair still looks like shit, and I bet he has bacne."

She laughed, and the sound of it fuzzed his head, easing his headache better than the Advil. "Well, now I need to check if he's been to the dermatologist."

Roarke tapped his finger against the side of his empty glass. "Pretty sure his bacne is not pertinent to this mission."

"Yeah, you're probably right." She actually sounded disappointed.

There was a beat of silence. This was his cue to speak up, but damn if his brain wasn't failing him. "So, how're you feeling about everything?"

There was a sound like she sucked in her breath. "Can

you narrow it down? Are you asking me how I'm feeling about Darren, this mission, or the fact that you almost kissed me and now want to pretend like it never happened?"

Welp, there it was. She was right to call him on his bullshit. Seeing as he was too weak to do it himself. "I guess we can go with door number three first."

This time she snorted and rounded it off with a growl. "Don't make me laugh when I'm mad at you!"

"I'm sorry."

"Sorry for what? Roarke, this is what I'm talking about. *Com-mun-i-cate.*" She emphasized each syllable, and if any other person had done that to him, he would have hung up on them.

She wasn't letting him off the hook at all, and his experience dealing with this kind of conversation was limited. He didn't date. If a woman ever put him on the spot like this, he would have walked. No attachments. Ever. He'd always thought it was his personality, but now he realized it was because he'd always been hooked to Wren. What a time to have this epiphany.

"Roarke?" she said, her voice rising.

He tried to talk quickly, worried that, if he slowed down, the words would dry up and he'd never get out all of what he needed to say. "I'm sorry for what happened at the coffee shop. I shouldn't have said what I did, or tried to kiss you, and I definitely shouldn't have left like I did. All of it was bad."

She didn't speak for a long moment. "Why do you think it was bad?"

"Because this can't work," he said. "If you were anyone else, I'd still be able to think clearly, be objective. But I'm already compromised as fuck when it comes to you. If I get my hands on you, then see Darren do it, I will bring this entire mission down. Do you understand what I'm saying?"

"Yes," her voice was almost a whisper.

There was something he wasn't saying that he should, he knew that for sure, but he couldn't figure it out. He glanced around his apartment, like the answers would spell themselves out on his brick walls. Then it hit him. "How, uh, do you feel?"

"I need to know first if you meant it."

"Meant what?"

"What you said at the coffee shop. That you cared then, and you care now." She paused. "And that you *wanted* to kiss me."

He closed his eyes and speared his fingers through his hair. Lying would be so much easier than telling the truth. "I meant it all."

She inhaled and exhaled slowly. "Then I'm feeling okay. Still confused about why this is all happening now rather than ten years ago."

He groaned. "Ah damn, Wren. Can we do that conversation another time? This is more talking than I've done in years."

She laughed softly. "Fine. So we have a truce?"

"Yeah. A truce." One that involved him keeping his hands to himself.

"So is there another reason you called?"

He was exhausted and hadn't even accomplished the point of this entire call. "Jock said you went shopping yesterday. I saw the work he did on your necklace, and the camera is undetectable."

She blew out a breath. "Oh great. Yeah, I got a dress and colored my roots. I'm all prepared to be his Korean Trophy Girlfriend."

Roarke cringed. "He fucking wishes."

"Well, he can keep wishing. So is that all? You just wanted to check in?" There were sounds in the background, running water and some metal clinking.

"What are you doing?"

"Making tea."

Those words took him back. Teenage him walking in on teenage Wren while she stood in her kitchen, wearing only underwear and a T-shirt. One bare foot was propped on the other as she waited for the water in her kettle to boil. She was swaying her hips to the song on the kitchen radio and didn't notice he was there. He didn't know where to look first, her purple-painted toes or her lean legs, or her cute little ass in the white briefs with small bows on the waistband. Her T-shirt was an old Nintendo one she'd found at a thrift store. Her hair had been piled up on her head, but a million strands escaped in a pretty black waterfall.

He hadn't thought about that sight in years, but as if the word *tea* was some weird code, his brain recalled it in an instant.

That might have been the moment teenage Roarke realized he had a massive, insurmountable crush on Wren Lee. She'd never even seen him because he'd slipped back out of sight silently.

"Roarke?"

Her voice brought him to the present, and he wondered what she was wearing now. Was her lavender hair up or down?

He shifted on the couch. "Uh, no, that wasn't all I wanted." He held the phone away for a moment and smacked his cheek to force himself to focus. "I wanted to make sure you understood that this mission could..." How did he word this? He didn't want her to go on the defense right away. "Could permanently affect your future."

She was quiet for a long moment, and in the background, her tea kettle whistled. Once it stopped, she spoke slowly. "I have thought about it."

She didn't elaborate, but the melancholy in her voice tugged at him. "You could still pull out. Cancel the date."

More clinking, and he pictured her stirring sugar into her tea. "I know that."

"Wren..." He closed his eyes, drawing on all the limited people skills he had. What would Flynn do? He was the empathetic one. "Talk to me. I'm not going to judge you for being scared or nervous. Hell, I'm scared and nervous."

Something clattered on her line. "Really? Because you're all business. All cold glares and gritted teeth."

He laughed. "You know me well enough to know that's what I've always shown everyone else."

"Everyone else?"

He swallowed. Tit for tat, right? He confided in her, and she confided in him. "Yeah. But you can open me up if you want to. All you'll see inside is grief and rage and a sick drive for revenge that will likely leave me gutted and empty afterward. So there you go. That's how I feel."

She was quiet for a long moment. "Oh, Roarke..."

No, no, he didn't say that to hear her soft voice say his name like that, all sympathy and longing. "Now it's your turn."

"Uh, I didn't agree to this exchange of emotional purging."

Ah, there was the attitude he loved. He smiled. "I'll get your signature beforehand next time. How about you give me this one freebie?"

She took a sip of tea, the sound of the hot liquid flowing

past her lips filling his ear. She gulped. "Okay, fine. I'm terrified. Not of Darren necessarily, but of how this mission will affect my life. I know that afterward, I'll probably have to leave. That I'll have to cut ties with Erick and . . . you . . . for years. It kills me to think about it."

"You can still—"

"No," she said firmly. "I'm committed. This means something to me, to you, to Erick. I'm committed to avenging Flynn and protecting others from Saltner. I've thought long and hard about this, I promise you, Roarke."

"If you're sure."

"We're all giving up a lot, I think," she said. "Right?"

Wren was the only woman he'd ever truly wanted. Seeing her now as a strong adult and knowing he couldn't touch her was giving up a fuck of a lot. "Yes," he answered honestly. "Sometimes it feels like too much."

They both fell silent, the air zinging with unspoken words. There'd be no future for them. Pursuing anything now would only make the time they had to be apart insufferable. He didn't know what he'd do once he got a taste of Wren. He didn't want to know what he'd be missing.

"I guess," she said slowly, "that timing will never be right for us."

There it was. The words they were both thinking. "I guess not."

He heard her swallow. "Right. Well, uh, thanks for calling. I appreciate you checking that I thought all of this through." Her voice was back to formal, and it killed him.

"Of course."

"I'll see you tomorrow."

For this fucking date. "Yep, rest up today."

Her laughter was a bit sad. "I will. Thanks again, Roarke."

"Anytime."

Once he hung up, his headache came back with a fucking vengeance. He took a minute to feel sorry for himself before picking up his phone to call Jock. The best way they could ensure this wasn't all for nothing was to keep up the work on their end. Over his dead body was Wren going to be hurt because they didn't do their jobs.

When Jock answered, Roarke started talking immediately. "I want everything on Belview. I want to know where the cameras are, and I want control of them. I want to know how many employees they have and the square footage of the place. Make a map of every inch of that restaurant. Down to how much oregano they put in their marinara and which employees are fucking in the freezer, got it?"

Jock, bless his no-bullshit heart, said, "Consider it done," before hanging up the phone.

Right, so now Roarke just had to get his shit together.

* * *

Wren walked into headquarters to the sound of clanking metal and Marisol's laughter. Her brother sat at a table with Marisol, eating Cheetos while Dade looked to be dozing in the corner. She'd come to be prepped by the team before her date that night.

A van sat at the back of the room. A nearby ramp led to a garage door that opened to street level. Roarke had wired it to open only with a special code on one remote. When the garage door closed, a corrugated steel door fell into place over it, which matched the wall of the building.

Marisol glanced up as Wren made her way over to her and snagged a Cheeto. Wren glanced around. "Where's Roarke?"

"He said he had a quick errand to do. He'll be here soon."

An errand? What, was he out of milk? Wren frowned at Erick, who shrugged. Right, this was stupid, getting her feelings hurt. Maybe this was how it was going to be the rest of the mission—Roarke avoiding her.

Erick rose to his feet, the scrape of his chair on the basement floor startling Dade awake. Erick walked over to her and, with a hand on her arm, dropped a kiss on her cheek. "Hey, Duck."

He'd called her that since they were kids, a play off her bird-related name and *ugly duckling*. But he didn't say it with the normal teasing tone that always made her smile. His voice was tinged with regret and sadness, and it seeped into her skin like poison.

Over his shoulder, Marisol had gone to go bug Dade, so they had a small moment of privacy. When she focused on her brother, he was studying her face, shoulders hunched and hands shoved in his pockets. She'd expected jokes about a date with the snake or sleeping with the enemy—his typical humor. This anxious Erick was fraying her nerves.

"Bro, you're making me nervous." She wasn't even in her dress yet. She was wearing a pair of sweats, sneakers, and an oversized T-shirt and her hair was in a ponytail. But Erick was acting like she was dressed to take a walk down death row.

"I told myself I'd hide this all well, but I guess I'm not doing a good job, huh?" He tried for a grin, but it just kinda looked like a grimace.

"No, you're freaking me out. Stop it."

"I'm sorry. I can't help that I want you to stay here and not go on this fucking date." She opened her mouth to protest, but he cut her off. "That's not what you want though. And I'm respecting that. Just know I'll be throwing up in the back of the van until you're safe." He shook his head and glanced down at his Jordans. "Already lost Flynn, and if I lost you…"

"Hey." She reached for his hand and brought it up to her cheek. "You're not going to lose me. It's just a date. You guys will see and hear everything." She touched the front of her neck, where the necklace outfitted with a camera and mic would go. "We have a plan to get me out if things go bad. But you have to trust me a little." She grinned. "I'm pretty scrappy and resourceful."

Erick's fingers curled around hers as he laughed softly. "Yeah, you are."

"Come on, brief me so I can go home and get pretty."

"Yeah, and we all know that takes forever."

She shoved him as she laughed.

He jerked his head toward the vehicle. "Come see what we did." He hopped up into the back of the van, and she followed. Jock was busy tapping away at an open laptop, big-ass body squeezed onto a little fold-out chair.

The driver and passenger seats of the van remained unchanged, but they'd torn out the entire back. Monitors lined one side. "That monitor," Erick said, pointing to one that was black, "will be your camera." He pointed to two monitors beside it. "These two will show street views outside Belview, and those three"—he pointed to three positioned vertically—"cover the entire dining area of the restaurant."

They'd had to hack the Belview security cameras plus cameras on the adjacent buildings to have access to all this. "I'm impressed."

A couple of headsets sat on shelves under the TVs, and several laptops were open on a table lining the other side of the van. Seeing all they'd done to prepare and to ensure her safety had her breathing a little easier.

"So we're wired for everything we need in here. We can hear what you hear and see what you see," Erick explained.

Jock twisted in his seat to face her. "Your primary goal is to get him to trust you. Ask him a lot of questions about himself and his family. Don't act too interested in cyber security and...sorry to say it, but play dumb about anything involving Saltner Defense."

She nodded. "Got it."

"You're a smart girl. If he starts talking about something that could give us info, ask more questions."

"'Course."

"And we talked about copying his phone files?"

"Yeah, if I can gain access to his phone, then I'll download what I can." That was for Flynn's mission *and* hers.

Jock nodded and grabbed a jewelry box off the table beside him and took off the lid. The bare bulb hanging from the ceiling in the van reflected off the diamonds of her necklace. They hadn't gone cheap, figuring someone like Darren could spot counterfeit jewels. Wren and Marisol had searched for a while to find a necklace that would be suitable for the dress and that could hide a camera lens.

He rolled it in his palm and pointed to a small black square on the back that was paper thin. "Camera and mic are here, and it's waterproof."

She had no idea why it would need to be waterproof, but she figured Jock had thought of everything. She took the necklace from him and looked at it from the front, twisting and turning it, but unable to detect the hidden camera. The job was impeccable. She handed Jock the necklace and leaned forward with her neck pushed toward him. He watched her warily, and she nodded to him. "I want to try it on and make sure it fits and looks okay with the alterations."

A muscle in his jaw ticked, but he ordered her to turn around. His movements were quick as the heavy weight of the necklace settled against her throat. There was a fiddling at the nape of her neck. "Done," he announced, and she raised her fingers to touch the stones.

"Looks great, Duck," Erick said from his seat in the van.

"It's gonna look so bomb with that fire dress we picked out." Marisol sat on the tailgate, one leg propped up while the other swung. "You'll have Darren kissing your feet."

Marisol grinned at her, and Wren smiled back even as anxiety raced over her skin like angry fire ants.

Dade joined Marisol at the bank of the van, his arms crossed over his chest. He cocked his head, gaze riveted on Wren's neck. "Look around. I want to see how it moves." She turned her head from side to side, looked down and up. The necklace didn't move from what she could tell, but she'd need a mirror to be sure. She held her hands out to the sides. "Okay?"

Dade made a begrudgingly impressed face. "Good work there, Jock."

With his unknown accent, it came out more *Shoke*. Wren knew there was animosity between Dade and Roarke, but she trusted Dade. She didn't trust him to save her skin over his own, but she trusted him to do everything he could before it got to that point. When they'd worked together, he'd told her, in no uncertain terms, that he preferred to work alone and that he put his life first. She respected him for that. At least he was honest rather than leading her into false security and stabbing her in the back.

"Wren." She turned at the sound of Erick's voice, which still wasn't quite normal. "If anything happens, things go south, and you need out, say *duck*. And no matter what, we'll get you out." She pursed her lips, and he pointed at her. "I'm serious, and if you act like you won't pull the trigger to save your skin, we're not sending you."

"Safe word is *duck*, I got it." She glanced around as the crew minus its leader watched her. "We done here? I need to go get ready."

As Jock unclasped the necklace for her and placed it back in the box, she thought about all the reasons she'd have to say the safe word. Would Darren try to sexually assault her? Would he take her somewhere other than the restaurant? Would he hurt her? By the time she'd shoved the jewelry box into her book bag and said her good-byes, she was shaking so hard that she feared she'd crash her bike.

Before leaving, she retreated to the bathroom. Once the door was shut behind her, she crouched down, not giving a fuck if her clothes touched the dirty floor, and took several heaving breaths. She'd never had a panic attack before, but she imagined she was feeling a pretty close cousin of one. Her heart beat in her ears like a base drum, and her throat felt like it was the diameter of a pin head. If the positions were different and this was Marisol—would she face it all with a smirk and sass? Wren couldn't imagine confident Marisol would be deep breathing in a bathroom.

But she wasn't Marisol. She was Wren. And she'd be okay. She just had to keep breathing and get through this. She needed time in private to come apart a little bit because that was the only way she could fit herself all back together. Once she left here, she was on the job. It was all business—a pretty dress and face full of makeup and game on.

Her hacker name—Seocheon—was taken from Korean mythology. The Seocheon fields were positioned at the border of this life and the afterlife, and flowers there held all kinds of powers, from bringing people back to life to destroying an entire army. Wren had always been fascinated by the story of Hallakgungi, the mythical deity who protected the realm. Wren's floral tattoos were a nod to the myth, and a glance at the colorful ink on her arms centered her.

She stood up, splashed cold water on her face, and took a look in the mirror. She pushed aside her anger over Roarke's absence and focused on what came next. This was her show now.

* * *

Lacy's apartment was on U Street NW and a little upscale for Wren's taste. She'd stocked it to look as lived in as possible. Now Wren tottered around the wood floors on three-inch stilettos, which was an Olympic event, especially with the silver straps digging into her skin. She was going to have blisters on top of blisters on top of welts. She used to be able to get around much better in heels, but she was out of practice—now she preferred her motorcycle boots.

As Lacy, she was decked out with diamond stud earrings, a set of bangles on her left wrist, and—of course—the necklace. The dress fit her curves like it had been made for her. Which it kind of was. On top of all her other talents, Marisol could sew. And so she'd made some slight alterations, which sent this dress from pretty to gorgeous.

Her face was full beat—smoky eye, red lip, and false eyelashes so long that they were obscene. She'd left herself a lot of time to get ready, but now she stood in the living room with an hour to kill. She didn't want to sit down and wrinkle the dress or even touch her face for fear of messing up her makeup. Her tattoos were hidden with cover-up, and it was always odd to look in the mirror and see herself uninked.

Her stomach growled. With her nerves, Wren hadn't eaten all day. Going into this on an empty stomach was probably a bad idea. Her blood sugar was dropping already—she could feel it. What if she ate and smudged her lipstick or got something stuck in her teeth? This was why she didn't date, but if she did, she sure as hell wouldn't go through all this trouble.

She made a whining sound as the doorbell rang. She frowned because, if that was Darren, then he was hella early. She walked to the door and stared into the peephole.

A dark head was bent, and it lifted until she looked right into the eyes of Roarke Brennan.

CHAPTER SEVEN

WREN took his breath away.

When she opened the door, all oxygen fled Roarke's body. It was a struggle to keep his face neutral, to not show that he was actually gasping for air at the sight of Wren Lee in all of her red dress glory.

The fabric fit her like a glove, skimming over her ample tits and full hips. The diamonds in her ears and on her neck sparkled. Her hair lay over one shoulder in soft waves. She looked like a million bucks. Nah, scratch that. She looked priceless. The only thing he mourned was that she'd covered up all her tattoos. They were too distinguishable for Darren to see.

Wren's weight shifted. "Hey."

His gaze shot to her face, to her black-lined eyes and rosy cheeks and perfect lips. He swallowed. "Hey."

She braced a hand on the door, the multitude of bracelets sliding down her arm to rest with a clink. "You took some time out of your errands to come give me a pep talk?"

She was going for sarcasm, but he heard enough real hurt in her voice. She must have thought he hadn't planned to see her before the date. Oh, he'd planned on it. He just hadn't wanted to do it in front of everyone else.

He gestured inside her apartment. "Can I come in?"

"Sure." She backed up a step in heels so high that he couldn't comprehend how she stayed vertical.

He shut the door behind him and faced her. The front door of her apartment led right into the living room. There was a couch with some pillows and a fluffy blanket set on an area rug. Along the wall was a TV on a stand with some cords and a few video games spilling out of the open cabinet.

It was clean and smelled a little like cookies, and he wondered if she'd made some or if the scent was from a candle. "You've done a good job making this place look like a permanent home."

"Thanks." She sighed. "I don't even keep a lot of my stuff at my real apartment—Erick has most of it. I try not to get too attached to any specific place since I know I'll have to move." She made as if to tug her lip into her mouth with her teeth and stopped herself. "Ugh, lipstick," she muttered.

He pulled a black jewelry box out of his leather coat pocket. "Sorry I missed you at HQ earlier, but I wanted to get you this."

She eyed the box before taking it from him with fingers tipped with pink nails. She kept her gaze on him as she flipped open the lid, deep brown eyes studying his face. His hands itched to reach out to her, to feel those soft lavender waves lying on her shoulder and to run his fingers along the soft curve of her elbow. To smudge the cover-up she'd rubbed into her skin and reveal her colorful tattoos underneath.

She finally glanced down, and when she saw what was inside, she sucked in a breath. With the tip of her finger, she stroked the teardrop diamond earrings and slowly lifted her head and cocked it to the side.

"Marisol told me where you bought the necklace," he explained. "So I went and got you the matching earrings."

"You didn't have to—"

"I know I didn't, but I wanted to so..." He shrugged, unsure what else to say. He took the box from her and pulled out an earring. He gestured to her ear. "Want me to help you put them on?"

It was a lame excuse to get closer, to get his hands on her, but she didn't protest, only nodded. Of course, this was stupid. This was the exact opposite of what he told himself he'd do. But knowing she was going on this date, he wanted something on her that was from him. His claim. It was fucking crazy, but that didn't stop him from taking a step toward her.

The front of his jeans brushed the side of her hip. He inhaled as he leaned in. She must have dabbed perfume behind her ear because the floral scent was intoxicating. He took out the diamond studs she had in her ears already and placed them in the box. "Remember when Erick and I took you to get your ears pierced?"

She laughed. "My earlobes were so small that the technician had a hard time with the piercing gun."

"You sat so still though." He slipped in an earring. "And we took you for smoothies and soft pretzels."

"It was a good day," she said softly.

He moved to her other ear and slipped in the new earring. He couldn't resist taking a moment to run his fingers down the rim of her ear. Except he didn't stop there. His fingers continued down the curve of her neck, and when her eyes slid shut and her lips parted on a gasp, he closed his hand around the back of her neck.

Her body swayed into his, her hip connecting with his groin and sending a jolt of heat up his spine. He leaned his forehead onto her temple, indulging in her scent, the warmth of her body, and the way the fabric felt under his hand where it rested on her other hip. "Promise me you'll be smart," he said into her ear. "Don't be reckless or the hero. It's still early in the mission, and we need you. *I* need you."

He hadn't realized he'd closed his eyes until a hand cupped his cheek. Wren turned to face him, and their gazes locked. "I promise," she said.

He thought she'd say more, and it was on the tip of his tongue to make promises back to her, ones he didn't think he was capable of keeping. But then something that sounded like a rumble reached his ears, and he pulled back and frowned at her.

Her cheeks pinked as she touched her stomach. "I'm starving."

He glanced at his watch. She still had about forty-five minutes before Darren arrived. See, he could be useful. He rubbed his hands together and took a step back. "Then I'll feed you." He turned on his heel and walked toward the kitchen. "Do you have food here?"

"A little. But what if I get something on my dress?" She protested as she followed him. "And I already put on my lipstick and lip liner and..."

He reached the refrigerator and opened it. "We'll put a bib on you if we need to. But as long as I'm breathing, you're not meeting that dickhead without something to eat."

"It's not that big of a deal."

He straightened up, holding a clementine, and kicked the fridge shut. He could feel Wren's gaze on him as he found a plate and began peeling the fruit. "It is a big deal. You need your strength and your brain firing on all cylinders. That's not gonna happen if you're hungry." He needed to do this as much as she needed to eat. He felt useful taking care of Wren, and he'd do it despite her protests.

When he had all the pieces separated, he picked up one and held it near her mouth. Her lips were the same color as her dress, and he wondered how women pulled off magic like that. "Open up."

She raised her perfectly arched eyebrows at him. "Excuse me?"

"Open. I place this on your tongue. You chew, swallow, and you won't be hungry. It's a simple human function."

She reached for the piece of fruit. "I can feed my—"

He held it out of her reach. "I'll feed you. That way I can make sure your lipstick stays on and nothing gets on your dress."

Her eyes narrowed, but finally she slumped against the counter. "Fine."

"Open and stick your tongue out."

She complied, and in that moment, when she parted her red lips and stuck out her pink tongue between white teeth, he realized he'd made a grave mistake.

He'd honest to God been trying to fill the woman's belly, to care for her. In his complete lack of romantic prowess, he'd underestimated how erotic it was to feed a woman by hand. He wanted to delete the entire last five minutes, but he was committed now, and so was she.

Wren looked up at him with those liquid eyes and long lashes. He shifted as heat raced down his spine and flooded his groin. He would *not* get wood standing in Wren's kitchen before she went on a date—no matter how fake—with another man. As much as he wanted to cover those red lips with his own, taste that mouth and stroke his tongue over hers, that wasn't going to make her any less hungry. *Focus on the job, Roarke.*

With one hand cupped below the other to catch any stray juice, he carefully placed the orange slice of clementine on her tongue and withdrew his fingers. "'Kay." The one word was a croak.

The situation in his jeans wasn't getting any damn better as Wren began to chew and swallow. He watched her throat work and had to look away. He glanced down at the plate. He had to do this, like, eight more times? Fuck his life.

But he did it. One at a time, he fed her the clementine until all that was left on the plate was one lone piece along with the peel. He reached for the last piece, but she grabbed it before he did. "Open up," she said with a grin.

He shook his head. "Not hungry."

She pouted, her bottom lip poking out. "Come on."

Heat raged throughout his body at the sight of her slim fingers holding the fruit in front of his face. "I'm not wearing lipstick. I can feed myself."

She blinked, and for a minute, a streak of uncertainty crossed her face. "Please?" Her voice shook a little. "Let me think about this moment while I have to pretend to be interested in that jackwagon."

Why were they doing this to themselves? The thought of her on another man's arm, a man like fucking Darren Saltner, made him see red. He wished he could get out of viewing and listening to the damn date, but there was no way. If she had to live through it, he could, too.

He opened his mouth and stuck out his tongue. When her fingers got close, he curled the end to tickle her thumb, unable to help himself from getting a taste. She laughed softly. Then he bent at the knees and leaned his head back so she could drop the slice in.

She did, her eyes sparkling, like this simple act was the best part of her day. Hell, maybe it was. It was the best part of his damn year. Maybe decade. He chewed, and the juicy clementine burst in his mouth.

She bared her teeth. “All clear?”

Somehow he managed to answer her. “Yep, all clear.”

She reached out, her thumb swiping the corner of his mouth. “Bit of juice there.”

The urge to kiss her, fuck up that red lipstick so it was all over him, all over her, hit him like a shot. “Wren—”

The alarm on his watch beeped, his warning to get the hell out of the apartment before Darren arrived. “Fuck.” He silenced it and took a moment to get himself under control. This sick feeling in his gut before a mission was new, but it was because this one involved Wren. They had backup plans upon backup plans, and over his dead body would he let anything happen to her. He met her gaze with as much confidence as he could pack into a grin. “Guess it’s go time.”

“Thanks,” she said, fondling an earring. “I love these. And thanks for making sure I have something for my stomach to work on.”

“Sure. Hope you at least get a good meal out of this.”

Her cheeks colored. “I totally staked out the menu, and you bet I’m getting market price everything.”

He laughed. “That’s my girl.” He dropped a kiss onto her forehead, reluctant to let her go but knowing he had to. He jogged to the window along her back wall and threw it open. Swinging a leg out, he paused half in and half out and glanced back inside. Her hand was on the back of her neck, where his had been earlier. With her other hand, she waved. He gave her a wave back before slamming the window shut and descending the fire escape stairs with his heart in his throat.

* * *

Why was that clementine the best clementine she'd ever had in her life? Wren had already had half the crate and none of them had tasted as good as the slices direct from Roarke's fingertips.

She regretted staying away for ten years. Maybe if she'd have come home sooner, they could have had the chance to *be* something. Instead of now, which was the worst timing ever. But she'd never had a reason to think he was interested. There'd never been an incentive to come home.

After their phone conversation, she couldn't say he was sending her mixed signals anymore. His signal was very clear, in an *I want you but we can't do this now or probably ever* way. She knew that, in her heart. This was not a job that afforded them the luxury of a regular life, especially getting mixed up with the Saltners. Who knew how long their reach was?

She wandered around her apartment for another ten minutes, straightening things that didn't need to be straightened and wishing she had a cat, then being glad she didn't have a cat because there would be fur on her dress. Then she spent several agonizing minutes despairing and wishing she could kiss Roarke. It was like she was in high school again.

When the doorbell rang, she was fiddling with her necklace, making faces at it in the mirror so the crew in the van could see her. She imagined Roarke trying not to laugh while Erick made faces back at her. Dade would roll his eyes, Marisol would whistle, and Jock would just be annoyed at life. That thought made her smile.

She walked toward the door, taking a moment to inhale and exhale and turn into Lacy—the woman that desired Darren. When she opened the door, Darren stood in the foyer. She noted he had no flowers, which was great, because she didn't want to have to invite him in to put them in a vase. Although she wasn't sure what was in vogue with dating in this, uh, decade. Were flowers on dates still a thing?

While she mused on this, Darren proceeded to look her over like a piece of meat. He reached for her hand, and she tensed her muscles to resist recoiling at his touch. With their joined hands over her head, he made her twirl. She winced when she heard his inhale at getting a glimpse of her backless dress. When she faced him again, his lips were turned up into a filthy smirk. "I like a woman who dresses for her man."

Oh gag me. She managed a smile. "Well, good thing I like red, too."

He smiled knowingly, and it took everything in her not to twist his fingers until she broke them. Which she could totally do because Dade had taught her.

He dropped her hand and gestured out into the hallway. "If you're ready, the car is waiting."

With one last look into her apartment to lament that she wasn't on the couch in her pajamas eating mac and cheese, she grabbed her purse and stepped into the hallway. After locking the door behind her, she turned to see Darren holding his arm out. Did they really have to touch this much? Well, it could be worse. He could walk with his hand at her lower back, touching her skin.

Number one mistake of the night was this damn dress.

So she took his proffered arm and forced herself to cut off the Wren who'd just been in that apartment with Roarke.

This was Lacy, with the skills of Seocheon. She was playing a game now, a game she intended to win. So she held her head up and she walked confidently in her high heels toward the elevator. She wouldn't let her crew down.

* * *

Out on the sidewalk, Darren led Wren to a black Lincoln Town Car. A driver waited nearby, and as they approached, he opened the door without a word. Darren helped her inside, and she slid on the leather seat, heart pounding. She'd never been claustrophobic, but as Darren settled into the seat beside her and slammed his door shut, panic clawed up her throat. She was at Darren's mercy now. He could drive her out to the desert—her irrational fear didn't comprehend there were no deserts in DC—and kill her and bury her body where no one would ever find her.

The black leather interior was closing in on her, cutting off her air. Darren's lips were moving as he talked to his driver, but she had no idea what he was saying. White noise roared in her ears, and a trickle of cold sweat dripped down her spine.

This was it, the moment she lost it. She scrambled for something to soothe her, to bring her back to the present, and lifted her hand up to her ear. She fingered one of the teardrop earrings Roarke had given her and inhaled deeply. Her hand shook, and she lowered her fingers to graze the necklace. The camera was like having the crew right there with her. Roarke and Erick wouldn't let anything happen to her. Dade, Jock, and Marisol would back them up.

She willed herself to stay focused. She was loved, and she had people who cared about her watching out for her. She closed her eyes for a moment as the tightness in her chest eased, as the sound in her ears began to dull.

She snapped her eyes open as Darren fiddled with his

phone. Most important, she was capable, and smart, and she just had to get her wits about her. She wasn't some amateur. By the time Darren slid his phone inside his jacket and turned to face her, she had herself under control, her expression poised.

She took some comfort in the fact that they had a driver. They weren't alone. Hopefully this driver had morals and was against things like kidnapping and homicide.

Darren's hand, bejeweled with two large rings, held a glass out to her. "Champagne?"

The bubbles rising to the surface in the crystal flute were oddly calming. She took the glass from him. "Sure, thank you."

She angled her body slightly so Darren would be in the frame of the camera. He poured himself a glass. Dom Pérignon. If only he knew she didn't actually like champagne and preferred Miller Lite. Erick constantly mocked her for her taste in beer, and she told him that his hipster IPA–ass didn't appreciate classics. The thought made her smile. So when Darren turned to her, he caught a glimpse of her showing real happiness.

He beamed, probably thinking it was because of him. He rested a hand on her knee, and the heat of it burned through the fabric of her dress in seconds. The urge to shove his hand away and pour her champagne on his head was real.

"So," he said, "tell me what you do, Lacy."

If she talked, she'd have an excuse not to drink the champagne. "I'm between jobs right now. I used to be a nurse in Dallas." Which was not true, but Erick had hacked into employee records so there she was—Lacy Kim, former ER LPN at Medical City Dallas Hospital. She even had a fancy degree from Baylor, courtesy of Erick's fast fingers.

Maybe Darren wouldn't bother to fact check but if he did, their bases were covered. "Are you looking for a job now?"

"I'm applying, yes."

"I know the head surgeon at George Washington. Would you like me to put in a word for you?"

Jesus Christ. "Oh, that's not necessary. I'm thinking of getting out of hospitals and maybe into private practice. No rush though. I have savings."

"I have contacts all over the city." He squeezed her leg. "Let me know if you need access to them."

Right, she needed to get him talking about himself. "So, do you like owning Alpha? It's got such a great reputation."

He was smug. "I enjoy it very much. It's not all I do, of course." He turned away to refill his glass and she took a minute to pour some of her champagne onto the carpeted floor behind the seat.

She shifted closer and placed her elbow on the back of the seat, letting her hand drape over his shoulder. The posture of an interested woman. "Oh yeah? What else do you do?"

"I'm the vice president of a cyber-security company."

She widened her eyes. "Oh, so what exactly does that mean?"

"We test software to ensure there are no weak points where data can be stolen. And we suggest ways for companies to improve their security."

"Oh, so like, making sure credit card information isn't stolen from the Target website or something?"

He smiled at her indulgently. "Sure."

"Good, I spend a lot of money there. That red card gets you five percent off." Okay, that was all true. She didn't even have to lie about her love for Target. "What's the name of the cyber-security company?"

"Saltner Defense," he said. "My father owns it."

Bingo. "Ah, so success runs in the family."

"It does!" His cheeks were flushed, either from the champagne or from the excitement of talking about himself. "I come from a long line of entrepreneurs. My great-grandfather was involved in creating the first electronic digital computer in the forties."

This was a cute family story for Thanksgiving and all, but she wanted him back on track. "So what do you do as vice president? That must be nice, you get to work with your dad."

"Well, it's a position that requires a lot of meetings. My father consults with me on any big changes that he plans to make within the company. Sometimes I visit the employees on the floor, make sure they know we appreciate them." He puffed out his chest slightly. "Saltner Defense is a great place to work."

Anger, swift and hot, rocketed a fireball up her spine to explode behind her eyes. A great place to work? A place that killed whistleblowers. He was either clueless or putting on a front. She couldn't be sure. He might not know a thing about what his father had done, but if she worked this right, he might be their ticket to more information. "That's really great. I'm sure your employees are grateful to work there." Had she kept the bitterness out of her voice? She sure hoped so.

Despite her hatred of champagne, she took a sip, because she needed something to put out this fire in her blood.

"We do very worthwhile work," he said. "But we don't have to talk about that boring stuff all night. I'd love to hear more about you."

"Oh, well, I'm rather boring." She lamented she couldn't get drunk.

Darren's smile was creepy. "I doubt that." He glanced out the window. "Ah, we're almost there, and I have something for you."

"For me?" She placed her champagne in the holder in the door.

He held up a slim black box, and her heart thudded in her chest. If that was what she thought it was...

He opened it, and sure enough, there sat a diamond choker with a massive ruby in the middle. "While there's nothing wrong with your necklace now, I thought we could do an upgrade."

Oh fuck oh fuck oh fuck. She remained motionless, worried one movement would show her panic, as he reached behind her neck to unclasp her necklace. Her link to her crew. All that was protecting her tonight. She didn't look at him, fear curdling her blood. She could say her safe word, just blurt it out, and get the hell out of this situation.

Then she thought of Flynn and of Fiona. She thought of the reason she was risking it all and giving up a future with Roarke. And the fear receded because the tide of revenge and anger was back. She was Lacy now, not Wren, and she had a job to do. This was just a date, and she could get through it alone. As the clasp on the back of her necklace gave way, her brain clicked back on. Darren couldn't see the back of her choker. She grabbed the front just in time before it fell into her lap.

She clutched it in her fist as Darren picked up the new choker. He slid it around her neck and clipped it into place. The comforting weight of the choker she'd had on before was now replaced by a diamond-and-ruby-encrusted noose.

She could do nothing but beat back the tears and slip her necklace into her purse.

"Let me see," Darren said, gazing at her with wonder.

He leaned down and pressed a kiss to her jaw. “Beautiful. This suits you much better.”

She closed her eyes and counted to ten before she opened them and flashed him a smile. “Thank you, it’s lovely.”

He made a contented grunt and laid his hand on her knee.

She was on her own now.

CHAPTER EIGHT

"MOTHERFUCKER!" Erick roared. He ripped his headset off and threw it against the back of the van where it cracked before crashing to the floor. He tore his hands through his hair so it stood up straight. "She's alone with that fucking monster!"

Other than Erick's outburst, the van was unsettlingly silent. Roarke glanced around at his team. Dade's face was red, Marisol was biting her nail, and Jock maintained a cold expression as he stared at the TV screens.

This wasn't ideal, Roarke admitted. But he had a backup plan. "Erick, sit down."

Erick's eyes bugged out of his head. "How are you fucking calm?"

"Sit. Down," Roarke said through clenched teeth. "Your screaming ain't doing shit but giving us all a headache."

Erick plopped down on his chair with a thud and a growl, crossing his arms over his chest and glaring at the dark screen like he could make it reappear with his mind.

Roarke pointed at the TVs. "We can see almost the entire restaurant. Yes, there are blind spots, but it's better than nothing." He tapped away at his laptop, eyes on the now-black screen that had been the camera feed for

Wren's necklace. He changed the input, hoping this all worked because he hadn't had time to test it. He unplugged his headphones and adjusted the volume. Within seconds, Darren's voice filled the van. "Have you ever been here before?"

"No," Wren answered. "But I've heard about its reputation so I'm eager to try it."

"Good," Darren said. "I know the chef, so we'll be treated well."

Wren's laugh was a little forced. "Of course you do."

Erick's eyes were huge. "Wait, how is the mic that good that it's picking up from inside her purse?"

"It's not the necklace," Roarke said, continuing to adjust the settings to eliminate as much background noise as he could. "It's—"

"The earrings," Dade said, his arms crossed over his chest. "You mic'd up those earrings you gave her."

Roarke whipped his head around to pin Dade with a stare. "How do you know I gave her earrings?"

Dade shrugged and picked at a piece of lint on his jeans. "I know everything."

This fucker grated on his nerves, and if Wren's well-being wasn't on the line, Roarke might have punched his smug face. He pointed a finger at him. "I don't have time for this now, but we're coming back to it."

Dade grinned at Roarke. "Looking forward to it."

"So wait," Erick said, drawing Roarke's attention. "You gave her earrings and mic'd them?"

"Yes, one of them. I was worried Darren would do this, or something would happen to the necklace, and I wanted backup."

"Does she know?"

Roarke shook his head. "I didn't tell her."

Marisol smacked him in the head. "Why the fuck didn't you tell her? She's probably freaking out right now."

"At the time, I didn't want to make her nervous. That necklace gave her security, and I didn't want her to think of how it could be taken away."

Marisol didn't look impressed. "Okay, but now her only security has been taken away and she has no idea we're still with her."

Doubt about his decision began to creep in. "I don't need a Monday morning quarterback, Marisol."

"Then don't treat her like a fragile woman, Roarke." She bared her teeth at him, all traces of joking Marisol gone. This was Marisol in protection mode. Maybe Wren brought that out in everyone. "She doesn't get to sit in this van with us tapping away at keys. What she's doing is mind over matter, and knowing she had backup would be really fucking great."

He didn't know how to answer her because she was right. So without a word, he turned away and slipped his headphones back on. He'd probably have some apologizing to do later. But for now, he couldn't do anything but listen.

"Sit, please," Darren was saying. Roarke searched the monitors showing the security camera feeds until he spied them in the far corner. Wren was mostly out of the frame except for her hands, but he could see all of Darren—including *his* hands, which had better not touch her more than they had to or he'd fucking break them.

A waiter arrived at their table to hand them menus, blocking them from view. Roarke tuned out Darren's dithering over his wine choices and checked out the rest of the restaurant. It was at capacity, and most of the diners were politicians. He squinted his eyes at a table along the far wall. Yep, there was a senator's daughter who was always in the tabloids now that her father was making a run for the Republican presidential nomination. He was a waste of space, and Roarke hoped he lost.

Once the waiter left Wren's table, Roarke focused on their conversation. Erick sat beside him, his headphones on and head down, ready to take meticulous notes.

"So are you close with your father?" Wren's voice sounded steady, and she'd even dropped it a note to sound sexier. Roarke shouldn't have doubted her.

"I am," Darren said. "I mean, we weren't always close. I had a little bit of wild oats to sow when I was a teenager."

Wren laughed. "Oh, I know that all too well."

Roarke smiled. Wren had been the perfect straight-A teenager. He wondered what she'd been like in college. All he knew about her were her good grades—data points. At the time, it'd been enough, but data didn't show all the ways Wren had grown up, her friends, her favorite hangover cure, or her preferred dining hall food. He'd missed all that, and he had no one to blame but himself.

Darren paused as the waiter delivered their wine. Roarke couldn't see him because the employee was once again blocking his view, but Darren was probably sipping and swirling his wine like some snob. Who cared how long it was in an oak barrel? Or if it had cedar notes, or whatever the fuck. Just drink the damn wine.

When the waiter departed again, two wineglasses full of dark liquid sat on the table near the candle centerpiece. "But we get along now," Darren continued. "The whole family is close."

"That's wonderful." Wren's hand lifted her glass out of the frame. She had informed the crew ahead of time that she wouldn't drink, but she would pretend to.

Darren launched into a spiel on the history of Saltner

Defense, and Roarke wanted to smash everything. Darren's voice was filled with pride in the company, and either he didn't know or didn't care that, beneath it all, Saltner was stealing from its clients and putting the greater population at risk. Oh, and committing homicide. There was that, too.

Roarke's brother had believed this spiel once. He'd sat in on a meeting with Arden and Darren and other top execs and believed in what he was doing, that he was using his skills to make the Internet a safer place. A better place. And it'd all been a goddamn lie.

Wren didn't say much, other than soft murmurs of interest here and there. She was playing her part and playing it well. Even though Roarke was sure that inside, she was a massive tangle of nerves.

Finally Darren stopped talking. "But that's enough of that. I'd love to hear why you agreed to go on a date with me. I've been watching you for weeks."

He leaned forward and covered her hand with his.

Oh fuck, Roarke was going to throw up in his mouth.

"He's the worst kind of fuckboy," Marisol muttered behind me.

"Shhhh," Erick hushed her.

She stuck out her tongue at him.

Wren delayed answering by once again lifting her wineglass. Roarke racked his brain to think of an ulterior motive as to why Darren would ask that question. Was it the narcissist in the guy? Or was he testing Wren?

"Well," Wren said as she placed her glass on the table, "when you first noticed me, it caught me off guard. I'd just ended a relationship before I moved here. And I wasn't looking to meet anyone so soon. But I guess..." She paused, and when she spoke again, her voice had dipped seductively. "You were persistent. And I've always been attracted to powerful men."

Marisol made a gagging sound from behind Roarke.

Darren seemed to like that answer. His grin spread over his face like an oil slick. "And you think I'm a powerful man, do you?"

Roarke was beginning to think Darren was just a narcissist.

"Of course," Wren said quickly. "You own Alpha, and now I know that you also help your father run his business."

"Yes, I do. A lot of people don't realize that, since we spend a lot of time at his home office, but I'm very involved."

She leaned forward so her hair and the tip of her nose were visible in the frame. "I can't imagine you have time for anything else. That would be truly impressive."

Darren's chest puffed out. "Oh Angel, you have no idea all the things I have my fingers in."

"Are they secret?" Wren was impressive as hell, sounding intrigued and turned on at the same time.

Darren tapped his rings on the stem of his glass. "Some are . . . unconventional."

"Wow," Wren breathed out.

It was like Darren couldn't help himself. "And one such venture just netted us a nice windfall, so that's something to celebrate." He held up his glass in a cheers gesture.

Pain registered in Roarke's brain, and it took him a minute to realize he was digging his nails into his thigh through the worn denim of his jeans. Fuck, his entire body was one tight knot. He had to relax a bit or he wasn't going to be able to move a muscle tomorrow.

"Well, congratulations," Wren said as they clinked glasses.

"He might be talking about the zero-day," Erick mumbled to himself. The sound of Jock's typing grew louder in the small confines of the van.

"In fact"—Darren took a sip of his wine and swirled it, studying her over the rim of the glass in a way that raised Roarke's blood pressure—"my parents are having an anniversary party in a week. I haven't asked anyone to accompany me yet, but I'd be happy to show you around. It's a very impressive estate."

Marisol whistled. "Bingo."

Roarke knew what this meant—an invitation to the Saltner house would give them access to Saltner's personal files. They could plant bugs, copy computer files, anything. Except it also placed Wren right in the mouth of the lion.

"I'd love to come," Wren said quickly, and Roarke felt some sort of door shut tight in his heart. "Thanks for asking me. I'm honored."

Darren then asked Wren some questions about her parents—well, Lacy's parents—who were dead. The rest of the van seemed to relax a bit as Wren filled in Darren on Lacy's made-up backstory. Roarke, however, fiddled with the cord to his headset, wondering why Darren was asking Lacy so many questions about herself. He didn't think the man actually cared about her. He was only interested in her devotion and admiration of him. So Darren must be testing her to be sure she was who she said was. Why else?

Roarke was going to go crazy second-guessing everything Darren did. He wasn't a complicated man, from what Roarke could determine. He didn't get the impression Darren respected women, but rather that he liked having power over them. Lacy was a perfect fit for him—a gorgeous, unemployed newcomer with no family.

The conversation was dull as they ate. The weather,

some brief political topics, in which Wren stayed neutral. There was an undercurrent to the conversation that rankled Roarke, made him wonder why Darren had taken such a liking to Wren. Yes, she was gorgeous, but there surely were other women Darren could find to hang on his arm.

Why Wren?

Darren also talked a lot about Alpha and his many partners, as well as the numerous investors in Saltner Defense, some who were silent investors, but Darren was on a roll, name-dropping politicians and other DC bigwigs. Wren kept him talking while Jock typed furiously on his laptop behind them. Some of these silent investors were rumored to have many illegal ties, so this gave them more ammo to bring down Saltner. Roarke planned to ruin his life, so the investors who didn't want to be associated with homicide? Well, they'd be hearing about this.

"Excuse me for a moment." Wren's body came into the frame as she placed her napkin on the table and ran her hand down Darren's arm. "I'm going to use the restroom."

She walked away from the table and out of the frame. Roarke darted his eyes over to another monitor and cracked his knuckles as he waited for her to make her way down the hallway. In his ear, her heels clicked loudly, and there she was, her hips swaying as she clutched her purse in front of her. There were no cameras in the bathroom so she was out of sight once she opened the door. Roarke leaned back in his chair and took off his headphones to give her some privacy.

He looked over to see Erick had done the same thing and turned around to face the rest of the crew. Dade's seat was empty, and Roarke frowned. "Where'd he go?"

Jock didn't even acknowledge the question, and Marisol looked up from her phone. "Uh, he said he was going to the bathroom, but..." She frowned as she checked the time. "Fuck, that was almost ten minutes ago."

Roarke hadn't even noticed Dade had left, he'd been so focused on Wren. He glanced at Dade's seat and at the monitor. Dade was a shady motherfucker, but he'd made it clear he cared for Wren. She was his protégé after all. No, he couldn't have...

With a deep breath, Roarke picked up his headphones and put them on.

* * *

Wren opened the bathroom stall and stood in front of the mirror. The necklace that Darren had given her was gorgeous—runway-worthy—but the longer it sat on her neck, the more it choked her. By the end of the night, she wasn't sure she would be able to breathe anymore. This hunk of metal and gems probably cost close to fifty grand, and she couldn't wait to donate its worth to charity.

A toilet flushed in another stall, and she busied herself at the sink washing her hands. She was stalling, soaping up twice, because she really didn't want to go back to that table. Darren hadn't been inappropriate yet, but she didn't know how far he'd push after they left the restaurant. She was surprised he'd been open about his other business opportunities, implying they weren't all legal. His desire to impress her was overriding his good sense. She wondered how he had kept it quiet all this time, but then maybe that was a good thing—he'd screwed up before, he'd do it again, and she planned to bring his entire business of exploiting women crashing down around his head.

While she dried her hands with an unnecessary amount of paper towels, the stall opened and out walked a tall brunette wearing slacks and a long-sleeved red blouse with a bow at the collar.

Wren was about to leave when the other woman blocked her exit. Wren tensed, unsure what fresh hell awaited her, but she'd go to battle in a bathroom in heels. She didn't have her Sig Sauer. She'd left it at home on Erick's orders, but she could do some damage with a stiletto. She took a step back to give herself some distance from the woman who was now staring her down. Wren braced as the woman lifted her hand to her face and, in a swift move, removed her wig. Wren blinked, her memory sorting through faces before it landed on one. Of course. The tension left her body in a rush, and she relaxed. "Dade," she breathed out with a hand on her heart. "Jesus, do you have to be so goddamned dramatic?"

He placed the wig back on and adjusted it in the mirror before swiping at a smudge of lipstick at the corner of his mouth. "Ugh, I don't like this lipstick. Looked better as a swatch. Anyway, why yes, Wren, you know I have to be dramatic. Because that's how I amuse myself in this shitty world." He leaned against the sink. "So, I decided to get dressed up and pop in to say hi."

Everything about Dade was over the top. But she kinda loved him for it. "Well, hi. I appreciate it, because I feel mighty alone, that's for sure."

He nodded. "Suspect you might, but you should know we've been with you this whole time."

She held up her purse. "Can you hear through this?"

"Nope." He reached out and tugged gently on one of her earrings. "But we can hear through here." He leaned in and spoke slowly. "Hello, Roarke, you big, fucking tool bag."

Wren's heart thudded, and she spun on a heel toward the mirror, leaning over the sink as far as she could to get a look at her earrings. "What the hell? Is there a camera in these?"

"Just a mic."

She glared at the offending earrings anyway. "Thanks a lot for telling me, Roarke. I've been freaking out here, but this whole time you knew I was okay?" She growled low in her throat. "I'm going to kill you when I see you again."

Dade clapped like this was a game. "Wonderful, this mission just got so much more interesting. I like it better when you two hate each other than when…" He winked. "You know."

"No, I don't know," she said through gritted teeth. "Did you come here to mock me or…?"

He pulled a phone out of his silver bag. "I came here to say that we can hear you, so don't go home and touch yourself while saying Roarke's name—"

"I swear to God, Dade—"

He pressed a couple of buttons on his phone. "Okay, the feed for your earrings is down for sixty seconds so the team doesn't hear. I'll make this quick. I also came here to tell you that you should probably make an excuse to catch a cab home."

She blinked at him. "I'm sorry, what?" This whole meeting was giving her whiplash.

"Make some excuse. Probably don't use your cat again, but anything else you can think of would be great. I'm not quite sure of his plans for you after this dinner, but from what I've gathered during my spying, they most certainly will require you to blow your cover for this mission to achieve that personal one of yours." He cocked his head, studying her reaction. In seconds, she was twenty again, her numb body stretched out on a dirty mattress in a dark basement. She'd been shivering uncontrollably as the drug worked its way through her system.

Fighting her way out of the flashback, she gripped the edge of the sink as a tremor rattled down her spine. Dade knew what had happened to her. He'd required full honesty before working with her. His voice was a little bit kinder when he spoke again. "And for reasons we can explain soon, we need you at the Arden estate, where you will be in a week if you don't mess this up tonight. You understand?"

Right, he was asking her to prioritize. And he knew what her answer would be. "Of course. I understand."

Heels sounded outside the door, and Dade cocked his head as a beeping sounded from his phone. "That's my cue. Feed is back on. If you need us, just say the word. Take care, princess."

He turned and walked out the door, holding it open for a woman who was entering.

Meanwhile Wren stood frozen in place. She fingered her earrings, glad the crew was with her even though she was going to kick Roarke in the balls over this. She pushed aside her feelings over what he'd done because that had to be dealt with later. She had more pressing matters, like getting out of here without being drugged and raped. She'd hoped to get access to Darren's phone, but not at the expense of blowing her cover for the team. As of now, Flynn's mission came first, and she'd deal with her own personal vendetta later. That was what she promised herself.

And right now, she needed to get safe. She'd scored an invite to the Saltner estate, so this night needed to end before she messed up her cover. *Think, Wren, think.* She needed an excuse to catch a cab. Something that wouldn't allow Darren to say no or offer to take her himself.

A medical emergency. A family member? A friend?

This performance was going to have to be pitch perfect or she'd find herself in a Lincoln Town Car on a one-way trip to Saltner's House of Black Market Porn.

No thank you.

Turning back to the sink, she dripped water down her cheeks and smeared mascara under her eyes. She held her breath until her face was red and smacked herself a couple of times for good measure. She tangled her fingers through her hair, messing it a bit.

She leaned back and eyed herself in the mirror. Yep, she looked frazzled and upset. Good. When she was really young, she had wanted to be an actress, and she was a huge fan of K-dramas, so this was her turn to put her fandom of the Korean shows to use and act like her life depended on it. It kinda did.

Wren walked out of the bathroom, jogging in her heels. She wanted to make enough of a scene that Darren wouldn't be able to argue with her. She burst into the dining room and managed to conjure a sob. Darren spun in his chair and stood up immediately. "Lacy? Are you okay?"

She glanced around, like she was searching for the exit. "I'm so sorry to do this, but I have to run."

"Wha—"

"I just heard from my friend who's in the hospital after a car accident. I have to go see her."

"I can take you—"

She shook her head, already walking away from him. "A cab will be quicker. I told you I have no family, and she's all I have here."

Darren's hand closed around her arm, pinching her skin. She looked around, but no one was paying attention. Did everyone turn the other way in this town? "Angel, sit down a minute. Drink your wine. I can call the hospital, and we'll see what's going on." He smiled at her and held the drink out to her.

A drink that was probably spiked.

Fuck, this wasn't working. And she didn't know how to insist without blowing everything. She couldn't do that, not with an invitation to Arden's house on the line. She took the glass from him and placed it on the table. He watched her movements, and a muscle in his jaw ticked before he smoothed over his features. She stepped closer to him, and his hand slipped down her bare back to rest at the top of her ass. His fingers teased under the fabric. "The doctors are doing everything they can, I'm sure. And you visiting her while you're this upset won't help her."

He was manipulating the fuck out of her, which might have worked if her emotions over this were real.

"Why don't we take a drive? You can relax a bit, then I'll drop you off at the hospital." He smiled at her, all teeth and charm. "I'm trying to be sensitive here, but with you in that dress..." He whistled softly. "It's been a bit of an uncomfortable night." He shifted, and she sucked in a breath as the hard bulge in his pants brushed against her. This guy couldn't give a shit about her or her friend; he just wanted her.

She bit her lip, trying to look coy. She ran her hands up his chest and rested them on his shoulders. "Would you agree to take a rain check? I want to spend more time with you, too, but I can't concentrate knowing my friend is all alone." With bile rising in her throat, she leaned up and whispered in his ear while pressing against his erection. "I'll make it up to you. I promise."

He groaned softly, and she took that opportunity to slip out of his grasp. He blinked at her, caught off guard, as she backed away. "I'll catch a cab. Thanks for dinner." She blew him a kiss and all but ran out of the restaurant. She felt like goddamned Cinderella, except nothing about this was a fairy tale.

She burst out on the sidewalk and immediately spotted a cab with the vacant sign lit. The driver leaned over the passenger side to yell out the window. "Need a ride, ma'am?"

"Yes!" She opened the door and all but dove inside, slamming the door behind her. Her blood pressure was through the roof and her body was beginning to shake. She glanced back at the doors to the restaurant, expecting to see Darren chasing her down, but there was no sign of him. She blurted out Lacy's address to the driver, who nodded and pulled away from the curb.

Only then did she lean back in the seat and take a deep breath. "Jesus Fucking Christ, that was close."

"What did Dade say to you in the bathroom?"

Roarke's voice filled the cab, and for a split second, she thought the earring had a speaker, but then she opened her eyes to see Roarke unfolding himself from the floor beside her. "What the fuck?"

He grunted as he slumped down in the seat next to her. "What, you think this cab just happened to be here? I paid him a thousand bucks to sit out here waiting for you. And he's going to your apartment, by the way, not Lacy's."

She glared at the driver. Traitor. He met her eyes in the rearview and shrugged.

"Well, thanks for the cab. Now you can see yourself out. Maybe while it's moving at sixty miles an hour." They'd gone from feeding each other clementines to wanting to kill each other, apparently.

Roarke narrowed his eyes. "We need to talk. What did Dade say to make you leave the date?"

The words jammed in her throat. With Roarke's hazel

gaze boring into her and the cab slipping in and out of traffic, she wasn't ready to blurt out everything. It hadn't impacted this mission yet. And it wouldn't. "Just that we had enough on him for the night, and I should go before Darren talked me into leaving with him."

Roarke didn't seem to be buying that. "Until we can dig into what *unconventional* things this guy has going on, I'm not comfortable with this plan. He's too dangerous—"

Oh no way, he wasn't pulling the plug on this. "We can chat tomorrow when we debrief and plan my next date with him. For now, I have to get these clothes and eyelashes off and get some sleep."

"Wren," he growled.

"Roarke!" she shouted back at the height of maturity.

"Why are you yelling at me?" He reached for her arm.

She yanked away from him and plastered herself to the side of the car, ignoring the hurt flashing across his face. "Why am I yelling? I'm yelling because this is the result of an adrenaline crash. Because I just played someone for two hours and I'm goddamn exhausted. And you pop up like you're my savior, telling me all of this is for nothing—?"

"I never said it was all for nothing. We got some great intel—"

"And we'll get more." She gritted her teeth. "Don't do this right now, Roarke. Do not. I'm pissed off and a little scared, and you're going to get the full brunt of my flailing emotions. Is that what you want?"

"If it makes you feel better to get it out, then bring it on."

"Oh, fuck you. I'm not doing this just so you can use it against me to show why this is a bad idea." She pointed at him. "And don't think you're going to get away without answering for this earring thing, you asshole."

"I didn't want to freak you out with ideas on all the ways the mission could fail."

"So what if you freaked me out? I'd get over it. In case you haven't noticed, I'm pretty damn capable. I got out of there without the safe word—"

"Barely—"

"So you can kiss my ass."

The cab stopped in front of her apartment building with epic timing, and she threw open the door, slamming it shut behind her and speed walking toward the stairs.

Roarke was right on her heels and caught her arm before she could make the ascent. Once again, she found herself trapped between Roarke's body and a brick wall. The lights of the cab faded as it drove away, and she lifted her chin. "Getting a little tired of men manhandling me tonight, Roarke."

His eyes flashed. "And now you're lumping me in with Darren Saltner?"

She huffed out a breath. "You know you're not like him. I'm making a point though that I've had it with guys who want to prove to me how big their dicks are."

"Men who are concerned with your safety?" His nostrils flared. "Men who want to see you live past thirty-five? Men who give a fuck about you?" His fist pounded the wall beside her head, startling her. He inhaled, eyes rolling back as he fought to control himself, and he flattened his hand against the wall and dropped his head beside hers. "Jesus, Wren, this is killing me."

He pressed closer, and she shuddered as his chest brushed hers. There wasn't much fabric separating the heat of his body from her hardening nipples. Why did her body always respond to him like this? She ached from keeping her muscles tense all night, from constantly being on guard, and she didn't have the energy to fight him anymore. To fight this.

She wanted comfort. She wanted to be lost in a feeling other than terror. After what happened in college, she'd sought out sex on her own terms, seeking to cover bad memories with good ones. So sex had always been an outlet for her, and although she knew intimacy with Roarke would be a web of complications, that didn't really matter right now. It was either this or go into an adrenaline crash that would last for days.

She'd rather have an orgasm.

She twisted her neck so that her lips closed over the hinge of his jaw, and she rolled her hips forward. His breath caught in his throat, and the hand beside her head scraped down the bricks until his fingers closed around her hip in a punishing grip.

Yes. Make it hurt a little.

She ran her tongue along his jaw and licked at the corner of his mouth. She leaned back a bit, just to study his eyes as she curled a finger in his belt loop. A dim light over their heads reflected in his light eyes. There was hunger there, too. When she rolled her hips again, his arousal was unmistakable, a thick bulge in his jeans, and she wanted to unveil the prize behind his zippered fly.

"Wren." That syllable was a warning and a dare and a plea all in one harsh burst of sound.

"You cut me off, and I'll just go rogue." She ran the tip of her tongue around the flower inked on his neck and tasted a bead of sweat that lurked among its petals. "But I'd rather have your support."

The five pressure points where he gripped her hip were spreading heat into every limb and pooling between her legs. She'd have bruises tomorrow, and she'd relish them.

He pressed his full lips against the corner of her eye, then her cheekbone. "You like seeing me cave, don't you?" His words sank into her skin like fishhooks. "You like breaking me in half, ripping me open, and getting me to show you what I'd never show anyone else."

She'd dreamed of this, of an emotionally naked Roarke desiring her. She wanted his respect more, his confidence in her that she could complete this mission. And while she didn't have that, and wasn't sure she ever would, she was able to make him putty in her hands. So she'd take that and run with it. So yeah, watching him cave, ripping him open, and picking at his insides would have to do for now.

She wouldn't get out unscathed though, and she hoped he took care of her once he inevitably saw all *her* ugly insides.

CHAPTER NINE

WREN was driving him out of his mind. Beneath his hands, her body was tight and hot, and his dick was painfully hard and pretty pissed off at his unyielding zipper.

This was a bad idea for a thousand reasons. He was already in over his head with Wren on this mission and if he finally got to taste her? He was going to be fucked.

But when she slipped those hands up the back of his shirt and scraped her long nails down his bare back, his brain went offline with an echoing click.

He'd thought many times about what he'd do if he ever got to touch Wren, and all his fantasies involved taking care with her, slow and easy with soft, whispered words and lots of affection. But that wasn't really him, and he was too far gone in a Wren whirlpool of anger and fear and desire.

He gripped both her hips and thrust against her roughly. "This the kind of support you want?"

She gasped, and her red lips, smeared with makeup, twisted into a smile as she let out a dirty laugh. "Well, I didn't think I was being subtle."

"We didn't agree to this. You're changing the code on me."

"Maybe I am." Those damn fingers scraped his back

again, teasing above his waistline. "You're not the only coder. Maybe I don't give a fuck about what's going to happen after this. Maybe I just want to live in the moment. With you. Right now. I've never been into beta testing. Let's just live it."

He was done with the torture—the wishing and wondering if she was as delicious as she looked. He yanked her off the ground with his hands on the backs of her thighs, and as her legs circled his waist, he dove in for a kiss.

She met him halfway, her hands gripping his face as she opened her mouth to meet him. They clashed in a mess of lips and tongue and teeth. He thought he tasted blood but it didn't matter, because holy shit this was Wren. *Wren.* The first girl he ever wanted. The reason he learned to hack, so he could get back at her cheating boyfriend. The woman he'd spent the last decade protecting from behind a computer.

Wren.

And fuck she tasted good. Their lips slotted together like puzzle pieces, and their tongues moved in sync. He wasn't aware he was thrusting against her until she let slip a pained whimper. He leaned back, and she winced, rolling her shoulders. Oh right, the brick wall, and her dress was backless.

He turned and slid down the wall until his ass hit the ground. Wren sat astride his lap with a filthy twist to her lips. "What a gentleman."

"Don't speak so soon." He pulled her dress off one shoulder so it exposed her bare skin. He ran his tongue along her collarbone. Then with a glance at her face, he slid her dress down to reveal a breast.

And oh fuck, she was perfect. Full and round with a dark nipple. He cupped the mound, kneading it slightly as

Wren's hips began to churn. He flicked the tip, and she gasped.

"You want to know how many times I jerked off as a teenager thinking of these?" He slid down the other side of her dress until she was fully exposed. Her left breast was slightly larger than the other, and he decided he liked that one the best. He pressed her closer and leaned down, closing his lips around the hard peak.

"Oh yeah?" she asked, her voice raspy. "I hope they live up to the promise."

It took all his willpower not to unzip his jeans and plunge into her right there. He closed his teeth around her nipple, just to test how she liked it, and she cried out, her nails tightening on his shoulders. He wanted to throw her on the ground, tug that dress up, and see how she reacted when he put his mouth between her legs. "They fucking exceed it."

While he could have stared at her tits all day, he wasn't sure if there'd be another chance to get his hands on her. No life was guaranteed, and the one they lived was rife with ways to be snuffed out.

While he kissed her mouth and sucked the skin on her neck, he ran a hand up her leg, over the cherry blossom tattooed from her mid-thigh to her hip. Under her dress, his fingers caught on a string. Just a string. He pulled back and lifted up her dress. What she wore underneath was tiny, a mere scrap of fabric covering her, held by thin string on each side. "Fuck me."

She squirmed on his lap, and he caught a glimpse of the damp fabric. Like a freaking beacon, he pressed his thumb there, feeling around for her clit. Her body jolted, and her head fell back as she thrust her hips against his thumb. Her responsiveness sent his arousal into overdrive. He'd never been one to talk much to his partners, but the sight of Wren had the words dripping from his tongue. "Oh baby." He smiled. "That's what you want, right? You want my hand on this heat?"

Her mouth was open, her hands braced on his chest. "Roarke," she gasped out.

He yanked the fabric to the side and stared down at the glistening curly hair around her folds. He sucked his thumb into his mouth and placed it right on her clit.

"Oh fuck," she cried out, and rolled her hips harder.

He was going to come in his jeans. The solid ridge covered with denim was wet with her arousal. He thought about pulling himself out and jacking off right there, but he didn't want to take his eyes off Wren or interrupt her desperate chase to get off.

He slipped two fingers inside her, and she gasped, stilling for a moment. She was picture perfect—tits out, skirt up to her waist, mouth open with kiss-swollen lips. A spot of red on the side of her neck, where he'd sucked up a patch, stood out against her light skin. Good, he hoped it was there for days. Weeks.

Her hips swiveled, and he curled his fingers, possessiveness for her slithering into his blood every moment she let him touch her. He didn't want to think about Wren with anyone else, but he had to know. "How long has it been, little bird?" he asked, his voice hoarse. "How long since you've been touched? Because I gotta say, you're a tight fit for two fingers." He slowly slipped a third inside, and she shuddered. "How long?"

"Months," she gasped out, a strand of hair sticking to her still-red lips. "But don't make me tell you how no one has ever touched me this good."

That's because no one cared as much as him. "You think

this is good? You haven't seen what I can do with my dick yet. But I want to see you come like this. I'm so fucking hard watching you."

She made a sound like a whimper and began to ride his hand. He could barely keep up, fascinated by the roll of her hips and her wetness coating his fingers and his lap. Her breasts bounced in his face, and he sucked a nipple into his mouth, clamping down with his teeth. Seconds later, her breath caught, her body shook, and her inner walls pulsed around his fingers.

He pulled back just to watch her face as she came, the way her eyes slid half-shut, the way her mouth rounded into a soft O, and he listened to the high-pitched moans falling from her lips. He was still hard, but his brain was now coming back online after its Wren-induced shutdown. It occurred to him that he'd just finger-banged the girl of his dreams in a dirty apartment stairwell. In public. She was topless about a hundred yards from the parking lot and although they were fairly secluded, this was all kinds of fucking stupid.

He righted her dress, covering her back up, and he took off his jacket and wrapped it around her shoulders. She was trembling, the spring air still cold, and the heat between them had cooled somewhat. Or maybe it was her adrenaline crashing. His hands were a little shaky, too. He tried to rationalize it all in his head that they could go back to the way things were. That this could be it, but he couldn't tear his gaze away from all the places he'd marked her with his lips and teeth.

They'd just rutted like teenagers. Maybe that was what happened when you finally touched the girl you'd lusted over for nearly two decades.

He helped her to her feet and rose next to her, discreetly

adjusting himself. As the realization of what they'd done sank in, he knew the truth—this would change things. It didn't matter if he tried to tell himself it was just sex. It wasn't.

"So," Wren said as she attempted to fix her hair, then gave up on it. "You agree to keep letting me do my job then?"

That comment made him flinch. Was her intention to give him a taste so he'd keep her on the team? His gut churned, and even though he told himself to walk away, to let it go, he couldn't. Not with Wren. She brought everything in him swirling to the surface like a damn magician. He leaned back against the wall and crossed his arms over his chest. "So Dade taught you how to use your body to get what you want, too? Thorough as fuck, that one."

She stared at him for a minute, like she couldn't believe what he'd said, and her eyes widened. She shrugged off his jacket, balled it up in her fist, and threw it at his face. "Fuck. You. Roarke."

She turned on a heel and took off up the stairs. For a minute, he thought about letting her go. If she was mad at him, if she wouldn't let him touch her again, then maybe it was for the best. But his feet were moving before his brain could tell him to get in his car and drive away. Wren had been hurt by his words. And he couldn't deal with that, so he took off after her. While she was damn fast in those shoes, he had the benefit of flat boots. "Wren! Wait!"

He finally caught up to her as she fumbled for her keys in her purse. She had the key in the lock and was opening the door when he reached for the knob. "Wait."

She whirled around and glared at him. *Oh fuck*, if looks could kill. She was furious, and the scrapes on her back from the brick wall made his heart ache. Her nostrils flared, and a bit of fight seemed to leave her eyes when her voice came with a little less heat. “Go home, Roarke.”

She slipped through the door and slammed it shut behind her.

He didn’t go home. With his palms flat on the door, he laid his forehead on the cool metal. “I’m sorry.”

He listened intently for any sounds inside, and there it was, something brushed the door, and a heel clicked on the tile in the foyer.

When she spoke again, her voice trembled a bit, even muffled through the door, and he wondered if she shut him out so he wouldn’t see her break. “How dare you?” She emphasized her words with a smack on the door, which rattled the hinges. “Like I can’t want sex or want sex with you on my own? It’s because I’m trying to manipulate you?” There was a pause. “I can’t believe you said that to me.”

“I said it as a reflex. What you said triggered me. It wouldn’t be the first time a woman tried to sleep with me or Erick to get what she wanted.”

“Men do it, too,” she snapped back.

Yeah, he knew Dade was a master at that. “I know. I’m sorry. I shouldn’t have said that to you.”

She didn’t answer for a moment. “Do you—is that what you believe?”

“No, of course not.”

“I’ve done it though.” Her voice was calmer now, more muffled as she spoke more softly. “And I never regretted it, not once. It was my choice. But tonight, you made me regret it. You made me feel dirty about it.”

He curled his fingers into fists and squeezed his eyes shut. “Let me in. I’ll say sorry to your face. On my knees. I’m sorry, Wren.”

“Do you date?”

The question came unexpectedly. "What?"

"Do you date? Have you had girlfriends?"

"No," he said, maybe too quickly, but it was the truth. "I've met some women on jobs, but it's always about release, and I usually drink first to loosen up."

"Why?"

He shrugged even though she couldn't see him. "I'm not interested."

"Was there anyone specific?"

There was a woman in France—Marie—sister of an art gallery owner he'd done work for. He visited her whenever he was in Europe. She called him *mon beau ténébreux*, which meant "dark soul," and put up with him when he dropped in unannounced. He was fond of her, but it didn't go much beyond like. "There's a woman in Europe I see sometimes. But you have to understand it's only about convenience."

"I see," Wren said.

He knew who she dated in college, but he asked anyway. "What about you?"

"I had a boyfriend during my first few years in college."

His names was Charles Hannigan. He had red hair and a mole on his neck, and he played lacrosse. "Did he treat you well?"

"Yeah, he did. We broke up because we just kinda fell out of like, I guess." Another scraping sound from behind the door. "Look, I'm not going to pretend Dade didn't teach me. But that was not the way it was with you. It'd never be that way with you. You understand that, right?"

He nodded, his throat suddenly thick. "I do." What had she had to do all those years when he thought she was happy and safe as a freelance columnist? Had she used men the way they wanted to use her? "I told you that you break me open. My reaction to you is a hair trigger, when normally I'm on lock."

"I get it. And that's why this isn't going to work. Not on this mission. We can't be doing this the whole time." She made a sound like a yawn. "So please go home now, Roarke."

Nothing was resolved. He could still smell her on his fingers and feel her under his palms. She was inches away on the other side of the door, but it felt like hundreds of miles. "You won't let me in."

"No."

Stubborn woman. He stared down at his boots. "Let me say this. If this mission kills me—"

"Roarke! Don't say that!"

"Or if I have to vanish and live in fucking Siberia, now I can go without regretting never learning how you taste."

"Roarke." Her voice was a hoarse warning. "Don't."

"Good night, little bird," he said, and walked away, running his hands over his lips as he jogged down the stairs. While he wanted to live in the moment—burst into her apartment and fall asleep with her in his arms—she was right. This was too much right now.

But if tomorrow brought Arden down on their heads, at least he had the memories.

* * *

Wren lay in bed staring at the ceiling, feeling paralyzed. She'd gone to bed last night with her stomach twisted in knots and woken up the same way.

Her life was a mess.

She should have walked away. Ignoring consequences and living in the moment with Roarke didn't work when she wanted that moment over and over again. And couldn't get it.

There was also Erick to think about. She suspected Erick had always wanted her to be with Roarke. But not like this, not when there was too much riding on the line and when their futures were so uncertain. All her life, no matter what happened, Erick and Roarke remained pristine and untouched in her mind. Her relationship with each of them was solid and understood. They were always there, and she knew that she could count on them if everything else crumbled around her.

Now lines were blurring.

She rolled onto her stomach and closed her eyes, her body heating at the memory of Roarke's touch, at the filthy words that dripped from his tongue like hot wax. Back when she'd had a crush on Roarke as a teenager, all she'd wanted to do was kiss him, hold his hand. Now she imagined how that dark head would look between her thighs and lamented she hadn't reached down to get a grip on what was in his pants.

Maybe she should have said fuck it and invited him inside—let him sleep beside her on this big bed. How she'd kill to see his tattooed hands gripping her pink sheets as he rolled over to press a kiss to her shoulder.

A knock at the door roused her, and she froze. Her phone buzzed, and she glanced at it to see a text from Erick. *It's me.* She smiled and climbed out of bed, throwing on a fleece robe and padding to the door. She'd texted him last night that she'd made it to her apartment safely. She should have known he'd show up in the morning to make sure. After a quick peek in the peephole to confirm it was her brother, she threw open the door.

He held a brown paper bag in his hands and wasted no

time gathering her in his arms. "Fuck, I'm so glad you're okay."

She closed her eyes and rested her head on his chest. "Of course I'm okay. I've got the best crew backing me up."

Erick leaned back and raised an eyebrow. "We're a pretty fucked-up crew, and you know it. I mean, we're capable as shit, but we got Dade sneaking into women's bathrooms without bothering to tell us, and Roarke putting a mic in random pieces of jewelry." He walked into the kitchen and began to pull bagels out of his bag. "Right now, Marisol and Jock are back at HQ fighting." He paused as he put a sliced bagel in her toaster oven. "Well, actually, Marisol is yelling at Jock, and he's ignoring her."

She tightened the belt of her robe. "Wait, what? Why are they fighting?"

"Because they are close to finishing the patch for the vulnerability, but they are disagreeing on how to launch it. Marisol wants to make a statement, and Jock wants to slip it in under the radar so whoever bought it won't know until they actually try to steal data." He placed a tub of strawberry cream cheese on the counter. "It's amusing to me. I think Marisol enjoys going at Jock because he's so stoic, but one of these days, he's going to blow like a fucking geyser."

Wren dipped her finger in the open tub of cream cheese. "I would pay to see that."

"Me too." He glanced at the toaster oven, then leaned on the counter. "So, you okay?"

She ate another scoop of cream cheese to avoid looking at Erick. "Yeah, I'm okay."

He was studying her; she could feel those brown eyes all over her. Finally, she looked up to see him smiling. "We're proud of you."

Who was we? Was Roarke included in that? "Thanks. I'm proud of me."

"I wish I'd known all these years... what you were getting into. Why'd you keep me in the dark?"

The toaster beeped and Erick slid the bagel onto a plate and handed it to her with a knife. She sat down at the breakfast bar and slathered it with cream cheese before taking a bite, needing the time to think through her words. She didn't want to lie to her brother, but she hadn't told him about what happened to her and Fiona. "Because I know you. And if I told you, then you would have tried to convince me to stop. Or blamed yourself for my interest. And sure, I wanted to learn some skills initially because I looked up to you and Roarke. But then when I started, I found I loved it. And I was good at it."

"You're good at playing a part, too," he said.

"I am." That had been Dade's influence. "You don't learn under Dade without some acting lessons."

Erick nodded. "Well, eat up. Then we need to get going. Roarke's got a slate of shit he wants to cover today."

At the mention of Roarke, her appetite fled. Would Roarke be angry at her? Distant? Friendly? She wasn't sure which reaction she wanted. Leaving her half-eaten bagel on her plate, she took a quick shower. After throwing on a pair of tight, ripped jeans, boots, and an off-the-shoulder black shirt, she walked out to the kitchen to find Erick cleaning her countertops. That was what he did when he was nervous. Clean.

She leaned against the wall and watched him. Her brother's hair was long in the front, strands catching on his eyelashes as he scrubbed at a stain. His mouth was set in a grim line, which hurt her heart. He'd always been the joker, quick to make everyone laugh, and now, every once in a while, that Erick came out, but much less frequently since Flynn's death. She knew they'd been close, but she suspected Erick was affected more than he was letting on.

"Bro," she said gently, "I think it's clean enough."

Erick froze, his shoulders dropped, and his head sagged. He braced his hands on the counter and twisted his neck to face her. Why hadn't she paid more attention to how much of a toll this was taking on him? She walked over and wrapped her arms around him from behind and rested her head on his back. "You're worrying me."

"I'm worrying myself," he whispered. "I'm terrified of what will happen to you. I'm scared about what this mission is doing to Roarke. I've never seen him this obsessed. And I'm spending so much energy on all of that, so I haven't taken the time to deal with Flynn's death. And it's fucking me up inside, Wren." His body shook, and she squeezed him tighter. "This feels like a mission that'll change everything. And I don't know if I want on this ride."

Deep in her soul, she felt that none of them would end this mission the same. She'd been changed by numerous events in her life, but this one felt monumental, like she was balancing on the edge of a cliff and there was nowhere to go but over. She had no idea how or where she would land. Deep in her heart though, she knew she wanted to leap while holding Roarke's hand.

Could she go five seconds without thinking about that man? Erick was confiding in her, and he deserved her full attention. She heaved a sigh. "Don't worry about me, and don't worry about Roarke. We're grown-ups, okay? And when this is all over, you need to take some time for yourself. Go on a date or something."

She thought he'd laugh, but instead his body tensed.

"Maybe I just need to get away from this all for a little bit. Take a vacation."

Sun, sand, and surf. That was her idea of a vacation. "We always wanted to go to St. Lucia. Maybe we can go there. Hide out in some hut with no Wi-Fi where no one can find us."

"That sounds amazing." There was a smile in his voice, and he reached up and squeezed her hands. She let go as he turned around and pressed a kiss to her forehead. "Thanks for listening to me. I think I've done enough soul-baring."

"You know you can always talk to me, right?"

His tongue teased the corner of his mouth before he said quietly, "Yeah, yeah I know."

As Erick drove to the warehouse, they sang along to the radio and forgot about the tension of the morning. She didn't think about Roarke for a blessed fifteen minutes, until Erick parked and she remembered she had to see him again.

When she walked inside HQ, the room was fairly silent. The white van sat in the corner, a reminder of the shitshow that was last night. Marisol was nowhere to be seen. Dade and Jock sat side by side, each tapping away at keyboards while concentrating on double monitors.

"Hey."

She and Erick turned around at the sound of Roarke's voice. He stood with his hands shoved in his jeans pockets, shoulders hunched in his plain white T. His hair was smoothed back today, and she remembered the way it had felt in her fingers.

See? This was why she didn't get involved during missions. Because it was a distraction. One hundred percent. She should have been focusing on the words coming out of Roarke's mouth, but all she could do was stare at the flower on his neck, the same one she'd licked last night.

Roarke's gaze took her in from head to toe. "You feeling all right?"

Anyone else would think he was referring to the date with Darren. But she knew he was asking about what came after that. "Sure, I'm okay. Didn't sleep great, but I'll live."

Roarke's voice was quiet when he spoke. "I slept like shit, too."

A small bit of satisfaction settled into her. At least she knew he was as affected as she was.

"So," Roarke said, his voice rising so the team could hear, "I wanted everyone together, because Jock cracked some shit overnight."

"Overnight?" Wren's brain engaged back into the mission. "Does the man sleep?"

"Yeah, Jock!" Marisol's voice called out as she emerged from the bathroom. "Do you sleep or are you part cyborg?"

Jock didn't even look up, just raised his middle finger.

Marisol smiled with glee, like his reaction pleased her. She walked over to Wren and pressed a kiss to her cheek. "Hey princess, happy as hell to see you well."

Wren squeezed her hand. "I'm good."

"Great, because we got work to do." Marisol raised her eyebrows at Roarke and sauntered over to perch herself beside Jock. "Hey, sweetheart."

Was that a smile on Jock's face? Wren did not comprehend their relationship, although it seemed very brother-and-sister antagonistic.

Roarke waved everyone over to where Jock and Dade sat at their computers. "Okay, so here's the latest. We know the zero-day sold, although we don't know who bought it. We've traced the sale back to its IP—which is Arden's home"—his dark eyes flashed to Wren—"where this anniversary dinner is being held."

Marisol made an explosion sound, and Dade rolled his eyes at her.

"I'm not comfortable sending Wren in there alone with Darren. So Dade—"

Wren blinked at Roarke. This again? He still didn't trust her. "Excuse me—"

"Nope, not Dade," Marisol said, swinging her legs just enough to kick Jock's chair. She smacked her gum and pointed to herself. "Me."

Roarke paused. "What?"

"Me. I'm going in with Wren." Marisol winked at her. "While Jock here did his job, I did mine. Meet the newest waiter for Jacie's Catering, proud to serve at the Saltner home."

Dade began to laugh while Roarke looked like he was going to blow a gasket. Wren was pretty damn pleased at this turn of events.

"Why didn't you speak to me about this?" Roarke said. "A heads-up? That would have been nice."

Marisol's gaze shifted quickly to Wren before snapping back to Roarke. "You had a long day. Didn't want to bug you. You needed your alone time and beauty rest, right?" Wren wasn't sure how Marisol knew about them but she did. She knew, and was letting Roarke know she did.

Roarke glared at her, his face reddening, while Marisol remained unbothered. Finally, Roarke heaved a sigh and rubbed his forehead. "Okay, fine, so you're going in with Wren to assist her."

"You bet," Marisol said. "Bitches get stuff done."

Dade laughed harder, and Wren had to press her lips together to prevent a giggle from escaping. Roarke was right—dealing with this crew was like herding cats.

Erick dropped his head into his hands. "I'm going to be sick."

Wren lifted her chin. Did no one have faith in her? Although the plan sounded simple in theory, she wasn't going to lie, she knew it would be anything but in action. "I can do it. Marisol and I will work on a plan. Right, Marisol?"

"You bet, princess. Multiple plans—A, B, C, D, E, and Fuck it."

Wren did laugh this time. She turned to Roarke, but whatever words she'd been about to say leaked out of her mind. Their eyes locked, and goose bumps raced over her skin. There they stood in front of everyone, acting like everything was normal, when she had vivid memories of what they'd done last night. This morning in the shower, she'd pressed on the lingering bruises on her hips, watching the color change and hoping they never faded.

Roarke's eyes softened a fraction. "This is going to be tough."

"I know that," she said. "But give Marisol and me some time, and we'll handle it. What choice do we have? We're not getting anywhere right now."

"I want detailed plans," Roarke said. "Last night can't happen again, where we don't have all the facts. Dade, I want you contacting everyone you know to find out who's buying zero-days. Study the market."

Dade's grin was the one he got when the game was just getting good. "You bet, Brennan."

"Erick and Jock, I want that patch deployed, rendering the zero-day useless as soon as you can. Anyone have any questions?"

"Yeah," Dade said. "What's your job, Roarke?"

Roarke speared him with a look that could kill. "I got Darren. By the time Wren goes into that house, I'll know everything about him down to what his sick brain is thinking."

His gaze shifted to Wren, and his hard stare was a vow that she felt on her body like a force field. "This time, I'm going to know absolutely everything there is to know about Arden and Darren Saltner. We're going in prepared." He broke her gaze and nodded at the team. "Get to fucking work."

CHAPTER TEN

Wren tangled her fingers in her hair while Marisol chewed the end of her pen. They stared at Marisol's laptop while it played video taken from the security camera in Arden's office. They'd hacked into Arden's home security company, so they knew the location of every security camera, every sensor, and every control pad. What they'd also found was that he had an air-gapped computer on his desk, so it wasn't connected to the Internet. There was no way to gain access remotely—so the only way to see what was on that computer was to get into that office.

There was also no way to get into that computer without a password. So they'd been watching footage for hours, speeding it up when the room was empty and slowing it down when Arden was there. What they needed was for him to sit down at the computer so they could analyze which keys he typed to log in. The zoomed-in footage was grainy, but Marisol said she was sure she could figure out the password based on the location of his fingers.

Stretched out on the six-foot table in front of them were the blueprints to Arden's house in intersecting black lines. The house was bigger than Wren had predicted, which was good and bad. Less chance of running into a guest when she was somewhere she wasn't supposed to be, but traveling from point A to B to C would take more time. If she was caught, she'd need a damn good excuse for why she was in a different wing of the house.

Wing. This place was like the White House.

"There!" Marisol shouted and pointed at her screen. Arden hadn't logged into his computer in days according to this footage, but he was finally sitting his ass down at his desk with his fingers on the keyboard.

He typed in his password, and Marisol's mouth stretched into an evil grin. It didn't end there though. She replayed the footage again and again, slowing the speed down and laying it over a program she'd designed years ago to detect passwords based on a person's finger movements.

Wren was studying the blueprints when Marisol threw her pen on the table and stretched her arms over her head. "Bingo."

"Got it?" Wren asked.

"Yep, it's a whole string of nonsensical numbers, letters—some capitalized and some not—as well as some symbols, so it took a long time for me to figure out." She cracked her knuckles. "Get me in front of that keyboard, and I'm in."

They spent the next hour looking over the blueprints, even if Wren's eyes were starting to protest.

"This rich bastard has a ballroom in his house." Marisol pointed to a large square space on the map. "A ballroom!"

"And a library," Wren added.

"I bet he pays someone to arrange them alphabetically," Marisol said. "If we weren't on a time crunch on this mission, I'd go in and move all his books around."

"He wouldn't be the one putting them back."

"Good point." Marisol picked up a Snickers and bit off

the end with a low growl of frustration. They'd been at this all day. Dade was gone, off doing whatever he did that usually resulted in some sort of injury. Jock and Erick were working side by side, fingers flying over their keyboards as they analyzed the scrolling code on a half-dozen monitors. An hour ago, Erick had left to get food and came back with pizza, soda, and a bag full of candy.

Meanwhile, Roarke hadn't moved for hours. He sat on the ground with his laptop, cross-legged, which pulled at something in Wren. Memories flitted through her mind of all the times she'd found him in Erick's room just like that. Roarke never liked working at a desk. He'd pile a bunch of pillows on the floor, prop his laptop on his legs, and get to work. Scattered around him were crushed Diet Coke cans.

"So," Marisol was saying, "I'll be there early with the catering company to set up. That gives me time to get the lay of the house and make sure nothing has changed from these plans."

Arden lived in a gated community and doubled down on security for his home. The place was more fortified than a bank vault. But Wren had the combination to walk right in the front door in the form of Darren Saltner.

"This catering job is no joke, by the way," Marisol said. "They ran a background check on me and everything. Good thing Carmen Esposito is clean as a whistle."

Wren popped a Sour Patch Kid into her mouth. "Carmen just wants to serve bacon-wrapped scallops to rich assholes."

"Lacy wants to eat those bacon-wrapped scallops."

"Carmen doesn't even know what recursive function is."

"Lacy hasn't updated iOS in a year."

Marisol gasped loudly before they both dissolved in

laughter. Marisol had to catch herself from falling off her chair. She wiped her eyes, smearing her eyeliner.

"Carmen and Lacy just want to live their lives, damn it!" Marisol grinned. "Anyway, you up for more acting, princess?"

Wren bit her lip and nodded. The plan was for Wren to play the part of a drunk date. She'd lure Darren into an empty room with the promise of sex, but with a perfectly timed drug slipped in his drink, he'd pass out before she ever had to lift up her dress.

Wren and Marisol selected a room equal distance between the ballroom and Arden's office. Once Darren was out for good, they'd head to the office. Arden's security system had installed cameras throughout the house, but they weren't manned round the clock. Because of the party though, the cameras would be recording and monitored by the security company.

"Jock can edit the footage from the cameras and play the feedback on a loop so anyone watching won't see us. They'll see a blank hallway that's already been recorded." Marisol said.

"Will they notice the glitch?" Wren asked.

Marisol shook her head. "Jock showed me how he does it. Seamless. So once Darren is out, we've got about two hours to get our shit and get out before he wakes up." She rubbed her hands together. "I gotta practice my lock-picking skills. I'm a little rusty."

"There's no separate security in his office at least," Wren noted.

"Well, it's not on the plans," Marisol said. "But we'll have to stay aware. I'm a little worried these could be outdated."

"So we get in, copy the files, and get out." Wren made

a face, her confidence flagging. "I'm sure that'll be super-easy and not nerve-racking at all."

"Getting into that computer will take most of our time," Marisol said. "And I'll be honest, I'm a little worried that's where we'll run into roadblocks."

Wren cracked her knuckles. "Leave that part up to me."

Marisol laughed. "Well, princess has confidence."

"I work well under pressure. At least when it comes to hacking. Peopling? Not so much."

"Good thing you don't have to hack into Darren's brain then."

Wren shuddered. "I don't want to know what's in there."

Marisol leaned back in her chair and propped her booted feet on the table, the silver buckles on the ankles clanging. "So you feel okay about this?"

"Sure. I'm glad you're going to be there." Wren didn't want to go into the lion's den alone, not with Darren. She trusted Marisol, and between the two of them, she knew they'd manage to get out of there with what they needed. Or at least go down fighting like mad. "I think I know a little bit more about how to handle Darren. That date was a nice trial run."

"And it got you this invite." Marisol shoved the rest of her Snickers in her mouth.

"It did."

"And you're okay with what you're going to have to do after the date?"

Wren had been reaching for a fun-size Twix but no longer felt hungry. When Darren woke up, she had to be gone. Lacy, Lacy's apartment, every trace of her had to be gone until Darren and Arden were brought down. And even then, she had to stay gone. She hadn't decided where she'd go yet. St. Lucia was sounding better and better. Once Wren and Marisol copied the files, Wren was a ghost. She sighed. "I guess I have to be okay with it, huh?"

Marisol nodded, her gaze steady. "Guess so."

Wren didn't want to be examined by Marisol anymore. She'd known the woman for a week, and already Marisol could read her like a book. Wren glanced around the basement and spied Roarke's dark head bent over his laptop. His shoulders were tight, inked fingers flying over the keyboard. "Roarke needs to eat," she muttered to herself. "He hasn't eaten, right? I mean, he should at least have a piece of pizza or something."

"Boy is fine with his caffeine," Marisol said, peering at Wren through her strands of blue hair. "You've known him longer than I have, so you know this is how he is when he's in it."

"I know but..." *It wasn't healthy*, she wanted to finish. What was she, Roarke's mother now? Well, hey, if he could worry about her life during this mission, then she could worry about his damn eating habits.

She picked up a piece of mushroom pizza—it'd always been his favorite—and carried it over to him on a ripped-off piece of the pizza box. Kicking a couple of cans out of the way to clear a path, she knelt down beside him. He didn't look up. She kicked another can, and he still ignored her. His eyes were glued to his computer screen, fingers tapping out a rhythm.

She couldn't deny it was hot to watch him work his magic, his brow furrowed, lips set in a determined slash. She wafted the pizza under his nose. He followed the scent, until those hazel eyes rose to her. She wiggled the pizza near her head with a smile. "Hungry?"

He blinked at her, and she could see the gears in his head switch from binary to English. "Uh." He blinked again, shook his head, and stilled his fingers. "What time is it?" He glanced around like he wasn't sure where he was, and his confusion was adorable. She knew what it was like to tumble headfirst into a project and lose all sense of place and time.

"It's kinda late," she said. "You haven't moved for hours, and I'm not sure why you haven't pissed yourself or why you haven't perished from lack of nourishment."

He took in the empty cans around him. "Huh."

"You went through a six-pack." She held up the plastic ring. "I'll take this and cut it before throwing it away, because I'm forever haunted by those pictures of wild animals stuck in these things."

The Roarke who was human finally smiled and reached for the pizza in her hands. "Ah, that's the Wren I remember. The one who cried over Animal Planet."

"I don't care if it's natural selection. I feel bad for the gazelles," she muttered.

"Nah, I always root for the lions."

"You're a monster."

"Survival of the fittest." He took a bite of his pizza and barely chewed before he swallowed it. "Shit, I was hungry. And I really do have to piss like a racehorse."

"How's it going over here?"

He stopped chewing and groaned. "Hold on. Let me finish this pizza before I talk about Darren and lose my appetite."

"That bad?"

"Worse."

She dropped to her butt on the floor next to Roarke while he finished eating. She wondered if he'd found out what she knew about Darren's other activities. She nibbled on her thumbnail while Roarke continued to eat. They were in relative privacy over in this corner of the basement. Marisol was busy at her laptop, and the guys hadn't come up for air since they'd eaten. Wren picked up Roarke's last can, rattled it to find it wasn't quite empty, and drained the rest of the Diet Coke. "You should probably get a new vice."

Roarke shoved half of the crust in his mouth. "Like what? Smoking?"

"No."

"Heroin?"

Wren rolled her eyes. "Shut up."

"Just saying, sweetheart. Could be worse. Let me have my Diet Coke, and I won't lecture you on the effects of hair dye fumes."

She glared at him.

He shrugged. "Heard it on NPR or some shit."

She smacked him. "You did not."

He grinned as he inhaled the last bit of his pizza. "I'm going to the bathroom, then I'll come back, and we can throw up what we just ate while talking about Darren."

"Romantic." Wren sighed dreamily and fluttered her eyelashes even though her stomach threatened to revolt. She didn't want Roarke to know yet because she knew he'd jeopardize this mission *and* hers if he did.

Roarke rose and winced as something cracked. "Fuck, I really need to take a walk and stretch or some shit."

"Pee first, stretch later," Wren said. "Old man."

He shot her the finger as he retreated to the bathroom.

She glanced around the room while Roarke was gone. Marisol sat hunched over her laptop, scribbling notes on a pad. Jock and Erick were pointing at something on Jock's screen and discussing it.

This was what she'd always wanted. A team. A crew. Working on a mission that fucking meant something as a gray hat hacker—she'd straddle the law if it was for the greater good. Stopping Arden from using his security company to sell vulnerabilities was definitely a greater good. How many breaches and data leaks so far were a result of his exploitations? How many deaths had he caused other than Flynn's?

But after this mission, there was no way to keep the crew together. They'd have to split up to protect one another. She'd be on her own, and that was if she made it through her own personal mission for Fiona.

Now that Roarke had finally begun to see her as a teammate and as a desirable woman, she'd have to betray his trust. From what she knew of Roarke, once he wrote someone off, they were dead to him forever. She had to operate under the assumption that that applied to her, too. Better not get her hopes up that he'd be okay with the fact that she'd lied to him all this time.

* * *

Roarke washed his hands, his stomach still rumbling. That one slice of pizza wasn't enough to fill him up, but the thought of eating another one made him nauseous. He should probably pay more attention to his diet rather than subsisting on Diet Coke.

He risked a glance in the mirror as he dried his hands. Yep, he looked like shit. Jesus. He was already a pale motherfucker, but the bags under his eyes were blue and purple, and his lips were discolored. He resembled a corpse, and while he'd never cared much about his appearance, it bothered him that Wren was seeing him so wrecked.

Maybe he'd try to work in some protein shakes before he keeled over from lack of nutrition. He splashed cold water on his face, ran it through his hair, and let it drip down his neck, soaking the collar of his white T.

He was known for keeping himself in check. Maintaining his cool. Erick dealt with difficult situations by making jokes. Roarke stayed ice cold. It was why he was known in hacking circles as only 6192—the melting point of tungsten, which was the highest of all metals.

Roarke didn't melt. He didn't even get close. But this situation with Wren... damn he was at least at 2,000 degrees. Losing his cool on the most important mission of his life wasn't an option. He shook his head and splashed more water on his face before rubbing it out of his eyes. She was in too deep to back out now, and at least this way he had a whole team keeping an eye on her.

When he left the bathroom, Wren was still sitting on the floor. She'd slipped off her high-top Converse and wiggled her toes in her mismatched socks. She glanced up at him as he walked over to her. Maybe it'd do him good to get out of this basement. "Hey, you wanna take a walk?"

She frowned. "Uh, I'd love to but are you sure? What if someone sees us?"

He shook his head. "I got a place. No one will bother us."

As she stood up, he called over to Eric and Jock. "Taking a breather with Wren. Be back in an hour."

The guys were deep into something because Erick barely glanced up. "See ya."

Marisol gave them a little salute. "Don't do anything I wouldn't do."

Roarke swore Marisol saw right through them, but she hadn't said anything yet so he let it slide. She could think what she wanted. He led Wren up the stairs and cut back through the building to a back door. Outside, his Mustang sat covered in a side alley.

As he took the cover off, folded it, and placed it in the trunk, Wren said, "Do you cover your baby so no one sees her or so she doesn't get damaged?"

He opened the passenger-side door for her before rounding the front. "Both."

She smiled. "That's what I thought."

Once he turned the ignition, the engine rumbled to life. He pulled out of the alley, made his way out of the city, and opened her up on the highway.

"You going to tell me where we're going?" Wren asked. She'd taken her hair down, and it hung in shiny waves around her shoulders. How did she look so good after spending hours in a basement huddled over a computer, eating pizza and candy?

"Just a small park," he said. "I need to clear my head, breathe in something that isn't that damn stale air."

"I hear ya," she muttered.

They drove in silence for a while until Wren turned on the radio. She tapped out the rhythm to a pop song on her thigh with purple-tipped fingernails. In this car, he could almost imagine what their lives would be like if they were normal. If they worked jobs that didn't require them to carry guns or constantly look over their shoulders.

"What would you be doing if you weren't doing this?" he asked as he turned down the radio a bit.

Wren ran her tongue over her teeth in thought. "Well, I know I went to school for journalism, but I think I'd want to be a social media manager."

"Really?"

"Yeah, I know it sounds weird, but I'd love to be in charge of a business's Facebook or Twitter page. Post funny memes and take down haters."

Roarke laughed softly. "I can see you doing that."

"Yeah? So can I. What about you?"

He hadn't given it much thought. In his mind, not hacking meant he'd have to wear a suit and work nine to five in an office with a briefcase, but he knew that wouldn't have to be the case. He didn't want coworkers. Hell, he hated most adults. A couple of times, he'd come into contact with young hackers, teenagers who reminded him of himself, who were getting into things they shouldn't have. He hadn't minded reaching out to them over the Web and setting them on the right course. "I think I'd want to teach computer science. At-risk teenagers. Show them there's a way out."

Wren was quiet for a while, and he stole a glance at her out of the corner of his eye. She was watching him, her face soft, lips parted. He startled when something brushed his hand. She squeezed his fingers gently where they rested on the gear shift. "I can see you doing that, believe it or not."

"Really? Thought you'd laugh at the idea of me standing in front of a bunch of scowling teenagers."

"No," she said with no hint of humor. "I wouldn't laugh at that."

He swallowed, surprised and touched at her belief he could be something other than a hacker consumed with a personal vendetta. Because he wasn't so sure he was much more than that. When he didn't respond, she patted his hand and drew hers away. His skin went cold at the loss of her touch. They drove in silence for a while more before he spotted the sign for the rest stop and pulled off.

"You need to use the bathroom again?" she asked, her lips turning up.

He shook his head. "There's a park behind the rest stop. No one stays long because they're pretty much just letting their dogs shit, then leaving."

"Sounds lovely," she muttered.

He bumped her with his elbow. "So we can mostly be alone and no one will bother us."

"Okay, that actually does sound lovely."

He laughed. "Told you."

There weren't many people there at all. The rest stop was mostly used by truckers, so large eighteen-wheelers lined the back parking lot, while the drivers inside got some rest.

After grabbing waters out of a nearby vending machine, they took a dirt path away from the main building, which housed a convenience store and bathrooms. Roarke chugged his water quickly and shoved the half-empty bottle in the back pocket of his jeans.

Wren walked quietly, her gaze on the ground. He wished he had the liberty to touch her, to grab her hand and press the back of it to his lips, to wrap his fingers around the back of her neck while she tipped those dark eyes up at him. He wished he could dip his head at that moment and kiss her. Last night, she'd thrown up road blocks. *Go away, Roarke.* And he had to stay in his lane. It was for their own good anyway.

As much as he enjoyed being with Wren, he wished he didn't have to tell her what he'd found on Darren. He took another sip of water before plunging in headfirst. "That password-protected forum? I made it in."

Wren's eyes widened. "Oh shit. You beat me then."

This wasn't a competition, but he was glad he'd made it in there instead of her.

"How'd you do it?" she asked.

"I figured out the identity of one of the admins—through befriending one of the pissed-off ex-admins—and was able to compromise his e-mail and recover the password."

"Ah," she said. "So what did you find?"

He sighed. "Look, I've seen worse men than *him*."

He took care not to say his name out loud. Just in case. "But he's right up there with some of the worst, I'm not gonna lie."

She nodded. "Okay."

"That subforum has instructions on how to access the Dark Web, where there is basically a female shopping list for sick fucks. Darren uses vulnerabilities to find data of"—he paused as he scrambled for the right words—"the more vulnerable of the population. Mostly single women. He offers them money to appear in videos doing whatever his subscribers order. If the women say no, he often doesn't take that as an answer and threatens them. His promises on how they will be treated in said videos are not kept."

Wren's face paled, and she swallowed on a nod. "Okay."

He'd never had a hard time reciting the crimes of the people he hacked, but looking into Wren's eyes while saying these words was proving to be difficult. He glanced around, but they were alone. He lowered his voice to barely above a whisper anyway. "He takes advantage of young women, or those with no families, or women who are here illegally. Sometimes he'll give them money, other times he'll just drug them. He films their assault, and he threatens to kill them if they talk. They usually have no recourse, no one to help them, and they can't go to the police. This is all done on the Dark Web and, as far as I can tell, he's been doing this for years."

Wren's brow furrowed. "Do you think Arden is mixed up in that?"

"I haven't found the connection yet, but I know it's there. When this is over, we're going after him, too."

She took a deep breath and looked away, blinking her eyes rapidly. No, Darren was her mission. His destruction would be by *her* hands alone. She needed it.

"Look, Wren…"

"That's not what he wants from me," she said.

He had to be honest with her. He hadn't been about the earrings, and he'd paid for it. "Then why was he asking you all those questions at dinner about your family?"

"Why would he take me out in public if he planned to rape me?"

"I don't know." Roarke gritted his teeth, his fingers itching to get back to his computer, to do more work, because the better job he did, the safer Wren would be. "I wish I had more time to flush this out…"

"The anniversary dinner is the last time I have to deal with him. We'll get those files, and I'll disappear." She turned a fierce glare on him. "Remember? That's why we're doing this thing where we pretend you didn't get me off in my apartment hallway."

"Jesus Christ, Wren."

"I have the crew and Marisol to protect me while I'm at the mansion. And I can take care of myself. He's not getting me, Roarke."

That sick feeling returned, lining his stomach like slow-acting poison. He speared his fingers through his hair. "That might be what you're telling yourself, but pep talks don't do it for me. I like facts, and the fact is, the Saltners are shady as fuck."

"The facts"—the color was back in Wren's cheeks now, reddening as she clenched her fists at her side—"are that Marisol and I know what we're doing. We're not just winging it. Jock is running the cameras, and I'm going to walk out of there even if I have to spike someone in the balls with my heel to do it. Okay?"

"I prefer a less violent backup."

She gave him a withering look.

He reached out and gripped her chin, tilting her face up to his. Her nostrils widened, and she stiffened before relaxing into his grip. Her eyelids fluttered as he rubbed his thumb over her bottom lip. "I'm not pretending anything," he said. He still remembered how she looked in his lap, the way she writhed on his fingers, the smoothness of her skin under her palms. And best of all—or maybe worst of all—he remembered exactly how she tasted. "You're the one who told me to leave."

She squeezed her eyes shut, and when she opened them again, they were wet. "Because it was the right thing to do. Neither of us are emotionally capable of figuring out what's happening between us."

She had a point. He could try to reduce what was happening between them to lust, but it didn't work. He couldn't separate how badly he wanted Wren from everything else he'd always loved about her, how she kicked in every protective instinct he had. His feelings for her were too overwhelming to combine into a mission that might take the last chunk of his soul.

Her mouth said one thing, but those eyes, those expressive eyes, were telling him to prove her wrong. For a moment, he thought he could. Kiss her, tell her they'd work it out, that it didn't matter if she had to vanish. But that line was a real, tangible thing to him, a wall between them that he could touch and scratch with his nails. Climbing over it would change everything.

So he dropped his hand from her chin and absorbed the disappointment that flashed through her eyes. "You're right," he said, his voice as dead as he felt.

She winced and turned away from him. They gave each other a few seconds to gather themselves, to back away from that wall, to retreat to separate sides. Finally, she glanced at him over her shoulder. Her expression was blank. “Ready to go? I think we both have more work to do.”

Right, back to the computer, back to where everything made sense, and he didn’t have to attempt to read horrible things like *emotions*.

They walked to the car in silence, a heaviness between them that hadn’t been there when they arrived. See? This was why he hated talking. It never did anyone any fucking good. Talking wouldn’t save Wren. His computer would, which was why he needed to get back to HQ as soon as possible.

CHAPTER ELEVEN

WREN fingered the jewels at the neckline of her dress as the Town Car made its way to the Saltner estate in Kalorama.

The bodice of her red dress was covered in sewn-in jewels—which was where they'd hidden the camera and microphone. There'd be no removing them in case of a gift from Darren.

She'd declined an earpiece, unable to fit it in her ear properly in a way that was undetectable. She wasn't blowing this just so she could hear Roarke's voice in her ear the whole night.

Darren was on the phone, talking business about Alpha. In fact, he had been since his driver came to the door to get her. If he was any other guy, she might have refused to even get in the car while his phone was at his ear—because *rude.* But with Darren, she was relieved. No awkward small talk. She could take a breather before she walked into hell.

While she knew Darren had been involved in what happened to her and Fiona, she hadn't known about the forum that Roarke had found. Hearing the words from Roarke's mouth back at that rest stop had made her physically ill. While Wren had escaped before they'd been able to film her, Fiona had not. Wren would never forget her friend's hollowed-out expression when she returned to college and promptly dropped out. The knowledge that Fiona's assault was probably ordered by some pervert online made Wren want to stab someone. Actually, not *someone*, but the man sitting next to her. The man responsible.

She hadn't told Roarke the truth even though she'd had the chance. This mission was his, his revenge for Flynn, and she knew, if she told Roarke what had happened to her, he'd be distracted. So she'd bide her time. Just like he wanted to avenge his brother's murder himself, she wanted to avenge Fiona's assault herself.

The car approached the entrance to the gated community, stopping for the driver to enter a numeric code before the gate swung open. She tried to see, but there were shields on either side of the keypad, like horse blinders. She knew the van holding Roarke and the crew was around somewhere, just outside the gate.

The car drove inside, and she turned slightly in her seat to see the gate close behind her. Why did the clang feel like a prison cell closing?

She turned around to see Darren slip his phone into the pocket of his tux. He sighed and faced her, his gaze raking over her body. "Sorry about that."

"It's okay," she said. "You're a successful businessman. I understand that means you work around the clock."

With the way he studied her, he seemed to be unsure if she was patronizing him. Which she had been in her head, but hadn't meant for it to come out like that. *Yikes*.

"I mean," she added, "I was a little put out you ignored me, but I guess you'll turn your phone off now?"

A grin spread across his face. He wanted her to be annoyed. Ugh, was he trying to play hard-to-get alpha male?

That would be the worst. He reached over and squeezed her thigh through her dress. "I can't turn it off completely but the ringer is off, and I'll only answer it if there's an emergency, how's that?"

"That's great. I'm sorry to be like that, but our date last time was cut short so..."

"Yes." He cocked his head, the shrewd gaze once again daring her to lie. "How is your friend?"

There was something off about his body language, his expression. He didn't believe her. She wasn't sure what he didn't believe. She hoped it was something minor, like her friend being in the hospital, and not something major, like—well, her whole identity. Her heart pounded in her chest, but she froze every muscle in her face so her fear didn't show through. Why would he still invite her if he was suspicious of her? He did give her that look often. Maybe that was just what his face did. *Act like nothing is wrong, be the pretty vacuous date.*

She smiled at him and hoped it didn't look forced. "She's fine. Thanks for asking. Some burns from the airbag."

"Ah, those things are nasty," he said, still with the smug grin, like he knew something she didn't know.

"Yeah, they are. And she has some bruised ribs."

"She'll heal." He peered out the window and rested his chin on his hand. "Tonight there won't be any accidents like that, I'm sure."

That sounded...like a threat. Inside, her nerves were blaring out a warning, but all she could do was smile and say, "Right, I'm sure there won't be."

He nodded, and she slipped her hand under her leg, digging her nails into the skin until the point of pain in order to keep herself from freaking out. She'd be okay. Marisol had confirmed she'd made it inside and was the model catering employee. Their plan was solid.

Wren took a couple of discreet deep breaths and smoothed out the long satin skirt of her dress. The top was heavy with beading but the bottom was light, with a slit that cut way up to the top of her thigh. Again, Marisol had come through with the wardrobe. Roarke had seen the dress but hadn't seen it on her. Which was probably for the best.

The car turned down a driveway, either side of the entrance framed with brick columns. They drove up a hill, and at the crest, the lights of the vehicle illuminated a mansion. There were several cars in front of a wide stone staircase that led to the front door, and multiple couples—women in long, glamorous dresses and men in tuxes—were exiting the cars. The driver parked the car along the bank of the long driveway and stepped out.

She'd seen the plans of the estate, studied every detail, yet there was nothing like seeing this much wealth spread out before her, brick by expensive brick. Columns stretched from the first to the second floor, and the third floor held a balcony that was already populated with drink-holding guests.

The mansion was sprawling and the yard—could something the size of three football fields still be called a yard?—was lined with tall trees. Although she knew the neighbors were not far because she'd seen their houses, the Saltner estate seemed to be in its own little world. She swallowed, the isolation pressing down on her like a hundred-pound weight.

Calm, Wren. You have Marisol.

The door to the car opened, and Darren exited first and leaned in with his hand out. Wren took it with a smile and slid out of the vehicle. The house was like something out of the movies, complete with several spotlights on an impressive fountain. Darren slipped her hand into the crook of his arm, and they began to walk toward the front door. Her heels slid a bit on the stone walkway leading to the staircase. Even if she hadn't been dreading this whole night, dressing up and attending exclusive parties in a mansion wasn't really her thing. She'd rather be home in sweatpants, eating pizza and watching Jason Statham movies on repeat. She steeled herself for introductions and small talk and everything she kind of hated.

The house was lit within with yellow light, and when they entered the double front doors, her heels clicked on black-and-white tile. The foyer was massive, laid out in front of a wide staircase that led up to the second floor.

She was distracted thinking how much fun it would be to slide down the bannister of the staircase when a tray of champagne was presented to her. "Champagne, ma'am?"

"Oh, I'm okay right now," she said, eyeing the flutes of bubbly, wishing she could have one to calm her nerves. But no, the last thing she needed was to be impaired.

"And you, sir?"

Darren took a glass with a slight nod. "Yes, thank you."

Wren smiled at the waiter, a pretty, brown-eyed Hispanic woman… *Whoa*, it was Marisol.

She wore a wig—that had to be a wig—of long, brown wavy hair, as well as contacts. Her name tag said Carmen, and she smiled back, completely in the role, before moving on to the next couple.

Wren tore her gaze away from Marisol's back before she gave anything away. She patted Darren's arm as he sipped the champagne. "Is it good?"

"Yes," he said, draining it quickly. "Could use some hors d'oeuvres though. Let's get some food."

"I could go for some bacon-wrapped scallops," Wren said.

Darren laughed. "Oh, this is a Saltner party. You'll be getting much more than bacon-wrapped scallops."

Wren wanted to roll her eyes at his you-silly-girl tone. Instead, she focused on the fact that she really loved food, and damn it, she was going to eat something before stealing all his dad's computer files.

He led her down the hallway, where they were stopped numerous times to make conversation. She was introduced to more people than she could count. Names that she filed away in case she'd need them later. She was probably the youngest one there, and if she saw another Asian or even someone with a shade darker skin tone other than Marisol, she'd be surprised as hell.

Eventually they made their way into the ballroom, and if she wasn't trying to behave, she would have yelled *jackpot*. The room was lined with tables of food, like a chocolate fountain, a swan sculpture made out of fruit, and an entire table of caviar. Hell, there was even a beef carving station. If Darren didn't let her eat, she might just kill him by the end of the night.

"Wow," she murmured. "This is the best smelling room I think I've ever been in."

Darren laughed. "You're impressed with the food?"

"Look, I like food," she said. "This ballroom is gorgeous, but the food makes it A-plus. Tell your dad your date is really happy to get some freshly carved prime rib with horseradish."

Darren turned them around. "You can tell him yourself."

She found herself face-to-face with Arden Saltner. She'd seen pictures of him, but nothing had prepared her to stand in front of the man. His tux was stretched over his wide stomach, and he looked down his nose at her. He had that puffy alcoholic look, but beneath it all, she could tell he'd once been a handsome man.

"Dad, this is my date, Lacy. And this is my father, Arden."

The man reached out his hand to shake hers, and she clasped it, swallowing the bile rising in her throat at the feel of his slimy skin. "Nice to meet you, Mr. Saltner."

He pursed his lips as they shook and dropped her hand. He took a handkerchief out of his pocket and wiped his hand and his face. "She's very pretty."

That was it, no direct comment to her. It didn't surprise her, as she'd met men like that before. And this time, she knew it'd be all the sweeter when they brought him to his knees.

"Your mother is around here somewhere. She'll want to see you."

"Of course." Darren preened, taking the compliment that Wren was pretty as a reflection on his character. "I'm going to get Lacy something to eat, and we'll find Mom."

"You have a gorgeous house," Wren said to Arden. "It's an honor to be here."

The man made some sort of grunt. "Yes, thank you."

A woman touched his arm, and he turned away from them to greet another guest.

That was it, her introduction to Arden Saltner. He'd written her off as a pretty girl in a dress. Sometimes it wasn't so bad to be underestimated.

Darren led them around the room, and she had to hand it to him because he was a decent date. He held her plate as she sampled all the delicacies in between sneaking bites of food himself.

Eventually they migrated to a high table, where an older

couple was standing. Darren introduced them as his aunt and uncle. They proceeded to talk about boring family things, like the latest cousin to have a baby, who'd moved, and who'd done something horrid and disgraced the family, like voting for a Democrat.

There was a lull at one point during which Arden commanded the attention of the ballroom so he could stand at the center, holding his wife's hand, to talk about their marriage and a lot of other things that Wren tuned out.

Marisol circulated the room, and Wren was impressed with how she'd transformed herself. She didn't walk with her usual saunter, and her smug facial expression was nonexistent. She was altogether very bland and blended in to the background. Even though Wren was aware of her every movement, Marisol was doing a stellar job at not drawing attention to herself.

It was probably killing Marisol to act like this. She'd leave this mission and torment Jock or go clubbing.

When the aunt and uncle walked off to grab another drink, a man approached their table. He gazed steadily at Wren before he turned and shook Darren's hand. "Good to see you."

Darren's smile was tight. "Good to see you, too, Franklin."

Franklin, what a name. He was attractive in the same way Darren was attractive, all-American with a strong jaw, clean-shaven face, and impeccable haircut. His tux was tailored to his body, and the blue shirt underneath was the same color as his eyes. Which were currently taking in her body like she was the freshly carved prime rib. "And your friend?"

"My date's name is Lacy," Darren said, his emphasis on *date* hard to miss.

Franklin didn't seem to care, still not taking his eyes off her. "Ah, and where did you two meet?"

Wren stayed silent, unsure of Franklin's story and careful not to draw the ire of Darren. Not tonight.

"At Alpha," Darren said simply.

Franklin cocked his head. "I guess I should be going to Alpha more often then."

Darren stared at him blandly, and Franklin shot him a grin that was all teeth. "Congratulations to your parents."

Daren said thank you, and the two men spent a few minutes in a tense conversation about the stock market, trying to one-up each other with knowledge. It was some weird privileged game of rich chicken that Wren had no interest in, but she did watch Franklin's body language. He held his back perfectly straight and continuously tapped some sort of college ring against his glass. He also met Darren's gaze directly in a challenging way that made Wren uneasy. He was either just an asshole or an asshole who was capable of evil. She'd keep an eye on him until she was sure which. Eventually he sauntered away, only after making an odd bow toward her with a barely hidden wink. Wren shuddered.

Two hours later and the ballroom was crowded with flushed faces, and the food had been forgotten in place of an unlimited amount of liquor. Wren had managed to avoid drinking all but a few sips of wine. She hadn't been able to get out of dancing with Darren though, and if he put his hand on her bare thigh one more time, she was liable to knee him in the balls.

She met Marisol's gaze over Darren's shoulder as they swayed along the edge of the dance floor. Marisol scratched the corner of her mouth with her middle finger. That was the signal to make her move.

"I'd love another drink." Wren shot Darren the most alluring smile she could. "And you're out, too. Would you grab us a couple?"

Wren's pulse pounded, the sound like a drumbeat in her ears. This was one of the riskiest parts of the mission, the most likely way they'd be caught. She and Marisol had practiced this over and over with Erick pretending to be Darren, and they'd perfected their moves to nearly imperceptible levels. Wren kept a smile plastered on her face and willed her hands to stop trembling.

Marisol moved toward them, holding a tray covered in champagne flutes. She didn't say a word as she held it out.

"Thank you," Wren said, grabbing two glasses before Darren could.

Marisol nodded and turned around, but not before stepping on Darren's foot. He yelped, and Marisol leaped back, still managing to hold on to her tray. "Oh, I'm so sorry, sir!" Marisol said, her hand out.

While Darren's attention was diverted, Wren pretended to adjust her bracelet. With a careful flick of her fingernail, she opened up the heart charm on her bracelet and angled her wrist. The powder contents dropped into one of the champagne flutes, and after a couple of swirls, dissolved completely.

There was safety in numbers this size. Everyone around them was drunk and singing along to Adele. No one was paying attention to her.

When Darren turned around with a frown on his face, clearly ruffled, Wren smiled and handed him a drink. "Accidents happen," she beamed, her grin growing as he snatched the champagne out of her hand and took a large gulp.

"I guess so," Darren said, still scowling.

He finished his drink a minute later, and Wren glanced at the giant clock above the ballroom doors. She had about fifteen minutes before the drug began to make him feel a little woozy, and another ten after that before he passed out.

This was going to be the hardest part of the night, where she'd have to let him take some liberties in order to prove to him that she wanted to be alone with him. Of course the thought made her want to vomit. The imprint of Roarke's hands were all over her body, the echo of his words in her ear. She hoped he was okay back in the van and not losing his mind over this mission. She imagined him hunched over in a chair, one hand tangled in his dark hair, the other holding the headphones to his ear. The dark ink on his fingers would stand out from his white knuckles. He'd alternate between sneering and wincing and cheering.

Well, he'd cheer as soon as she said the next sentence, which was her confirmation Darren had ingested his drink—along with the sleep aide. "This house is gorgeous by the way, at least from what I've seen."

Darren's eyes narrowed a minute before his lips stretched into a grin. "Why don't I take you on a little tour? It's crowded in here anyway."

He held out his arm, which she took as they began to walk toward the exit. He'd taken the bait, like she knew he would. Darren wasn't going to pass up a chance to be alone with her.

He did, in fact, give her a small tour, which surprised her because she figured he'd just shove her in a bedroom. But he led her through the state-of-the-art kitchen with four ovens and into a massive library, where the books were indeed alphabetized.

They approached the stairs, and Darren's grip tightened on her arm. His pupils had begun to dilate, his grin became a little crooked. Despite the knowledge that he was drugged and couldn't hurt her, it didn't stop her heart from racing as they ascended the marble steps leading to the second floor.

Every click of her heels on the floor echoed through the empty foyer. Everyone was concentrated in the ballroom so no one was around to see her and Darren.

"My mother has theme rooms," Darren was saying. "I can show you a couple. They are kind of ridiculous, but she loves them."

"Theme rooms?" Wren tried to act interested and not like every single nerve in her body was firing warning signals to her brain with high-powered rocket launchers.

"Yeah, like she's got an ocean room, a desert room, et cetera."

Oh, that actually sounded kind of cool. He led her down the hallway, which was carpeted with a long dark runner. He opened the door to a room on the left and led her inside.

Oh, he wasn't kidding. One wall was lined with saltwater fish tanks, little Nemos swimming around inside along with some weird crab creature. Another wall was painted with an ocean mural—a sperm whale surfacing. This seemed a little out of character for such an expensive house, but hey, what did she know about being rich?

Darren's body swayed into hers, and she wasn't sure if that was him or the drugs. But either way, she had a couple more minutes until this man slumped to the floor—

Suddenly she was slammed into the wall behind her, so hard that her head thunked loudly, scrambling her brain for a few seconds, which Darren took full advantage of. He caged her in, his hands on either side of her head, his chest smashed against hers. Oh God, she could feel how hard he was because his dick was pressed against her belly. She swallowed against her gag reflex as Darren began to suck on her neck.

Her entire body screamed at her to push him away, fight back, but she couldn't. She had to play the part, unsure if he'd remember this or not, but if he did, he couldn't blame her when he passed out.

"Lacy," he moaned, his wet tongue swirling along her skin, "been waiting a long time to get my hands on you." He ran his fingers up her leg, where her dress split, and with a firm grip on the back of her thigh, yanked it up. She sucked in a breath as he ground against her, his lips leaving her neck to make their way to her mouth. "Little body like this, I bet you're tight as fuck, aren't you?"

The only reason she didn't scream or start crying was because she knew Roarke was listening. *Be strong, Wren.* "Why don't you find out?" she breathed, slipping her fingers down his back to clutch at his ass. She thrust her hips against him. "It's been too long since I've been fucked by a real man."

Darren groaned and pressed his lips against hers. Oh fuck, she was going to be sick. He was moving his mouth, seeking entrance into hers, and if she had to feel that lizard tongue meeting hers, she might just blow this whole damn mission.

But then the pressure began to ease up as Darren's grip on her thigh went a little slack. With a stumble backward and a hand to his head, Darren blinked at her before his eyes rolled back in his head and he collapsed on the floor with a thud.

She breathed hard as she stared at his slumped body. She shuddered, thinking about how narrowly she'd avoided having to make out with Darren. "Done," she whispered to her crew, knowing they'd notify Marisol.

She rushed forward, feeling his pulse, which was light but steady. It was a struggle in her dress and heels to drag his deadweight body away from the doorway. She propped him up in the corner in shadow and smacked his face a couple of times. He didn't move.

She stood up, considering grinding her heel into his balls, when Marisol waltzed into the room. Her bow tie was loosened, and she gazed down at the unconscious figure and eyed Wren from head to toe. "Did he paw you too much?"

Wren shrugged. She didn't care, not really, although she would have given anything for Roarke to be there, for him to take her mouth and grip her thighs to remind her what it felt like to be touched by a real man. Not fucking Darren Saltner.

She resisted the urge to spit on the unconscious figure. "I'm fine, but we need to get moving. We have about two hours, and we've got some breaking and entering to do."

CHAPTER TWELVE

WREN wiped her clammy hands on her dress as adrenaline coursed through her body. Before they left the room with a passed-out Darren, Marisol glanced at her watch and whispered over her shoulder, "Got confirmation that Jock cut the cameras."

Good timing. Wren slipped off her heels to pad barefoot down the hallway while Marisol walked on silent, soft-soled shoes. Because of the size of the house, the sounds of the party could barely be heard as they made their way to Arden's office. Still, a sudden spike of female laughter rattled Wren, and her heart pounded as a trickle of nervous sweat dripped down her back. Darren had led her to the same wing that housed Arden's office so at least the trip to their destination was short.

Within minutes, they were standing in front of a large oak door. There was a security camera in the office as well, which Jock had cut along with the hallway cameras. Other than that, there was no extra security to Arden's office. Marisol rattled the knob with a gloved hand. It was locked, as they'd expected it would be. She unbuttoned her shirt and pulled a thin piece of wire out of her bra. With a wiggle of her eyebrows at Wren, she picked the lock. Wren glanced down the hall, wary of every single raised voice, every clink of a glass.

At the satisfying click of the lock, Wren exhaled.

Marisol pushed the door open, and they crept into Arden's office—the lion's den. Moonlight shone through floor-to-ceiling windows, spotlighting the computer that sat on the massive mahogany desk. An antique globe on a waist-high stand sat in the corner in front of a lush potted plant. Bookshelves, full of tomes with thick embossed spines, lined one wall.

Wren closed the door but stayed nearby to listen for anyone coming down the hallway. Marisol immediately sat in the giant chair, running her hands down the leather arms with an impressed nod before giving it a little spin and placing her hands on the keyboard.

Wren's heartbeat was now so loud in her ears that she feared she wasn't hearing anything else. She wished she weren't wearing satin, so she could wipe her damp palms on the fabric to dry them. The bobby pins in her hair were digging into her scalp, and the beaded bodice of her dress was scratchy. She curled her toes into the carpet, all her senses heightened as she met Marisol's gaze from across the pristine office.

For the first time since she'd met Marisol, a wariness crossed over the woman's face. Her bottom teeth came out to scrape her top lip. Then she spoke into the microphone hidden in her bow tie. "We're in the office. I'm at the log-in screen."

A bead of sweat dripped down Wren's neck, and she wiped it away. They'd watched the footage up until yesterday, and Arden accessed his computer with the same password. Still, Wren worried he'd changed it at the last minute.

Marisol's fingers moved across the keyboard. She'd memorized the password, not trusting to write it down anywhere. Her fingers stopped, and Wren clenched her fists.

"I'm in," Marisol said a little breathlessly, and Wren exhaled.

Marisol uncapped a lipstick from her pocket and popped off the waxy red tip to reveal a flash drive underneath. She plugged it into one of the USB ports on Arden's machine. "Copying his files now."

Wren alternated between holding her breath and panting like she'd run a marathon. She knew they had time. Darren would be passed out for a while, but that didn't stop the hair on her arms from rising like she'd been shocked. Anyone could come up here, and she was sure they'd be snuffed out without a second thought…

"Fuck," Marisol said, and the sound of typing ceased. That one word sent Wren scrambling behind her to look at the screen.

Marisol's hands were balled into fists over the keys, but she unfurled one to point a shaky hand at a password-protected folder. It had an innocuous name—school pictures. But with an extra password on it, they were sure it was anything but school pictures. "Jock, I have a password-protected folder here." Marisol glanced up at Wren. "He's going to look through the footage to see if there's a time Arden accessed this file but…damn it." Marisol's expression darkened. "I guess I can just copy it, and we can figure it out later, when we have time."

Wren glanced at her watch. It'd been ten minutes, although it felt like hours. They had time, but the sooner they got out, the less chance they had of getting caught. Jock had planned to review the files tonight, not spend his time gaining access to a locked folder.

She nibbled at her nail, her mind racing. Something told Wren that Arden had made this one personal. What was he most proud of? His family—

"EDC," she blurted out.

Marisol turned around slowly with raised eyebrows. "I'm sorry?"

Wren flapped her hand, her mouth moving too slow for her brain. "Type in variations of EDC, or electronic digital computer, maybe with the numbers 1946, when it was invented. Or his anniversary date. A family member was involved in the invention of the electronic digital computer. Darren mentioned it, and apparently it's the pride of the family. They claim entrepreneurship runs in their blood." She gestured at the screen wildly, unsure her words were making sense.

Marisol was already typing, the letters almost a blur as they appeared quickly in the input box. She tried about ten variations, with numbers interspersed among the letters. "Damn it," Marisol said. "At least it hasn't locked me out yet."

"Try Darren's birthday with it," Wren said, rattling off the date.

Marisol shrugged. "Worth a try. If this doesn't work, I'm saying fuck it and letting them take a crack at it back at HQ."

Wren wanted the team to spend time looking through the files, not hacking into the file. "Try it."

Marisol typed in a couple passwords, and on the fifth try, her pinkie finger slammed down on the enter key and the password input box disappeared.

The file opened.

Wren thrust her arms in the air in silent victory. They waited, watching the progress bar for the copied files creep from 0 to 25 percent, then to 50 percent. And as it slid to 90 percent, voices sounded down the hall along with the distinct click of heels.

"Come on, come on," Marisol whispered, pumping her fist in the air in a silent gesture to hurry up.

Wren scrambled to the door, pressing her ear to the cool wood as the voices drew closer. She widened her eyes at Marisol, who was bent at the waist to retrieve the drive from the computer. After replacing the lipstick on top to hide the USB port, Marisol wiped the computer's activity log and turned it off.

She rose and carefully placed the chair back where it had been, which she'd marked with small strips of tape. After pulling up the tape and slipping everything back into her pockets, she took her place next to Wren at the door. She mirrored her position to listen to the sounds in the hallway.

"Shh," a woman's voice said. "We're not supposed to be up here."

"Who gives a fuck?" the man said. "I want inside you."

The woman moaned, and Marisol made a gagging gesture. The women stared at each other with widened eyes as the voices reached the door and...kept going.

The slam of a door farther away echoed down the hallway, and the voices were no longer heard. They waited a minute longer until they were sure the couple was occupied. *Very* occupied.

This was where they had to part ways. Marisol had to finish out her shift so as not to draw attention to herself. "Go on, get out of here. I'll take care of Darren when he wakes up to explain why you left."

Wren nodded. That was the plan, for her to fake food poisoning and ask the driver to take her home. Marisol was to tell Darren about Wren's *illness*. "Be safe," she said.

Marisol grinned. "Never." Then her smile faded. "Good luck, okay?"

Wren nodded, knowing this escape would not be easy. Because she wasn't going to stick with the plan. She had other ideas. "I will."

Marisol opened the door, and they slipped out. After locking it behind them, Wren slipped on her heels. They turned to each other, and Marisol gave her a quick hug. "You did good, girl. I'll see you soon."

With a sloppy salute, Marisol turned around and took off down the hallway.

And this . . . this was when Wren went off script. Marisol had the files secure in her pocket. She'd make it back to the crew okay. But Wren? Wren had a mission of her own to complete. Of course, she hadn't told anyone because Roarke would have shut it the fuck down. Actually, so would Erick. And Marisol. And Jock.

Even Dade would have tsked her and told her it wasn't the time. She was aware of that, but it didn't change the fact that she was going to be really fucking selfish right now. Darren was passed out with his phone in his pocket, and Wren wasn't letting that go without copying the SM card. And doing a little digging of her own.

Once Marisol was out of sight, Wren dipped her chin so her lips were as close to the mic as possible. "Sorry boys, got some things to do. I'll catch you back at HQ." Then she turned off her camera.

* * *

Roarke blinked at the dark screen a couple of times while the van erupted around him. Even Jock stood up so fast that he slammed his head on the roof of the van. Erick was banging on the screen, chanting "motherfucker" over and over again, like the video feed would come back to life if he smacked it enough.

Roark slowly rotated in his chair to see Dade watching him steadily, those eerie slate gray eyes all-knowing. He pulled the pen he was chewing out of his mouth. "She's good, but this is stupid. And worse, I think she knows it and is doing it anyway."

Roarke closed his eyes slowly and pressed his headphones into his ears, muffling the sound around him. He had no idea why Wren was doing this, where she was, what she was doing, if she was safe. Nothing.

Just silence and a black screen.

This was worse than when she'd been with Darren on his date, way worse. He'd at least been able to hear her, and she hadn't gone fucking rogue.

Jock was back in his seat before Roarke could tell him what to do, and in seconds, the screens were back on, the security cameras showing real time. In the corner of one of the hallway camera frames, Roarke spotted Wren slipping back into the room where she'd been with Darren.

Roarke tossed his headphones on the table in front of him and rounded on Dade. "Why?"

Dade was quiet for a moment, rolling the pen between his teeth. "She's got a mission of her own against Darren. You think he just happened to notice her in a crowd full of hot chicks? I mean, Wren is bangable as fuck—"

Both Erick and Roarke growled.

Dade rolled his eyes and kept going. "But it's a little coincidental Darren picked her out of everyone, right? She played hard to get, but trust me, she wanted this to happen. She's using you as much as you're using her."

Roarke surged forward, aiming for Dade's neck, but

Jock held him back with a biceps the size of a tree. "Settle the fuck down," he snarled.

Roarke was amped up, his nerves tingling, ready to fight, punch, kick, anything. This wasn't how he acted during missions, but this one wasn't like any other. It involved every goddamn thing that was personal to him. His cool demeanor was shot through with flaming arrows. "Explain this shit to me, Kelly."

Dade shook his head. "Wren can tell you. I don't run my mouth about other people's business. Right now, I'm sure she's copying his entire phone, and she'll be on her way like you all planned. As long as this little setback doesn't throw timing off."

Why did he seem so unconcerned? Roarke flared his nostrils, inhaling as much oxygen as he could, hoping it settled his blood. He was reacting emotionally, a feeling that didn't sit well in his gut, but he couldn't ignore it. He could, however, still think smart.

Erick leaped up. "I can go in. I rode her bike here and hid it outside the gates for her, so we have a quick getaway."

Roarke studied Erick's flushed face. Gone was his calculated friend. Erick was riding on a knife's edge of panic, his hands shaking so badly that he shoved them in his pockets when he caught Roarke looking at them. Roarke shook his head. "I don't think so—"

"So we're just going to wait to see what happens?" Erick was red-faced and sputtering. "Darren is going to wake up, and when he does, Wren needs to be out of there. Don't you care?"

Roarke steadily met Erick's gaze with a level glare. "Don't question how much I care about Wren. Do. Not."

Roarke's tone must have penetrated Erick's hysteria because his expression fell and he slumped back into his chair, letting his head fall into his hands. "Then what are we going to do?"

Roarke stared at the empty hallway on the screen. He closed his eyes, imagining Wren in that mansion full of rich snakes who had enough money to make her disappear forever. She might have thought she knew what she was doing, but he'd be damned if he left her there alone.

He trusted every person on his team, but he trusted himself the most. Roarke grabbed his coat and slipped it on. "Get the van back to HQ. I'm going in myself."

Erick's face paled, and Dade made a snorting sound. "So you're going to rush in like fucking John McClane and likely get her killed?"

Roarke ignored the jab. "John McClane liked guns more than me," he said, opening up the back of the van and hopping out. "He liked ethics more, too. See you, fellas." He smacked the van on the back panel and darted into the hedges lining the street.

As Roarke weaved his way among bushes and weird topiaries, he shook his head. Rich people loved their landscaping, and he appreciated the multitude of shadows to conceal his lanky frame.

He'd scouted this wall several times, knowing there was a blind spot on the security cameras to the far right. Once he was there, he pulled a pair of small climbing suction cups out of his book bag. They soundlessly aided him over the wall, and he fell to a silent crouch on the other side. He was inside, the soles of his boots sinking into plush sod that probably cost more than most people's salaries.

He pulled his phone out of his pocket and pulled up the program he'd developed to give him access to the gated community's security system. The company used security cameras only at various points along the walls surrounding the homes, aimed toward each yard. He'd already recorded hours upon hours of night footage for each camera to loop on a feed should he need to enter the gates. With a few quick taps of his thumbs, he engaged the system to run his prerecorded footage so he could pass undetected. He hadn't done that outside the walls, as the guards monitoring the cameras would notice more quickly if the same cars kept passing into the frame. But here? Where there was no activity but a few squirrels? No problem.

Just like when he'd slipped Wren the earrings, he'd come prepared for this night. Not that he didn't think Wren could handle it. If Roarke had learned one thing over all the years he'd been 6192, it was to be prepared for everything and anything. Every backup plan needed a backup plan. And that backup plan needed a backup plan.

Once his system was running to hide his presence, he ran as swiftly as he could, crouched, toward the Saltner house. The small Glock in his boot holster dug into his ankle. He rarely carried a gun. In fact, he fucking hated guns. But sometimes in his profession, they were necessary. So he kept himself armed and hoped like hell he didn't have to use it.

The Saltner house loomed ahead, lit up like a goddamn Christmas tree. He could see figures in the floor-to-ceiling windows of what must be the ballroom, which took up the whole back of the house. His eyes immediately scanned for a red dress, even though he doubted Wren was in there. She was busy doing shit they hadn't agreed on. How the fuck was he supposed to help keep her safe if she went off-script? She'd had plenty of times to explain her own personal agenda against Darren or the Saltners. Had she not trusted him? Was this whole thing between them a distraction she'd planned?

He had to shut this anger off, stuff it down. Now was not the time to let it overtake him. The number one goal was her safety, and secondary was the success of this mission. A very, very distant third was his feelings over her decision to hide something from him.

He stood behind a large maple tree with a trunk as thick as his body and weighed his options. He couldn't go storming in there like some vigilante. They'd probably shoot him, and he'd blow everything. But knowing Wren was in there right now, possibly in danger, was making him ill. He shifted his weight from foot to foot, hands clenched at his sides. He pulled a ball cap out of his back pocket, pulled it low over his eyes, and was about to call Jock when he got an incoming text. All it said was the word *tracker* along with a link.

He opened it and a blueprint of the Saltner house unrolled on his screen. And there, in a side room on the first floor, was a red blinking dot. Jock must have put a tracker on Wren.

Roarke smiled. "Gotcha."

He kept to the shadows as he rounded the house, creeping closer to that red dot—and Wren. Why was she in that area of the house? Darren was on the second floor so if her only mission was to copy his phone, why would she be in a small room on the first floor?

He stopped once he was within ten feet of the room and crouched behind a hedge. Saltner had his own video security for his house, but Roarke didn't want to take the time to deal with the outside cameras, not while Wren was so close. Alarm bells in his brain told him to *get her safe now*. In the back of his mind, he knew this was dangerous, that he should take his time, but this was what Wren did to him. She made him take risks.

He glanced around for security cameras, and made a cursory glance at Jock's diagram. This seemed to be a dead spot, so he should be okay. With a deep breath, he made a dash from the safety of the shrubbery to the wall of the house and flattened himself against it, turning his head to listen. He was beneath the window, and when he strained his ears, he could distinctly hear voices. Plural.

A man's voice, so low that it was muffled but still detectable through the thin glass of the window.

Then a higher-pitched voice. Wren. He'd know her cadence anywhere.

He heard no other voices, just those two, and his heart began to thump in his throat at a rapid, parading beat, threatening to choke him.

Wren's voice grew louder, and he could pick out words here and there. "Wasn't feeling…well…Resting…driver…me home."

The male voice again, this time tinged with…Roarke's blood boiled. This guy was trying to pick her up. And from the sounds of it, Wren wasn't free to leave. Her voice was more insistent now. Irritated.

Roarke crouched and slid under the window. From there he checked his phone again. She was against the far wall, so most likely the guy had her cornered. He held his phone up and angled it so it would show what was going on inside the room, and he took a quick picture. When he checked the picture, sure enough, the man's back was facing the window.

Roarke lifted his head inch by inch until he could see inside.

Wren stood with her back against the far wall. Roarke could barely see her because most of her body was blocked by some suit with slicked-back hair. He had one hand propped on the wall by her head, the other casually stroking her arm.

Roarke took a chance and flashed the light on his camera. Wren's eyes darted toward the window before she looked away quickly to cover up. The man kept talking, oblivious to what was going on as Wren slowly lifted her gaze again and met Roarke's.

She shook her head, just a slight jerk, before once again focusing on the man in front of her. She held up one finger at her side, close to her body. And Roarke sat tight. He knew Wren wanted him to trust her to get out of this situation, and while he trusted her abilities, he didn't trust her judgment, not with this off-script stunt.

"...Hard to get...," the man said. And he gripped her neck and went in for a kiss.

Roarke saw red. He grabbed a rock on the ground, intent on breaking the damn window—detection be damned—when the man dropped to the floor with a thud, holding his hand between his legs. He shouted, *"Bitch!"* as Wren leaped over him, her dress billowing around her as she sprinted to the window. She unlocked the window and threw up the sash. "Get me the fuck out of here," she growled as she threw a leg over the windowsill and slid out.

Roarke caught 110 pounds of satin and crystals and a warm, whole Wren. He wanted to wrap his arms around her, hold her close, and breathe her in, but there wasn't time. He closed the window with a bang and grabbed her hand before sprinting off into the shadows.

Wren kept up surprisingly well in her heels. Her hand clutched his like he was her lifeline, and no fucking way was he letting her go. Any second, he expected to hear sirens, wondering if that man saw him or just thought Wren was some crazy woman who kicked men in the nuts and leaped through windows when threatened. Darren had been due to wake up minutes ago, and Roarke was sure he'd call the police, depending on how well Wren had covered her tracks. As of now, she was his date who went home after he passed out. Whether he believed that was another story.

She panted along beside him, and he swore their breathing was so loud that they'd clue everyone in to where they were.

They ran the entire way to the wall of the gated community. He pulled out suction cups from his backpack and handed them to her. Their eyes met for a brief moment, and he had to clench his jaw to keep from asking her what the hell she'd been doing.

A bit of guilt flashed in those brown eyes before she scaled the wall and threw the suction cups back down to him.

Once he dropped down on the other side, she whispered, "Where's the van?"

He shoved everything back into his backpack and grabbed her hand again, leading her to a shadowed yard. "It's gone."

"Gone? Are we walk—"

He pulled her bike out from behind a white pine in the yard of a nearby house. "No, we aren't fucking walking. Now get on so we can get the fuck out of here."

Her mouth dropped open, and she turned a glare on him just as they heard sirens. "Fuck," he whispered, hopping on the bike and starting it up. Wren grabbed the helmet he handed her, gathered her skirt, and hopped astride the bike. As soon as she wrapped her arms around him, Roarke sped off down a side street, narrowly avoiding the police cars.

CHAPTER THIRTEEN

WREN'S bike vibrated between her thighs as she clung to Roarke's chest. She curled her fingers into the worn leather of his jacket as the cold zipper rasped along her palms.

She'd underestimated Roarke. She never thought he'd hunt her down at the Saltner estate. And everything would have been fine if Franklin hadn't cornered her when she was almost out the door.

She might have done irreparable damage to her cover, but she wasn't about to go along with whatever Franklin wanted, not while Darren was minutes away from coming to. She'd texted him to let him know she wasn't feeling well and left, and made a chastising comment about him drinking too much.

She'd tried not to be terrified when Franklin had her back against the wall. She had some self-defense skills, but the smell of whiskey on his breath and the press of his body against hers had sent her nerves into overdrive.

Roarke had come for her. He was furious, evidenced by the tight clench of his jaw and his slightly reckless driving of her bike. But he'd still come for her.

She thought they'd go to HQ, but Roarke wasn't driving in that direction. Instead, he turned down a side alley and coasted the bike onto a small concrete pad next to his Mustang. Were they at his place? He turned off the bike and twisted at the waist, jerking his thumb to tell her to get off. She swung her leg over and pulled off her helmet, still confused as to why they were here and not HQ. She opened her mouth to ask why, but he was already striding toward the door, his boots crunching on the loose macadam. With her head down, she followed him as he opened the door.

The adrenaline was still fueling her, and nerves skittered over her skin like ants as they walked into a large room—his apartment. He tossed his keys on his kitchen counter, tore off his jacket, and with an explosive overhand throw, whipped it at the wall.

It hit with a slap, and she jolted at the sound as he turned on her. "What the fuck, Wren?" He gripped his white T-shirt over his heart. The veins in his neck stood out and strands of his hair fell over his eyes. "We send you there to get information, and you go dark on us? Do you even understand what it felt like when that camera shut off? When I had no idea if you were okay or not?" She'd never seen him like this—emotional and vulnerable and so damn wrecked. Now that he was in the light, she could see his lips were ravaged from biting them, his eyes bloodshot. As he stared her down, his entire body was shaking. "And fuck, I show up to pull you out of that hellhole, and some rich asshole has you pinned in an empty room." He tore his hands through his hair so it stood on end. "I don't trust any of them. They could have taken you to another location—"

"I'm sorry," Wren blurted out. Her heart felt split in two—her promise to her old friend warring with the need to soothe Roarke.

"Are you?" he asked, his tone vicious and accusatory, his words spat at her like daggers. "Because Dade said you had this planned all along, that you're using this mission as a vehicle to carry out your own—"

"That's not true!" Roarke could say what he wanted about her, but how dare he act like her love for Flynn wasn't the driving force behind this. She flung a finger at him. "You don't get to make up shit in your head or listen to Dade. The truth is that yes, I've been casing Darren for a year. Yes, I caught his eye on purpose. But my number one priority is Flynn's mission. Marisol already had the Saltner files, so I was free to get what I needed."

"What. Do. You. Need. Exactly?" Roarke spoke through clenched teeth.

"I can't..." No, she'd promised. "I can't tell you."

Roarke's dark brows lifted almost to his hairline. "You can't tell me?"

"I promised a friend, a very good friend, that I'd get evidence on Darren for her."

Roarke spread out his arms. "Do you see anyone here? Anyone? It's just me, Wren. You can tell me. I can help you. We can help you." His face changed, from incredulous to determined, as he began to stalk toward her. "Because I'm going to make one thing very clear, Wren." She had to back up because he wasn't stopping. "You're not going to put yourself in a situation like that again."

Her hackles went up. "Oh, so this is where you tell me what to do again—"

Her back hit the wall, and his chest bumped hers. "You have a crew now, an entire crew at your back." He clenched his jaw as his gaze dipped to her lips. His warm hand cupped her neck, thumb brushing along her jaw line, a heated touch that shot hot flares through her body like lightning. "And you have me. You've always had me."

This was the same position she'd been in less than an hour ago with Franklin. But how she felt now as compared to then was night and day. Roarke's body molded against hers, the desire that sparked in his dark eyes stoking the flames of arousal in her veins.

She turned her head slightly so her mouth brushed his palm. His breath caught in his throat as she opened her lips and placed a damp kiss on the heel of his hand. With a moan, he tilted her chin up and took her mouth, his lips opening immediately to sweep inside. Her pulse raced as she clutched his face to draw him closer, needing more. She kicked her leg out of the slit in her dress and hooked it over his thigh, wanting maximum contact as all the emotions of the night culminated into *must lose myself in Roarke.*

He tore away from the kiss on a frustrated growl and buried his face in her neck. His warm hand gripped her thigh, digging into the skin, as he spoke tersely. "How come I can't stop touching you? I tell myself to stay away—"

"Don't want you to stay away." She thrust her chest against his, grinding against the hard length in his pants. "You're so mad at me? Take it out on me then. Fuck the secrets out of me."

He jerked his head back and held it inches from her face. "That a dare?"

Maybe it was. Maybe she was bluffing. All she knew for certain was that she was going to combust if Roarke didn't make her forget this whole night. She bit her lip and looked at him from under her lashes. "Maybe."

With a snarl, he hoisted her up in the air so she had to wrap her arms and legs around him. She crashed their mouths together, and he stumbled backward until he hit something solid with a curse. He spun them around, making her dizzy, before laying her on a hard surface. She had a moment to realize it was his kitchen table before he was hiking her dress up to her waist.

She rolled her hips as he stared down at the small scrap of fabric covering her. His nostrils flared as his thumbs rubbed the skin above the waistband of her underwear, dipping lower and lower at a maddeningly slow pace.

She was about to tell him to hurry the fuck up when he slipped the thong down her legs and tossed it behind him. Then his fingers were on her, rubbing over the heated, wet flesh, circling her clit.

"Yesss," her voice broke on a hiss, and she closed her eyes as he kept up the stroking and the swirling with those talented fingers. "Those fingers can penetrate a fire wall *and* make me come." She opened her eyes and grinned a filthy smile. "Got me a man who can do both."

With a bark of laughter he kissed her again as he fumbled with his belt and jeans. "Fuck, Wren," he said. "Wanted to take this slow, draw it out—"

"Tonight's not the night for that," she murmured.

He pulled back, his hair in his eyes, tongue snaking out to taste her on his lips. He turned up his mouth into a smirk as he pulled his hard dick out of his pants. She reached down, wanting to get her hands on that hot, hard length. She rubbed her thumb over the head, wet with pre-come, while Roarke stood with his hands at his sides, letting her play. She stroked him and rubbed the tip over her wet folds. He was so hot, and her body ached from being empty.

Roarke's head was back, eyes closed. "Let me get a condom," he mumbled.

"It's fine. I'm on the pill," she assured him. He met her gaze steadily, and she added, "I don't make it a habit, but I know you wouldn't put me at risk."

"Never," he said through gritted teeth. He fisted his cock and entered her in a smooth thrust. She was wet, but his size was still a shock, so she squirmed as he fell onto his hands over her. His eyes were squeezed shut, lips parted. Once he was fully inside her, he froze. She did, too, the sensation so overwhelming, so much. Too much.

Oh fuck, was she going to cry? How many times had she dreamed of this moment, when Roarke wanted her so bad that he fucked her on the first available surface? When he would open up those dark eyes with the depth of infinity and stare into hers? "Wren," he said on a choked whisper.

"Roarke," she answered.

Then his hips snapped back, and he rocked into her. Once. Twice, then a steady pace that shoved her higher on the table, that caused the entire thing to squeak on loose screws. That had her crying out with her back arched as he gripped her hips and pounded into her.

This. This was what she'd been missing all her adult life.

She lifted her hands and gripped his wrists and met every thrust with one of her own. Soon they were in sync, the apartment filled with the sounds of flesh hitting flesh, Roarke's grunts and her high-pitched cries.

Roarke placed a hand on her lower stomach, his thumb right over her clit, which he began to swirl and press and rub. She could feel her orgasm building, that tell-tale prickle in her toes. She slapped a hand on the table, the sensations so overwhelming that her first instinct was to get away. But Roarke growled again as he changed his angle, and that was it. The big bang. Lights flashed behind her eyes, and her body jerked as she screamed out the orgasm currently sweeping through her body like wildfire.

She vaguely heard Roarke say, "Aw fuck," before his hips stuttered and his cock pulsed inside her.

When his thrusts stopped, she didn't move for a moment, unsure if her eyes were open or closed because she wasn't seeing anything anyway. Then she blinked them open just as Roarke's head thunked down onto her chest.

She lifted a weak hand and ran it through his hair as he clung to her, his back heaving. He was still inside her, and at this point, she wasn't too eager to change their positions. It took a minute or two for the postorgasmic bliss to dissipate, and she began to feel the hard wood at her back, the ache of her thighs. "Baby," she said softly.

He lifted his head slowly, and there was a brief moment when he let every guard drop. When those eyes weren't full of secrets, and everything he was feeling was right there, floating to the surface for her to see.

* * *

That wasn't supposed to happen. This entire night had gone right to shit. He stared at the crack between the bathroom door and the floor, watching the shadows shift as Wren moved about inside.

She was here, in his apartment, and he hadn't thought this through, hadn't planned this out. Nothing was black and white, and it was killing him. Why couldn't all of life be in binary?

He wasn't used to involving himself physically in missions this much. There was less control this way, more room for error. He preferred the logical lines of code, the clicking of a keyboard that dictated how things would go.

Hell, he preferred that in his personal life, too. Which is why he'd defaulted to quick Tinder hookups or, lately, porn. Porn was always a safe standby.

But Wren wasn't safe, and he couldn't control how things went anymore with a little extra programming. This was real, and the entire thing was making his chest tight. He retreated to his kitchen counter, where he poured a glass of water. He chugged the entire thing immediately. The door to the bathroom opened just as he wiped the back of his hand across his mouth and turned around.

Wren stood barefoot in front of him. "Um, could you unzip the back for me?"

He set the glass down on the counter a little harder than he meant to. The sound made Wren flinch, and he forced a smile to cover it up. "Sure."

On the way to her, he grabbed the backpack with her spare clothes and dropped it at her feet. He made the sign for her to turn around, and she did. He flexed his fingers, telling himself not to maul her, before he swept her hair to the side to reveal the zipper of her dress.

Her pale shoulders trembled slightly as he pulled the zipper down to where it stopped at her lower back. When she glanced at him over her shoulder, all dark, smoky cat eyes, he lost the battle with himself and leaned down to press a kiss to the top of her shoulder.

"Roarke," she whispered, as his lips moved their way up her neck. "Let me wipe off this tattoo cover-up, then we'll talk, okay?"

He closed his eyes and pulled away from her skin, even though every part of him wanted to devour her again. "Yeah." His voice was hoarse. Where was this going? What were they doing? How much was this going to hurt when it got even more fucked up than it already was?

She retreated to the bathroom. After he chugged another glass of water and proceeded to spill it all over himself, he took his shirt off with a frustrated grunt. He stripped down to his boxers and was rummaging around for a pair of sweats when Wren emerged from the bathroom. She wore a pair of leggings and an oversized shirt, her tattoos once again visible, her skin pink from where she'd rubbed off the cover-up. She stood just in the doorway of the bathroom, watching him as he stepped into his sweatpants.

She placed one foot on top of the other, leaning against the frame as she fidgeted with the hem of her shirt. Her hair was pulled up on top of her head, and her lips trembled slightly before she took a sharp intake of breath. "I was a freshman in college when I asked my roommate to go to this event at a local club. She didn't want to go. She was tired because she'd been studying for a test, but I was in the mood to drink and dance. So she agreed."

He wasn't sure where this was going, but he crossed his arms over his chest and settled in to listen.

"So we went, and it was really fun. These guys were paying attention to us, and they were hot, and so we went with it until…" Wren bit her lip. "Until I stopped remembering."

His heart slammed against his ribs, and he clenched his jaw to keep from roaring at the image flashing through his mind of a vulnerable Wren. "What do you mean you stopped remembering?"

"I mean I blacked out. I woke up to my friend screaming. We were in a house, and they were dragging her into a room, where I could see a dirty mattress on the floor and a"—she swallowed—"a camera set up in front of it, on a tripod."

"Jesus fucking Christ," Roarke spat.

"I couldn't do anything. My limbs weren't working right. My head was pounding. One guy was watching me, and I asked to go to the bathroom. He let me, and I managed to crawl out the window and run away. I called the police immediately, but when they went to the house, it was empty."

Roarke stared at her, unable to contain his horror or stuff down the bile rising in his throat. "Your friend—"

"She came back," Wren said. "A month later. She was addicted to drugs, weighed about twenty pounds less and..." Her voice failed as tears fell down her cheeks. "She went to rehab and therapy and got clean. She fakes being okay, but she's not okay. I found out they still terrorize her and send her the videos they made of her and threaten her if she talks. She has no family, no one really." She swallowed. "Except me."

Wren wiped vigorously at her face. "That's when I started learning to code. I'm determined to get back at these assholes and shut down this shit. I want revenge for her. And I have guilt on top of it because I made her go to that club."

Roarke didn't bother telling her it wasn't her fault. He knew all about guilt, and how someone telling you it wasn't your fault did jack shit. "What does this have to do with Darren?"

Her chin lifted. "It took a long time to follow the tracks, but they lead to him. Or at least, he's as far up as I've gotten at this point. He uses his clubs to find girls."

Roarke's stomach roiled. He couldn't get the image of Wren's unconscious body out of his head. "Did they... did you...?"

She shook her head. "No. I went and got checked. Just drugged."

He was going to implode as his brain raced through everything he'd done over the last ten years, all the small clicks he'd made to help Wren be nothing but safe and successful. "How did I not know about this?" His voice was hoarse.

She tilted her head. "How could you know? I didn't tell anyone."

"Hospital records?"

"I gave them a different name. Said I was insured and paid in cash."

"B-but you…No!" At his shout, she jerked, even as the volume of his voice surprised him, too. "But I watched you. I knew when you got a sinus infection; I knew when you went to Planned Parenthood for free birth control. Fuck, I even knew when your profs entered your grades… everything. I knew goddamn everything, so how the fuck could I not know about this!"

She stared at him, frozen with wide eyes before her face screwed up, and she stalked toward him. "What did you say? What do you mean you knew all of that?"

He wasn't thinking of self-preservation. He just wanted to know how he missed this, what he could have done to prevent it, to make it better. "You haven't been alone for ten years," he said. "Because I was always one click away."

Her mouth dropped open. "I'm sorry, what?"

"I oversaw it. Sometimes interfered."

Her face went from disbelief to rage in about two seconds. "You hacked my life?"

"I was trying to help you."

"By spying on me!" She trembled, tears pooling in the corners of her eyes as she stamped her bare foot. "What kind of interference?"

Why had he confessed? *Because I love her.* "Small things."

She spoke through gritted teeth. "What kind of small things?"

"A raise here and there at your campus jobs." Her eyes bugged out, but his confession was on a roll. "And that one time you entered to win free gas for a year."

Her face was thunder. "You mean you made me win that?"

He held his ground. He hadn't done anything *really* wrong, had he? "Gas was expensive that summer."

"Oh my God, Roarke!" She spun around, her hands in her hair as she stalked over to the backpack and shoved her feet in her boots. With a huff, she slung the bag over her shoulder and clomped back over in her unlaced boots. Her finger was out, pointing right at his chest, and he knew he'd fucked up. How did he explain it'd grown into an addiction? He had no excuse. He'd wanted the best for her, and somewhere along the line, it'd all gone awry. "Wren," he said, "I'm sorry, but I can't take it back now—"

"Fuck you, Roarke." She stalked past him on the way to the front door.

"Wren—"

She whirled around. "I'll finish out this mission for Flynn, but you need to promise me you'll stop. You'll get out of my life. It's not your life, Roarke! How could you do this?"

Tears streamed down her cheeks now, black, mascara-tinted rivers, and with them his dreams of ever holding on to Wren. "I'm sorry."

A sob burst from her lips before she covered her mouth with the back of her hand. "What am I to you?" she whispered. "An avatar or a real person?"

His heart cracked open like a split coconut. "You're—"

"Never mind," she said, straightening her shoulders. "I

don't give a fuck." She opened his front door and stalked out to her bike.

He knew she was beyond reason, but he couldn't stop himself from saying, "At least tie your damn boots before you get on your bike."

She froze with her helmet halfway to her head and turned a glare on him that he felt on his face like a rattlesnake bite. "Sorry, Roarke. Guess you didn't enter the right coding for me to lace my boots. Error five-oh-five," she said in a robot voice.

Then she shoved the helmet on her head, straddled her bike, and roared away.

He watched the taillights of her bike as they grew smaller and smaller until she turned a street corner and vanished. He somehow managed to drag himself into his place and shut the door behind him before he slid to the floor with his back against the wall.

This place still smelled like her, and when he glanced into the open door of the bathroom, he saw her dress lying in a crimson and beaded puddle on the floor.

He wasn't perfect, he'd never claimed to be. Flynn always said Roarke needed to quit living life through the Web and actually dialogue with people. *Be relatable*, Flynn always said. That was the problem though, because Roarke didn't know how to be. During all the crucial years in his life when he maybe could have developed some sort of damn social skills, he'd been behind a computer.

He'd intended to check on Wren only to make sure she wasn't getting screwed by people and to double check inaccuracies that would harm her. He'd never actually meant to...affect her life. Until he'd done it that first time, then another time, until he was making tiny changes all over the place.

Love was watching over people. And if that meant from behind a computer, then that was what he did. That *was* love, right?

He wasn't sure how much time passed with him sitting on the floor when his phone buzzed with a text from Erick. *Wren's here, where are you? Got news.*

CHAPTER FOURTEEN

WHEN Roarke strode into the basement, the room was full of quiet murmurs and the click of keys.

In the corner, he spotted Wren and Marisol. Wren didn't even look at him, but as he approached, her body went tight. Fuck, the memory of them together was still vivid. He could still taste her skin on his tongue, and now he had to pretend like nothing had happened.

He could do this. He had to.

He clapped Marisol on the shoulder, and she elbowed him affectionately. "Hey boss."

"Glad to see you back safe. You killed it in there."

"I know." She'd taken off her wig and already changed her clothes, slipping back into herself effortlessly. "Wren here smashed it, too."

Roarke forced himself to look at her, and when her brown eyes lifted to his, there was hurt there. Maybe a little regret, too? Regret about what they'd done? She might as well have punched him—it would probably hurt less. He steeled himself and said, "Yes, she did."

Something flickered over Wren's face, and when he looked back at Marisol, she was frowning. She opened her mouth to say something, but Erick beat her to it.

"Get over here!"

Roarke spun around. Erick beckoned from where he stood hunched over Jock, who was squinting at the computer in front of him. As Roarke walked toward them, he spotted Dade in the corner, the light of his laptop illuminating his face.

"Did you find anything?" Roarke said as he drew up a chair next to Jock.

Erick seemed too hyper to sit down, his face flushed. "He kept a lot of documentation."

Roarke squinted at the lines of code. This was his language; he had an easier time reading it than something written in English. It was the way his brain worked. He didn't have to translate code in his head, it was a language all on its own, and the one his mind preferred. "Do we know when the zero-day sold?"

"Day after Flynn was killed," Jock said in a monotone.

Roarke wiped his hand over his face. "So Arden needed him out of the way to get his payday."

"Yup," Jock said, his fingers moving across the keyboard in a blur.

"Excuse me," Dade said from his corner. All heads turned to him, as if they'd forgotten he was there. Roarke kinda had.

"What's up?" Roarke asked.

Dade plunked down a wireless speaker on the table and projected it out to the rest of them, and Roarke stood.

Dade settled back in his chair. "Looks like Arden recorded some conversations for insurance." Dade dramatically pressed his finger down on the keyboard.

A voice garbled by a distorter filled the room. "I don't have time for your *research* anymore. My deadline is tomorrow, and I need him gone or I'm out millions. I'm not paying you to spy on him. I'm paying you to kill him."

Roarke sucked in a breath; the words were like a kick to the solar plexus. This had to be Arden, speaking casually about killing Flynn. Roarke braced himself on the table in front of him.

"And I told you, I'd have it done by your deadline." The second voice wasn't distorted, and Roarke assumed Arden kept this conversation in case the hired hit man turned on him. "It's been hard to get him alone. As soon as his boyfriend leaves tomorrow, I'm on it. Unless you want me to kill him, too?"

"No, I'd prefer less bodies," Saltner's voice said. "You mean that Asian guy?"

"Yeah," the hit man said.

Dade stopped the recording, and the room plunged into a deafening silence. Roarke's ears were ringing, his mind reeling. So this wasn't about Flynn. This was in reference to the other guy they offed, because Flynn didn't have a boyfriend…

A muffled sob reached Roarke's ears, and he jerked his head up. Erick stood by the door, his hand cupped over his mouth and a single tear slipping down his face as he met Roarke's gaze.

That was when Roarke's mind went blank, when human emotions and words jumbled in his brain because they didn't add up to clear data. "Wait." Roarke's voice didn't sound like his. It sounded deeper, miles away. "What's going on?"

Erik dropped his hand as his eyes darted from Wren to Roarke. "I'm sorry. We were gonna tell you. All of you. Soon. But…" He shook his head, and the tears were coming harder now, dripping off his chin as his slender shoulders shook. He turned and ran out the door, Wren at his heels, her hair streaming behind her as she called for Erick to wait.

Jock muttered under his breath, “Shit,” and Marisol stood with her hands on her hips, her eyes wet as she stared after Erick. Dade simply raised his eyebrows and went back to typing.

Meanwhile, Roarke couldn’t move, frozen in place by the brand-new information that Flynn and Erick had been together. A couple.

Hell, he hadn’t even known either of them were into men. Why hadn’t they told him? His mind tried to flip through his past words and deeds, wondering if he ever gave either of them the impression that he wouldn’t accept them, but he came up empty. Had they not trusted him?

He shook his head—his feelings were secondary though. All this time, he thought Erick had been grieving for a friend. But he’d been mourning a *boyfriend*, and he’d kept it all inside. He must have been hurting so badly. How shitty of a friend was Roarke that he hadn’t even picked up on it?

So he was fucking up left and right with the Lee family. He should just head up to Erie and do something to piss off their parents while he was at it.

“I…” His tongue wasn’t working right. He needed to get out of here, to be alone. There was too much that wasn’t making sense, too many people and thoughts and feelings, and it was more than he’d had to deal with in years. He licked his lips and tried again. “I gotta go.”

He made his way to the door and vaguely heard Marisol call his name, followed by Dade’s bored tone. “Let him go.”

When he slammed the door behind him, they were arguing. Whatever, they were adults. He had his own shit to unfuck.

He sat in his car with the engine running for a long time, fingers hovering over his phone's keyboard as he thought about what to say to Erick. Was it just fooling around? Did they love each other? Roarke's head pounded, wishing Flynn was in the passenger seat of his Mustang, bitching about the vents blasting cold air on his face and the way his knees always knocked the dashboard.

Roarke would growl at him to quit being a diva, and Flynn would grin that effervescent smile that dripped with charm. And Roarke would grin back. No one could resist smiling around Flynn.

Roarke squeezed his eyes shut, the grief once again threatening to drown him, to take him under. He'd been able to ignore it for so long because revenge had been the one overriding thought as soon as he'd heard about Flynn's death. It had taken on a life of its own, evolving from a loaded noun into its very own emotion.

He couldn't let the grief win right now. He couldn't retreat to that time right after Flynn died, when he realized he had no one. No mother, no father, and now no brother. No fucking family and only Erick to cling to. But Erick had been distant, lost in his grief. And now Roarke understood why. If Roarke let himself go back to that place, he'd never be able to finish the mission. With his heart in his throat, he finally typed to Erick, "You're still my right hand, man. This doesn't change anything."

He sent the text and waited. No response. He thought about driving to Erick's apartment and banging down the door until his friend answered, but the guy had been through enough. It was probably better they both talked again after a good night's sleep.

Except Roarke knew his sleep would be anything but good. On the way home, he picked up a bottle of Jameson.

He'd already broken the seal by the time he parked his car and took his first swig as he unlocked the door.

He didn't think after that, not about Wren or Flynn or Erick or about smashing Arden's face. He drank and he drank until the room spun and the bottle slipped from his numb fingers.

Only then did he pass out on his bed fully clothed and dreamed the dreamless sleep of the drunk and broken.

* * *

Roarke woke up to the sound of his ringtone. With a pounding headache that blurred his vision, he fumbled around for his cell, not even caring who was calling. He just needed that goddamn bleating sound to stop.

His hand closed around his phone and he swiped blindly with his thumb before croaking, "What?" into the receiver.

Jock's voice came over the line. "Patch is deployed. Data is safe. Whoever bought that zero-day is gonna be mighty disappointed."

Roarke blinked, waiting for his brain to catch up. "Good work."

"Orange juice and Advil," Jock said.

Roarke wasn't in the mood for puzzles. "What?"

"For your hangover." Then he hung up.

Roarke took his phone from his ear and stared at it for a moment. Jock was a fucking oddball and way too damn observant for a person with no emotions.

He rolled over onto his back, wincing at the soreness of his muscles and the crick in his neck. His mind was moving at turtle speed, but it managed to conjure up last night. Wren storming out his door. That distorted voice. Erick's face. Roarke's stomach roiled and he dry heaved. He had to get up, eat something, get his shit together.

He stumbled out of bed, used the bathroom, and trudged into the kitchen in his boxer briefs. He opened the refrigerator, staring inside, unsure what he came in there for in the first place.

"Orange juice is on the top shelf," Erick's voice filtered through his headache.

"Oh, cool." Roarke grabbed it and froze, his head still in the fridge. Wait, how had he heard Erick's voice? He stood up and shut the fridge door, before spinning slowly on his heel to see Erick sitting at his island.

His hair was a mess, sticking up at angles. He scratched his blotchy face and peered at Roarke with bloodshot eyes. "Hey."

Roarke stared at him, then the front door. He returned his gaze to Erick. "How'd you get in here?"

"I copied a key one time."

Of course he did. "Um."

Erick gestured to a glass in front of him. "For your juice."

"Oh. Right. Thanks." Roarke tugged the glass in front of him and poured a full cup of orange juice. He chugged half of it before wiping his hand across his mouth and staring at his best friend. He wasn't sure what to say. Did Erick want validation they were okay? Of course they were okay. Sure, Roarke felt a little rocked that his best friend and brother hadn't been truthful, but Erick was a visible wreck, and Roarke wasn't going to rail on him for keeping his relationship private. "Um, I don't know what to say here. Did you get my text?"

Erick was staring at his clasped hands on the counter. "Yep."

Roarke swirled his orange juice, and downed the rest of it. "Do you want anything? Water? Coffee? Eggs—"

"I loved him." Erick's voice was reed thin, riding a wire.

Roarke dropped his glass onto the counter with a clatter. "Erick—"

Erick lifted his head, tears leaking from the corners of his eyes. "We had it planned when we were going to tell everyone. Remember that barbecue we were going to have? The one where Flynn got mad because I wanted to grill turkey burgers?"

Roarke smiled at the memory of the two fighting. "Yeah."

"That's when we were going to announce everything."

"Look." Roarke wished he didn't have a blood alcohol content while having this conversation. "I'm not mad. You don't have to assure me I was going to know soon. But if you want to tell me, I'd love to know how this happened. I didn't know Flynn was gay. Or you."

Erick ran his hands over his face. "Flynn was Flynn. I'd never been with a guy before, even though I'd thought for a long time I was attracted to them." Erick bit his lip and glanced at Roarke, who kept his face neutral. He didn't want to spook Erick into shutting down. "Flynn had been with men before, and you know, Roarke...he's so...he was so damn charismatic." Erick's shoulders seemed to lose tension as he lifted his head to stare at the ceiling before dropping it back down to meet Roarke's gaze. "So we started *us*. And it was the most perfect thing in my life."

Roarke started toward him—to hug, to console, something—but Erick held up a hand to stop him and took a deep breath. "We had plans. We were going to travel and get a dog, maybe a cat. I wanted a Nemo fish. So many plans." Erick's voice deepened, growing rougher. "He took the job with Saltner Defense for me." He pounded on his chest. "He was going legit so we could settle down.

Pay taxes. Be productive members of society." His hands clenched. "So it eats at me like a fucking cancer every god-damn day that Flynn is dead because of me."

In two strides, Roarke was at Erick's side, clasping him against his chest as Erick let loose a torrent of sobs that he'd valiantly held back. Erick's entire body shook, his gasps sounding painful as he soaked Roark's chest with tears.

A part of Roarke wanted someone else to blame for Flynn's death, but he could have blamed himself, too. He was the one who started programming, who encouraged Flynn to do it, too. They wouldn't be in this mess at all if Flynn had gone into nursing or teaching or something fucking legal.

Instead he'd followed in his big brother's footsteps and paid for it with his life. So no, Roarke couldn't blame Erick. Not one bit.

"It's not your fault," Roarke said. "I know you know that. But guilt is a motherfucker."

"I'd give anything to have him back," Erick said, his voice a bit clearer.

"I can't believe you kept quiet about your relationship this whole time. How are you not angrier?"

Erick pulled away. "I *am* angry. I'm fucking pissed. But I can't live like that every minute. This mission is the reason I'm not still in a blanket fort in my apartment. This revenge gave me life again."

"I know the feeling," Roarke said grimly.

Erick's smile was wan. "Yeah, I know you do."

Roarke sat down heavily on the stool beside Erick, his legs not supporting him as well as he'd like. "I wish I would have known. Was he nervous about telling me? Did he think I wouldn't have understood?"

"He was nervous, but he didn't think you wouldn't accept him. He was worried it would affect your relationship with him, that it would affect your friendship with me. No matter what, this would have changed the way the three of us interacted, you know? Not necessarily in a bad way, but it would have changed."

Roarke tried to imagine family dinners with Roarke and Flynn sitting together at the table, kissing, holding hands. He could have seen all the joy they brought to each other's lives. He could have been a witness to their love. And instead it had been taken from him. From Erick. From all of them.

That fire in his blood, that driving need for revenge, was still there, brighter than ever, pushing through the haze of alcohol.

"I'm sorry I never got to see how happy you were together," Roarke said.

Erick's lips twitched. "Me too."

"Was he, uh, was he a good boyfriend?"

Erick's smile was genuine now. "The best. He used to..." He paused. "Do you want to hear about us?"

"Yes," Roarke said quickly, wanting Erick to keep talking, to remember the good times. And to remind Roarke why they were all putting themselves at risk.

Erick nodded. "If he spent the night at my place, he'd leave me notes on my bathroom mirror. Dumb shit that made me laugh, like 'I hate your smile. It's really bad and doesn't make me want to kiss you at all.'" Erick's cheeks were reddening, his breath quickening as his eyes grew brighter. "Or 'You should do more squats. Your ass definitely doesn't make me want to fuck you.'" Erick blushed.

A hole opened up in Roarke's heart, thinking of his brother joking with the love of his life. He rubbed his chest, squeezing the skin painfully as grief scratched and clawed at his heart. "That sounds like Flynn."

"I wasn't sure what to do when he died. You were grieving, too. I didn't want to place all this on you. The time wasn't right. I loved him, but so did you."

All Roarke could do was nod. Fuck, why did this have to be so painful?

Erick blew out a breath. "I'd built this all up in my head so much."

"Telling me?"

"Yeah. And now I have, and it finally feels like I'm not constantly drowning." He slapped Roarke's cheek gently. "We're cool, right? No secrets now."

"We're cool," Roarke said, then swallowed because there were secrets. There were definitely secrets, and it was probably time to spill it all. "But there's probably something you should know."

"Are you gay?" Erick said, his brows furrowing.

Roarke barked out a laugh. "No." He scratched his head and let his hair fall into his eyes. "Your sister and I have a thing."

Erick's expression was frustratingly neutral. Roarke waited until Erick bobbed his head. "And…?"

"You want details?"

"Well, what's a thing?" Erick stood up and turned on the Keurig machine to make a cup of coffee. He didn't turn around. "When did it start?"

Roarke listened to the hum of the machine starting up and stared at Erick's back. "I think you know I've always had a thing for Wren."

Erick paused with his hand halfway to the cabinet to get a mug. "Yeah, I think I did."

"Look, man. I don't want you to be angry. We tried to resist what was happening between us. Hell, that was half the reason I didn't want her involved."

"I thought it was a little sister–protective thing, I guess." Erick placed a pod in the Keurig, slammed the lid shut, and pressed the button.

"Sure, it was that when we were teenagers. Maybe. I think I was always half in love with your sister," Roarke admitted. Maybe the alcohol last night was a truth serum because this was more than he ever talked about himself. Wren was the one thing he kept locked up tight. Confessing his feelings for her, even to her brother, was like releasing a bird from its cage. It could fly any which way or smash into a window. "And now she's back, all grown up and so damn... fiery. And brave and smart."

Erick pulled his mug from the Keurig and took a sip before turning around. He leaned back on the counter behind him, his eyes on Roarke over the rim of his mug. "You seem conflicted, like you don't want to do this."

"I don't," Roarke said quickly, and Erick's body stiffened. "That came out wrong. I do want your sister. More than anything. But I don't want to get involved with her. Our lives are not normal, and staying together after this mission would be dangerous for us both, but mostly for her. How can I live with that?"

That seemed to hit Erick where he was vulnerable, because he flinched. "So how did this happen?"

"It happened because we want each other. Although maybe it's over before it began. She's pissed at me now. Stormed out of here last night before we came to HQ."

Erick seemed a little amused. "What did you do?"

"Uh, I might have told her about all the times I interfered electronically in her life."

Erick blinked at him, heaved a sigh, and set his mug on the counter. He rubbed his forehead. "For fuck's sake, Roarke, I told you to stay out of her life."

Roarke felt officially cowed. "I know, but I couldn't stop."

Erick didn't look convinced by that explanation. "You couldn't stop."

"No. Once I started, it was like an addiction to keep track of her, to help her—"

"By pressing buttons on her life."

Roarke snapped his jaw shut. "You make it sound like I'm a creeper."

"No, I don't. If that's what you think I'm saying, that's on you. This is *her* life, Roarke. You can't just press buttons and change things. You don't know the reasons behind her decisions." Erick shook his head. "This is where you and I always see our job differently. You think everything can be controlled with a key stroke. It can't. It's not human.

"I know Wren's had a crush on you since we were teenagers. You think love is protecting her from beyond a keyboard. Meanwhile, all she ever wanted was a scrap of your attention. A tiny bit of emotion. She wanted words out of your mouth, not a change in her coding."

Roarke's mind replayed Wren splayed on his table, her warm lips on his, her nails on his back. Then her harsh words when she found out all the shit he'd done behind her back. His stomach roiled again, and this time he couldn't stop his body's revolt. He stood up and tripped his way to his sink, where he vomited up all the orange juice and whatever else was leftover in his stomach.

Erick took a step away but watched him while casually sipping his coffee. When Roarke was done upchucking, he rinsed his mouth out and wiped his face with a towel. "I hate throwing up. I, uh, drank a lot last night."

"No kidding," Erick deadpanned. He finished his coffee and placed the cup on the counter and crossed his arms over his chest. "My words hit home?"

"Well, yeah. You didn't mince words, asshole."

"She's my sister, of course I don't."

Roarke sat back down on his chair. "I'm sorry."

"Don't say sorry to me. Here's the thing—I always thought you two would make a great couple. A little volatile, but it'd keep life interesting. So say sorry to her. You have my blessing, even though you didn't ask for it. Worst friend ever." He winked.

"Pretty sure she'd go postal if I tried to get your permission to date her," Roarke said with a smile.

"Damn straight. Now sober up and go apologize."

Roarke groaned. "I need a shower."

"You do smell."

"Fuck off."

Erick grinned and surprised Roarke by wrapping his arms around him from behind and squeezing. Lips brushed Roarke's temple. "I'm going to leave then. Love ya, man."

Roarke watched Erick walk to the front door, that ache in his chest blooming again. "Hey, Erick."

His friend turned around with his hand on the doorknob. "Yeah?"

"Is it…is it hard? To see me? Because of Flynn." They'd always been told they looked alike.

Erick's smiled faded, and his face softened. "Sure, sometimes. And sometimes it's like…having a little bit of him still around." He grinned again, but it was tinged with sadness. "So don't die on me, okay?"

Roarke saluted him, even as his stomach lurched. "I'll do my best to keep my heart beating."

CHAPTER FIFTEEN

THE ceiling fan rattled. Well, it would start silent, and, after about five rotations, it would rattle before falling silent again. Lather, rinse, repeat. Wren wondered how secure it was, because she wasn't all about a rotating ceiling fan crashing down on her in the middle of the night.

She was now an expert on her ceiling fan because she'd been staring at it for about eight hours—give or take—while her mind spun like an overheated laptop. Sleep had been elusive last night, all because she'd been unable to shut off her mind. She'd considered taking something to help her sleep but didn't like the idea of being incapacitated in case of an emergency. Like her ceiling fan crashing down on her.

Last night, she'd followed Erick out of HQ, where she'd tried to console him. Although she knew her brother wasn't straight—he'd confided in her years ago—she hadn't known about Flynn. Erick had kept all his happiness inside when Flynn was alive, and now all of his grief after Flynn's death.

That flayed her. Ate her up inside. They'd hugged, and he'd trembled in her arms. Then he told her he needed to be alone. She understood and watched him leave with a heavy heart.

With everything that had happened with Roarke, she was burned out. She'd always loved how deeply she felt things, how she never let a computer screen and lines of code make her forget there were real people being affected by her key strokes. But right now, she wanted to cauterize every emotion until she was numb. That desire scared her. What was this mission doing to her? To the people she loved?

She rolled onto her side and blinked blearily at the clock: 9:00 a.m. She needed to get out of bed and get shit done. Check in on Erick. Make sure Marisol knew everything was okay.

Roarke though? She wasn't sure what the hell to do about him. After slipping out from under the thumb of her controlling parents, she'd loved being on her own, making her own decisions. Everything she'd earned had been hers, or so she thought. So finding out that Roarke had a hand in her life, had pulled strings…it didn't make her feel loved. It made her feel manipulated.

She couldn't listen to his intentions now. While mostly good, his actions still hurt her. Yet, he was Roarke. A man she'd known almost all her life. A man who looked at her like he wanted to give her the world.

And the way he touched her…She squirmed, remembering his lips on hers, the feel of his hair along her palms, the way his tattooed fingers gripped her naked thighs.

Her stomach warmed, and she moaned into her pillow. She wouldn't touch herself thinking about him. No. He was a jerk. But a jerk who could make her body sing.

She glanced at her phone. Darren had texted her earlier to apologize for "drinking too much" and had asked to see her again. She wondered if Franklin had told Darren about their run-in, but she suspected the man's ego was bruised, so he'd kept her rejection to himself.

She hadn't texted Darren back yet, thinking that Lacy would be appropriately furious and would give Darren the cold shoulder. Wren could worry about replying to Darren later. She had his cell phone files, and he didn't blame her for his brief slumber, or so he said. She didn't have to leave town—or Roarke—yet.

A pounding echoed from the door of her apartment. She lifted her head off her pillow, frowning. Glancing at her phone, she saw no messages. Erick probably would have texted if it was him. She slipped out of bed, careful not to make a sound. She threw a robe on over her tank and underwear and opened the drawer of her nightstand to take out her Sig Sauer P220. A gun she'd only ever had to use at the firing range. She flipped the safety notch and made her way out of her bedroom and down the hallway, walking silently on the balls of her bare feet. The pounding started again. If someone wanted to break in, they'd just break in, right? Her mind went right to Darren. Despite his text this morning, she couldn't be sure she'd gotten away scot-free. But he didn't have *this* address; he only had Lacy's.

Her heart pounded as she drew closer, her gaze zeroed in on the doorknob, waiting to hear the scrape of a lock clicking.

Then a deep voice came from the other side. "Wren, it's me, Roarke." A deep sigh followed. "Put down the gun, little bird."

Relief swept over her, annoyance on its heels. She placed her gun on the table near the door. After a quick peek in the peephole to confirm it was Roarke, she unlocked the door and swung it open.

He stood with a forearm braced on the frame beside his

head, looking fucking amazing for 9:00 a.m. He was wearing jeans, hung low on his hips, unlaced motorcycle boots, and a tight black T-shirt beneath his ever-present leather jacket.

For a second, she considered slamming the door in his face, but then she looked closer, spotting the dark circles under his eyes and the pale color of his skin. His lips were raw and bitten. Seemed like he'd had a night even shittier than hers.

So she swallowed her protests and stepped aside in silent acceptance of his entrance. He brushed by her, and she closed and locked the door behind him. Then she leaned against it. He took two steps into her apartment before he turned around to face her, running a hand through his hair to sweep it off his face.

She wished her body didn't respond to him, that her heart didn't skip a beat, like it had when she was a teenager and every time since whenever he said her name. There was a magnetism to Roarke that made her believe that she could make him happy and that he would love her unconditionally. That he'd cherish her. She'd never felt cherished, not until she stepped back into Roarke's life weeks ago.

His eyes dipped briefly to scan her body. Oh yeah, she wasn't wearing much. In fact, she hadn't bothered to tie her robe. She wore no bra beneath the light blue tank top that was a little sheer, and her matching underwear was bikini-cut.

His gaze heated, and even though her blood pumped hot, she snapped her robe closed.

He flushed and dropped his eyes to the floor. "Sorry," he mumbled.

"Sorry for what?" she asked.

He lifted his head. "Uh, hold on, let me start over. I have a thing planned."

"A thing?"

"Yeah, a thing..." He blew out a breath. "First, thanks for letting me in and not slamming the door in my face. I know you wanted to."

"I didn't..." Her voice trailed off as he raised his eyebrows. "Okay, I did for, like, two seconds."

He smiled a little and licked his lips, his tongue rasping over the frayed edges. "I went home last night and got drunk. Then passed out. Because I didn't want to think about Erick, or my brother. Or you. This is..." He swallowed, his throat clicking, like words were failing him. "Shit, why is talking so fucking hard?" His voice cracked on his last word, and Wren's annoyance began to fade. Why couldn't he be a bad person? Why couldn't she hate him?

She stepped forward, grabbing his hand and pulling him down her hallway.

"Wren?" he queried.

"I have an idea." She marched into her bedroom, Roarke in tow, and stepped into her walk-in closet. It wasn't huge, but there was enough room for two bodies to fit between the racks of clothes lining the walls.

She shut the door, plunging them into darkness. Their hands were still entwined, and the only sounds were Roarke's harsh breaths. She squeezed his fingers, and he squeezed back.

"Okay," she said quietly, breaking the silence. "Now talk."

"Uh..."

"It's easier in the dark," she said quietly. She'd learned this from Fiona, who'd been able to talk about what happened to her only in the dark. They'd do it often, huddle in their closet, before Fiona dropped out, and spill everything they couldn't in the light.

Roarke shifted his weight, rattling some hangers. For a while, he didn't speak, and she wondered if this had been a stupid idea. It always helped her, to talk her real feelings into darkness. She was about to call it all off and open the door when he said hoarsely, "I never felt like he paid for what he did."

The words froze her breath in her lungs. "Who?" she whispered.

"It wasn't enough." Roarke spoke above her, his breath tickling the loose hair around her forehead that had escaped her ponytail. "He took my parents, he took Flynn's parents. Left my baby brother an orphan. And he went to jail but it still wasn't enough." He swallowed, the sound of his throat working loud in the confined space. "I used to lay awake at night thinking of things I could do to him. To make him pay for what he did."

Wren had never heard this ache in Roarke's voice. It chilled her to the bone and cracked her heart open. Had he ever shared this pain with anyone?

"I took computer courses and taught myself how to program, then hack, because as soon as my skills were good enough, I was going to break in to the prison system. Fuck up his medications. Anything to make him suffer."

Her stomach bottomed out. He'd been only a teenager then. "You didn't..."

"I did, but it didn't matter because he'd died years before that. Aneurism. Passed out peacefully in his sleep, unlike my parents. Unlike my dad, who was stuck in a car with my mom's dead body while he bled out."

She hadn't known those details about the drunk driver

who killed his parents. "I'm sorry," she whispered, stepping closer to him.

His hand tightened on hers, his other one pressing against her lower back. She leaned into him, not sure if he wanted the physical contact but not knowing what else she could offer. His body was trembling slightly, and when she splayed a hand on his chest, he shuddered.

"I see now that what I did to you was wrong, and I'm sorry for it," Roark said. "I justified it in my mind by telling myself that I was finally protecting someone I cared about, that I had the upper hand, that no one could hurt you if I was looking out for you." His voice shook now, and he fisted her shirt at her back. Everything in his body was tight, like a coiled spring, and she wasn't sure what was going to happen in this enclosed space once that coil snapped. "I've always been in over my head with you, and I still am. I lost my parents, and I lost Flynn, and every time one of them died I felt like I lost a piece of myself. I lost what makes me human." He buried his face in her neck, his breath hot on her skin, and he clutched her like she was sand slipping through his fingers. "I'm terrified there'll be nothing left of me if I lose you, too."

"Roarke." She spoke into his hair as his body shook in her arms, and she clung tighter. She didn't want to say anything to spook him, but her heart was breaking at his pain. He'd always been cool and aloof, unbothered, uncaring. To know he'd been harboring these feelings made her want to sob and rage at the same time. "I'm not going anywhere. And don't ever give anyone the power to take away who you are. No one." She was glad she couldn't see him and that he couldn't see her, because silent tears were slipping down her cheeks. Her robe felt damp on her shoulder where Roarke rested his head. "Just hold me. Remember this moment, because it's real and human. No computers or wires or code. Just me and you."

He clung harder, and she felt his arousal brush along her lower stomach. Her head was spinning, the darkness making it harder for her to know what was up and down, right and left. All she knew was that Roarke's lips were moving against her neck, sucking on her skin as his tongue did delicious things. She moaned, and Roarke surged forward, sending her into hangers of flannel shirts until her back hit a wall. With a grip on the back of her thighs, he hoisted her up so that she clung to his shoulders as his lips smashed into hers. He groaned, his hips grinding between her thighs, and Wren was lost.

The heat of Roarke's body was spreading through hers as his hands squeezed her thighs with his fingertips close to the edge of her underwear. She'd asked him to fuck her last night so she would forget about what had happened to her, and now she was returning the favor so he'd remember who he was. Her entire being focused on him, on getting her hands on as much of his skin as she could, to show him that she was real, *this* was real. She wouldn't let him lose himself—over her fucking dead body.

His hips pressed into hers. God, she ached, she ached so much. Last night hadn't nearly been enough. She'd never get enough of this man, especially now that he'd let himself be vulnerable. He'd let her feel him.

She fumbled to the side, reaching for the door. "Out," she muttered against his lips.

He froze and pulled back slightly. "Out?"

"Out of the closet," she said. "There's a bed, like, five feet away!"

He snorted against her cheek as he turned them around, her legs still wrapped around his hips. He found the doorknob and swung it open. She blinked at the sudden light, her eyes watering. Roarke strode to the bed and dropped her onto it with a bounce. She lifted herself onto her elbows as she watched him shed his jacket and shirt. She wasn't going to let him out of her sight, not when everything felt so precarious, not when he'd shown how much he needed her.

Stripped down to his jeans, he crawled over her, eyes latched onto hers. His boots thunked to the floor as he toed them off on his way up to her.

She gripped his face, his scruff rubbing her palms as he kissed her, tongue sweeping inside in a possessive claiming that lit up her blood like fireworks. She arched against him, and the rough denim of his jeans chafed the insides of her legs. This was frantic, and after last night she wanted something slow, something less desperate…

Roarke abruptly pulled back and dropped his forehead to her chest, his back heaving as he sought to catch his breath. She laid a tentative hand on the back of his neck, the pads of her fingers resting on his inked flower. Maybe he was having second thoughts, maybe that confession had not been an indication he wanted to be with her…

"Give me a minute," he said, his voice pained.

"Are you okay?"

He nodded, then shook his head and nodded again.

She had to laugh. "What is that supposed to mean?"

He collapsed between her legs but kept most of his weight to her side. He laid his cheek on her chest, pillowed by a breast, and lifted his eyes to look at her. Her tank top had ridden up, and his hand was hot where it lay on the bare skin of her stomach.

"You know I used to stay over at your house when I was a kid, and I couldn't sleep knowing you were nearby." This Roarke who confided in her, who told her childhood stories, this was the Roarke who made her heart soar, the Roarke she always knew was in there.

She ran her hands through his hair as he kept talking. "Sure, I beat off as a horny fifteen-year-old, like, a million times thinking about you, but I also just wanted to hold you." He scooted up so he was lying beside her, their heads even. His fingers began to swirl over her skin, making her breath catch. "I wanted to touch you, watch the goose bumps rise on your skin, hear that little hitch in your breath. I wanted to hold your hand and run my fingers through your hair. And I wanted you to just fucking smile at me. So I'm telling myself to take that time now. Not rush it."

She tried to smile, but it was hard with the tears building in her eyes at his naked confession. "Why didn't you say all these things years ago?"

"I never thought I was right for you. I thought you'd marry some doctor who'd look at you like you were precious, and I'd run a background check on him and make sure he never did you wrong. That was how I saw our lives."

That was a nice thought, but it had never been her dream. "How come you never asked me what I wanted?" Wren picked up his hand off her stomach and kissed the back of it.

Roarke's hazel eyes watched her movements before lifting to meet her gaze. "Because if you said you wanted me, I'd never let you go."

"I want you," she whispered, opening her lips to turn the kiss on his hand a little more erotic.

"Wren," he said on a groan.

"No, you got to control everything for over ten years. Now it's my turn. What about what I want? Will you give it to me?"

His breath was shallow. "You know I will."

She tilted her chin and repeated, "I want you."

His fingers, the ones that said OVER, slipped into her hair, cupping the back of her scalp as his thumb rubbed across her cheek. "Little bird, you have to understand, I'm fucked up. You tell me you want me, then that's it for me. I don't want anyone else. I never have. It's always been you. So if you say that you're going to give me you, then you're stuck with me. I'm embedding myself like a motherfucker."

She turned her head to the side to press a kiss to the heel of his palm. "Good, make it permanent."

With a grip on his wrist, she ran his fingers between her breasts, then over her stomach. She locked eyes with him and slid his hand into her underwear. He let his head drop to her temple on a muttered curse. She withdrew her hand, wanting him to take over, and he did, his fingers continuing down until they dipped into her wetness.

"Oh fuck," he said against the side of her face as his fingers swirled around her opening. "You are so wet, Wren."

"You've been grinding your dick against me," she mumbled, already starting to lose coherent thought as he worked delicious torture on her. "Of course I am."

With a yank, he tore her underwear down her legs. She sucked in a breath as he slid down and positioned himself between her thighs. He met her gaze and blew gently on her heated, wet flesh. She cried out and wiggled, but he clamped his hands on her thighs and kept her right where she was. In front of him.

He moved a hand to tease her folds, running a finger over her clit and blowing on it again. She was bare, exposed, more than she'd ever felt in her life, and Roarke was staring her down like he planned to devour her. She was pretty sure that was his plan.

She squirmed again, wanting his mouth on her, but he was in no rush, his focus on what his fingers were doing. "I knew you'd have a pretty pussy, Wren," he said with reverence. "I used to try to imagine how you'd feel, and smell, and taste, and this is so much better than I fucking imagined, especially now that I know what you feel like on my cock."

Her chest heaved. "You didn't taste me yet though."

His finger left her, and she watched with fascination as he slipped his finger in his mouth, closing his full lips around it. When he pulled it out, he grinned at her, all teeth. "Fucking delicious."

Then he lowered his mouth and sucked her clit.

Pleasure swamped her as he ran the flat of his tongue against her, and her mouth opened on a scream. She flailed a hand behind her, bracing herself on the headboard while the other hand gripped his hair. She bit her lip, trying to hold back more screams, and squinted her eyes shut.

He pulled back and blew on her again. She made a growling sound in her throat.

"Wren."

"Mmm-hmmm," she said.

"Open your eyes."

She did and blinked at him with heavy eyelids. His grin was cocky as hell. "You don't have to be quiet, and you don't have to lay still. Scream, fuck my face, I don't care."

"My God, Roarke," she gasped.

Then he was back at it, not letting up this time as his hands kept her thighs apart while he did delicious things to her with his tongue. Actually not just his tongue. This was full service. He used lips, teeth, nose, and chin. He must have been coated in her, which only turned her on more.

She'd never been able to come from oral sex—she'd always felt too exposed, too vulnerable, and a little empty. But when Roarke lapped at her clit with the tip of his tongue and slid two fingers inside, crooking them at just the right spot, she saw stars.

The orgasm hit her like a bullet, speeding down her spine to explode in her belly. Aftershocks rocketed through her body into every limb, and she was cursing, wailing, and shouting Roarke's name so loud that the neighbors surely heard.

CHAPTER SIXTEEN

HE wanted to record Wren saying his name in her pleasure-soaked voice and play it on a loop. He wanted to live, breathe, and die listening to the rasp of syllables on her tongue while he made a home between her thighs.

Her legs were trembling, her chest heaving. One strap of her tank top had slipped down her shoulder during all her writhing, exposing a breast topped with a dark nipple. He suddenly needed his mouth on it, so he slid up her body and attached his lips to the hard peak. She made a squeaking sound, and her fingers slipped into his hair again.

"Roarke." There was his name again, dripping from her lips, tinged with awe. He didn't want anyone else to say his name ever again. Only her.

He wasn't done with her breast yet. He cupped it, thumbing the nipple as she squirmed, and he placed a chaste kiss on it. He tugged her other strap down, revealing both breasts. Fuck, she was perfect. All that tawny skin laid out on lavender sheets. All for him.

He was hard as a rock but wasn't in a hurry. Wren was obviously sated, her movements a little lazy as she ran her nails down the back of his neck and the tops of his shoulders. He made figure eights with his tongue around her nipples, he nipped at the sensitive flesh, and he gave Wren time to recover. She would come again, this time when he was inside her.

He kissed the inside of her elbow, her belly button, and the soft skin of her hip while she watched him with half-lidded eyes. He was moving back up to spend more time with her fantastic tits when she planted a foot on the bed and rolled them over so he was on his back and she was looming over him.

She made quick work of his pants and boxers and the rest of her clothes, throwing them on the floor. His dick twitched as her hair brushed his balls and sensitive shaft. She kissed the head of his cock, her mouth tipping up at the corners, before she crawled up his body to straddle him.

Now that she had come, she was slick as hell. She sat so her pussy rested on the underside of his dick. She rolled her hips, and he sucked in a breath, clamping his hands down on her thighs. "Fuck, Wren."

She raised her arms over her head, arching her back as she continued to torture him. The head of his cock nudged her clit over and over, and her wetness coated his shaft, his groin. He was drowning in the smell and feel of her. He was unable to stop himself from thrusting up into her, seeking her heat.

But she was content to tease him, grinning down at him with a smirk. Through gritted teeth, he said, "I'm going to come like this if you don't stop. And you don't want that, do you? You want me to fill you up."

She moaned long and low, falling forward so she braced herself with her hands on his chest. The obscene sounds of her wet flesh working over his shaft filled the room. He was going to lose it right there, all over his stomach, before getting inside of her.

"Tell me," she said, biting her lip as she slowed her hips. "Tell me how badly you want inside me, Roarke."

Yep, she was trying to make him lose his mind. "Can't get you out of my head. I dreamed of seeing you beneath me, dreamed of you saying my name when I came, but the reality is so much better." His hips were moving again even though he tried to lie still; his cock was a heat-seeking missile and her pussy was the target.

She lifted onto her knees and held his cock so only the very end touched her entrance. "Don't forget, don't ever forget, that you don't get this behind a computer screen, understand?"

His voice was failing him, so he nodded as he lost himself in her dark eyes. He clenched his jaw and held his hips still. He loved this fucking torture, lived for it. Wren could edge him all night, and he'd fucking worship her.

She lowered herself, taking just his tip inside, and paused. He threw his head back, his self-control hanging by a thread. He was panting like a madman, his chest heaving, and he was sure his veins were standing out on his neck as he sought to stay still.

She swirled her hips, and his eyes rolled back in his head. "Wren…"

"You could have had this for the last ten years."

How did she sound so in control? He blinked at her through unfocused eyes. She was so goddamn beautiful, and his hands slid up her thighs to clutch her waist. He'd give her anything right now, whatever she wanted. He'd been so fucking stupid for so goddamn long. "I'm sorry."

Her hips swirled again. "You were wrong."

"I was wrong," he choked out.

"But now you have me. And I have you." She tilted her head to the side and lowered another inch. Her thighs shook slightly at the effort to hold herself in place. "So anytime you feel your humanity slipping and you think it's okay to retreat behind a screen, you remember this, okay? You remember what it feels like to be connected to me."

With a sharp inhale, she sank down all the way onto his cock.

Her tight heat sent flames roaring through the rest of his body. He felt her everywhere, from his eyeballs down to his toes. She began to ride him, and it took a couple of seconds for his brain to come online. Then he joined her, and the rhythm of their bodies slapping together filled the room. Her tits bounced with each thrust of his hips, and she was crying out, bracing herself on his chest, eyes closed. He lowered a thumb to her clit and found the hard peak. She moaned his name and dropped her head forward. The ends of her hair brushed his chest, raising goose bumps all over his sensitive skin.

He was already feeling the orgasm barreling down on him, his will power to make this last failing him after all the teasing.

"Wren...," he gasped out. "I'm going to come." She lifted her head, eyes unfocused, and her mouth dropped open as she came.

Her inner walls clamped around him, and that was the last sensation he needed to tip him over the edge. He shot inside her, and she continued to ride him, milking his cock. He tugged her face to his, and he slid his tongue into her mouth as the last of his orgasm rippled down his spine.

She went limp on his chest, and he clutched her to him as they both sought to catch their breath.

He blinked at the ceiling, watching the ceiling fan spin, letting the air cool his heated skin while Wren's hair tickled his neck. There was really no going back from this. He'd been fine observing her from afar, but that was because he hadn't known how explosive they were together. Now he knew. And there was no way he could let her go now.

"I'm sorry," he said, his voice hoarse. "I'm sorry I avoided this for so long. I thought protecting you from afar was what I needed to keep myself sane. Now I know it was only keeping me from knowing what it was like to finally let myself go all in."

She shifted to the side so that he slipped from her body, and she lifted a sheet halfway up their torsos. Her lips were red and swollen, her eyes bright, and the best part was that she looked so fucking happy. Her smile hit him right in the chest, so much so that he had to reach out and brush her lips with his fingers. Yep, that smile was real and directed at him.

She kissed his fingers, her nose scrunched adorably. He drew them away and laid his hand behind his head. Her nails traced the tattoos on his chest. "You had to know I had a crush on you before I left for college, right?"

Yeah, he did. And he'd ignored it. "I remember the way you looked at me, yeah. It's one of the reasons I got the hell out of town as soon as Flynn graduated. I thought you were too young…" Her eyes narrowed. "What? I'm being honest. I thought you were too young to really know if you wanted to tangle with me. You had stars in your eyes because I was older than you."

"And hot."

"Whatever. I wanted you to go to college happy, not trying to be with me, or broken-hearted when it didn't work."

Her nails dug in a bit, and he winced. "How do you know it wouldn't have worked?"

He blew out a breath. "Because I didn't know a damn thing. I still don't, but back then I was especially clueless. I had sex for the first time when I was fifteen and drunk. I'd never taken a girl out on a date. I wasn't comfortable with the way you looked at me. I didn't deserve it. I still don't feel like I do, but I'm too old to run. And I'm too stubborn to give up."

"Well"—her voice softened—"I'm too old to think I don't deserve you. I do, damn it. I deserve you, and you deserve me. And if we have to flee the country after this, we do it together."

He rolled to his side and slipped his fingers into her hair. Her eyes fell shut, and her breath hitched as he leaned in and rubbed their noses together. Her breath panted across his cheek. "Roarke."

"I love the way you say my name," he said, running his lips over her jaw, darting his tongue out to get a taste of her skin. "You make it sound like two syllables, and you draw out the first part, and click the *k* with the back of your tongue."

"I can do other things with my tongue," she purred.

He laughed. "And I look forward to that."

"Let me feed you," she said. "Did you eat breakfast?"

That would be a no. "Not really."

She smiled and slipped out of bed. After grabbing a fresh pair of underwear out of her drawer, she tugged them on, along with sweats, a bra, and an old T-shirt. "I make amazing omelets." Her hair, which had long ago slipped out of its tie, was still stuck in the back of her shirt, and standing there fresh-faced in a big T-shirt, she looked so young.

"You want help?" He sat up and looked around the room for his clothes.

"Nah," she said, grabbing a hair tie and pulling her hair up again. "Just get dressed and meet me in the kitchen."

She turned to walk away, but he wasn't ready to let her

go yet. This moment hadn't lasted nearly long enough, and although he told himself they'd have many more, he wanted one last kiss. He reached out and grabbed her wrist. She halted and raised her eyebrows at him. He puckered his lips, eyes wide in the international give-me-a-kiss expression.

She laughed and wrapped her arms around his neck, pressing their lips together. He didn't try for anything more because her lips on his, her hair surrounding them, her body against his, was enough. Could this be it? Could he always have this? He imagined them traveling, sneaking kisses on a plane, renting a condo on the beach. He didn't think about all the security measures they'd have to take in the future. He'd have her, and that was all that mattered.

Finally, she pulled back, and her flushed cheeks let him know she enjoyed that as much as he did. "How was that?"

"Nothing wrong with it." He grinned, recalling their conversation in the off-track betting parking lot.

She rolled her eyes, stuck out her tongue, and bounded out of the bathroom on bare feet. He stared after her for a while, listening to her clanging pans around and opening the fridge. The guilt over her involvement had been weighing on him this whole time, and he had to let it go. It had been her decision, and although he felt responsible for her, she was a grown woman. She had her own revenge plan, and he was damn well going to help her with her mission as well. Kill two worthless, criminal Saltners with one key stroke.

He hauled himself out of bed, stretching his sore muscles. He liked the pain because it reminded him of how she'd challenged him to maintain self-control. Payback might be in order sometime. How long could he tease her? He pulled on his jeans with a grin as he thought of running a cube of ice down…

His phone rang, cutting off his fantasy. He spotted Marisol's name on the screen and answered the call. "Yo."

"Brennan, we got a problem."

He hesitated at the urgency in her voice. "How big of a problem?"

"Uh..." Her voice trailed off, as if she'd taken the phone away from her mouth, before it returned stronger. "Big. Potentially huge. Saltner's guys found me."

"What?" Roarke said. Wren's voice filtered down the hallway as she sang along to the radio. "Are you okay?"

"Yeah, I'm fine. I have a hidden panic room at my place." Of course she did. "So they didn't realize I was home. But one of them was the guy in the phone conversation with Saltner. I saved part of the recording, then ran a voice recognition program while they were tossing my apartment."

"Goddamn it." Roarke's mind raced.

"I'll call the guys. Want me to call Wren?"

Wren. If they'd found Marisol...

Marisol was still talking in his ear, but her words were just gibberish now. He had to get Wren out of there and somewhere safe. He tossed his phone to the side and raced down the hallway.

"Wren!" he hollered.

"What?" she yelled back.

He burst into the living room to see Wren slide an omelet onto a plate. "We need to leave."

She stared at him with wide eyes and opened her mouth, but whatever she said was drowned out by the shattering of a window to Roarke's right.

He covered his head from the glass shards as Wren screamed. The shrill terror in her voice sent a ball of pure fury right up his spine to explode behind his eyes.

Two men leaped through the window, cutting off Roarke's access to Wren. One man grabbed her around the waist, and while she fought him, the second man was coming for Roarke, gun at his side.

A gun. He had to get Wren's gun.

He ignored the broken glass digging into his bare feet as his entire world narrowed to the ten feet he had to travel to get her gun on the table by her front door. He took off at a dead sprint, pumping his arms. He heard Wren still screaming, along with the sounds of flesh hitting flesh. The sounds were breaking him apart inside, but he was no use to her, bringing fists to a gun fight. His feet pounded the wooden floor, his grip tenuous as he slipped on his blood, as booted footsteps followed him.

"Get her out," the man behind him yelled. "I'll take care of the boyfriend."

"No!" Her panic-filled voice reached his ears. "Run, Roarke! Get out of here!"

Like hell. He slid into the table, scrambling for the gun. The man in pursuit slammed into him, and they crashed to the floor in a pile of limbs and gun metal. Roarke tore out of his grasp and closed his hand around the grip of the gun. He brought the weapon around to take out the man, but he was too late.

He was staring down the barrel of a revolver. He threw himself to the side just as a gunshot echoed through the apartment. Pain exploded in his head, and Wren shouted his name on a broken sob one last time before everything went dark.

* * *

Wren screamed through the gag they'd stuffed into her mouth. The sounds she was making were ineffective as hell, and she knew in the back of her mind that she should be saving her strength, but they'd *fucking shot Roarke.*

She closed her eyes, remembering his blood spraying her wall and his body going limp. That image would haunt her forever. She refused to believe he was dead. He'd spun away at the last minute, so maybe, just maybe, he'd be okay.

She wouldn't cry in front of these bastards, and she fought them the whole time they took her down the fire escape and smuggled her into the backseat of their car.

Her hands were tied at her back, and after she spent the first part of the car ride slamming the front seat with her bare feet, they stopped the car and threw her into the trunk.

Good, she didn't want to hear their stupid voices anyway.

She lay in the dark, taking stock of her body. She had good aches, those from the morning with Roarke, and bad aches, which were where the rough hands of those assholes had bruised her body.

In the darkness of the trunk, she let herself cry, her tears falling to soak her hair, T-shirt, and gag. They couldn't see or hear her so she took the time to fall apart before she had to face whatever was next. She assumed they were taking her to Saltner, but she couldn't understand why. Why didn't they just kill her? She had a feeling she'd wish she were dead in the very near future. The car ride was even for a while, the hum of the engine steady, so they were probably taking the highway out of DC. Toward the end, the ride got a little bumpy, and she braced herself as she rolled around, crashing into the sides of the trunk.

She lost all track of time, but it seemed forever before the car rolled to a stop. Car doors slammed shut, and a key turned the lock in the trunk. They opened the hatch, and she blinked up at the two men staring down at her.

"She looks good all tied up, don't she?" one of the men grunted.

Wren narrowed her eyes and said, "Fuck you" but with the gag on, it sounded more like *fumf oo*.

"Aw sweetheart," said one of the men, hauling her out of the trunk. "I'm sure you were just trying to say how hot I make you, right?"

She decided to stay silent this time. She was pissed and hurt, but she wasn't stupid.

"That's what I thought," the man muttered.

She winced at the heat of the blacktop on her bare feet and wished she could shield her eyes from the direct sun. With a hand on her elbow, they marched her toward a large metal building that looked like an old warehouse. It was the only building in sight, tucked into a small forest. There were a couple of parked cars with Maryland license plates that looked like they'd been there awhile, but she couldn't be sure she was in Maryland.

She didn't bother fighting the men as they dragged her through a large metal door into the warehouse. They didn't stop, continuing to march her over dirty concrete toward voices on the far side of the large room. A few broken windows shed some small patches of light onto an upper loft, but other than that, the only light came from a few caged bulbs hanging from the high ceiling, which made visibility difficult.

She tried not to think about what she was stepping on—urine, blood, maybe dirty needles. God only knew, but she figured, in a few minutes, the dirty floor would be the least of her worries. The adrenaline was wearing off, and her body was shaking. The only reason her teeth weren't chattering was because of the gag shoved in her mouth. This whole mission, she'd taken for granted having a team as her backup—because now she was all alone, and she wasn't sure she was getting out of here alive.

They rounded a large column and plunked her down into a single chair. As they tied her to it, first her hands behind her back, and her ankles to the legs, the male voice she'd been hearing drew closer. Out of the shadows walked Arden Saltner, a phone pressed to his ear.

She could make out two men behind him, so five men in all. Those were horrible odds.

"I have her," Arden said into the phone as he stopped in front of her. The collar of his white button-down was stained with sweat, and he mopped his brow with a handkerchief he pulled out of the back pocket of his suit pants.

One of the men behind her spoke up. "She had a man with her. We took him out."

Those words were a knife to her gut.

"Who was the man?" Arden asked his henchman.

"Some tattooed guy."

The voice on the other end of the line was a deep rumble through the receiver. She couldn't make out what he said, but Arden's gaze narrowed. Shit, whatever that other guy said hadn't made Arden happy. Could he get off the phone? She didn't need him to be angrier.

Arden dropped the phone to his side and shot a meaty hand out to pull down her gag. He gripped her chin painfully, forcing her head back. "Who were you with at your apartment?"

"Just some hookup," she managed to say, despite his grip on her jaw.

His lip curled. "You fucking liar." He let go of her chin only to backhand her across the mouth.

Pain exploded on the right side of her face, and her ears rang. Her mind reeled for a bit, and she forced herself to focus through the agony. It was the taste of blood in her mouth that brought her back to consciousness. If he was willing to hit her over that, she was in deep shit.

Arden was speaking to the men behind her, furious bursts of sound, something about how they weren't supposed to kill anyone.

She heaved in a breath and glared at him while a deep laugh emanated from the phone at Arden's side. She froze, because she knew that laugh. Every fucking hacker knew that laugh.

Maximus.

Only the most infamous, faceless criminal hacker. A constant presence in the online black market and the Dark Web.

Only a person who could make her disappear forever.

He used a voice scrambler, but it was always the same—a deep alien-like voice that instantly sent ice cascading down her spine.

"Arden," the deep voice said, "I've talked to you about this. You can't break teeth or hands, okay? Don't damage the collateral before we get to use it."

God her jaw ached, but worse was that she couldn't control her body anymore. She was trembling all over, visibly. She was a scared, beaten woman in a chair surrounded by five men who would surely not care if she died.

And Roarke...

She couldn't think about him now. *Stay alert, stay smart, Wren.*

"So what do we do?" Arden said.

"I don't do anything." Maximus sounded bored. "I paid my money to you, and you failed to deliver the goods. So it's up to you to get that patch removed, because I'm not spending my resources on it. Figure it out. You have until sunset, which is when I plan to start using the zero-day. Got it?"

"But how—"

"You said there's a crew. Use her to get them to remove it, and we're solid again, understand? I don't have to tell you what happens if we're not solid."

So Maximus didn't seem to know who she was or who was in her crew. Arden swallowed and pulled out his handkerchief again, this time running it over his forehead and the back of his neck. "Yes, I understand."

"Good, get to work."

Arden glanced at his phone and slipped it into his pocket. He clenched his fists at his sides as he studied her. She hoped he took Maximus's advice and didn't damage the goods too badly.

Arden inhaled deeply. "Since Maximus tried to use the zero-day and he realized it'd been rendered useless, I haven't been having a good time."

Yeah, well, life for her was just jolly now, too. He wasn't getting sympathy from her.

"So my team did some digging and found a lot of interesting information. I wish we had more time, but we don't. Which is why you're here. Because you're going to get this fixed, or I'll cut off each finger one by one and mail it to your parents in Erie. Right, Wren Lee? And maybe Marisol Rosa's family will get a piece of their daughter as well, too."

She wasn't surprised to hear her and Marisol's real names, but the sound of them hit her like a smack all the same. How had he figured them out? All she could do now was nod, unsure what to say, and not wanting her big mouth to get her into any more trouble—and pain—than she was in already.

Arden smiled a sick smile. “Great, glad we agree.” He waved his phone in her face. “You will call your friends, and you will get them to remove the patch.”

If she called the crew, then Flynn—and maybe Roarke—would have died for nothing. Saltner would win, Maximus would win. And actually, she’d be dead, too. She glanced up at him, knowing timing would be everything—that she had one shot to make this count. “I can remove it.”

Arden’s eyebrows went up. “You expect me to believe that? You were the valentine, sent to distract my son and enter my home. You met my wife,” he spat at her.

Survival was the only thing she needed to focus on—that, and keeping the rest of her crew safe. “I can prove it to you if you get me a computer and a Wi-Fi signal,” she said. “I have to call my crew first though.”

Saltner’s eyes narrowed. “Why can’t you just have them do it?”

“Because I don’t want this on them.” She had to protect them. If he didn’t know her personal stake in all this, then he didn’t know the other dirt they had on him. “We’re just black hat hackers fucking around. We didn’t know the stakes in this.” If he didn’t know this was personal, maybe he’d let her go and wouldn’t go digging. She’d rather have him think she and her crew just liked to make messes and cause problems.

He shot her a withering look, and she didn’t know if it was of hate or disbelief. “How long will this take?”

“What time is it?”

He answered quickly, before realizing she had no reason to ask the current time. “Noon.”

She remembered when she’d been in the kitchen, the

radio show she liked was ending, so it would have been around 10:30 a.m. So the drive had taken a little over an hour.

She needed to leave that much time. "It'll take maybe an hour and a half."

He looked like he didn't believe her, but the fear caused by Maximus's threat was visible in every line of his body.

After cutting her hands loose, he handed her the phone and ordered someone to bring her a laptop and a hot spot for Wi-Fi.

She stared at the phone, weighing who to call, who would keep a level head, and who would understand her coded words. Finally deciding, she typed in the number and pressed SEND.

And she hoped like hell it would work.

CHAPTER SEVENTEEN

HE couldn't be gone. He didn't believe in an afterlife so, if he was able to think, then he must somehow be alive. He tried to open his eyes, but they wouldn't budge. There was a bright light just beyond his eyelids though, and something was jostling the side of his face, poking and prodding.

Oh fuck, maybe there was an afterlife.

The pain didn't register right away, but when it did, it slammed into him like a Mack truck. His head wasn't intact, there was no way. Maybe half of it was here, in the afterlife, and the other half was still lying on the floor of Wren's apartment.

Wren. He tried to part his lips to say her name, but they were stuck together, so he only made an *rrr* sound. A voice trickled through the agony. "Jesus, can someone wipe his face? His lips are stuck together with blood."

That was... that was Marisol?

Something soft wiped his lips, and fingers slipped through his hair. "Roarke, I'm going to fucking murder you when you wake up."

Erick. So if he planned to murder him then... "'live?" he mumbled.

The movement on the side of his face stopped. Then Marisol spoke again. "What was that?"

"Am I 'live?" he managed.

Something brushed his face, and a hand touched his forehead. "Yes, sweetheart." Marisol's voice no longer held that mocking tone. "You're alive, thank God, or I'd be in jail again."

He tried to laugh, but it didn't work. His chest was tight, and even the slightest movement of his lips caused a piercing pain.

"Wren," he said again, clearer this time.

"We're trying to find her." Erick didn't sound okay, not at all. Roarke fumbled with his hand, searching for his friend, and blinked his eyes open. "You never hung up your phone so Marisol heard everything. We came as fast as we could, but we only found you."

"In a pool of blood, and that wasn't fucking cool!" Marisol hollered.

Ah God, the yelling. He couldn't handle the yelling. "Well, I'm alive," he mumbled.

Erick was leaning over him, his gaze studying the side of his face. The side where Roarke had been shot. Roarke tried to lift a hand to touch the wound, but someone smacked him. "I'm almost done stitching you up. Just sit still."

Marisol? "You're stitching me up?" He glanced at her out of the corner of his eye. She was hunched over, brow furrowed.

"Yeah, my brother is a nurse. Taught me all kinds of shit."

"Why don't I feel the stitches?"

"Local anesthetic."

"You put a needle in me?" He tried to sit up, but Erick placed a firm hand on his chest.

"Shut up, you big baby," Marisol said, her tone once again mocking, which he preferred. Emotional, concerned Marisol freaked him out. "Just a scratch. You must have done some crazy *Matrix* bullet-avoiding moves."

He'd ducked. That's it. Roarke met Erick's eyes. "Where's Wren?"

Erick's expression cracked, just for a second, before he tightened it up. "We don't know."

Marisol taped a gauze pad over the stitches. "Done."

Erick helped him up, and while the room spun, Roarke closed his eyes and gritted through the pain.

With Erick's help, they shuffled over to a computer, where Dade and Jock were hard at work.

"Any leads?" Roarke asked. "Goddamn anything?" His pulse beat loudly in his head, and he could have sworn his skull had been ripped off. He didn't think this was normal or healthy. Was it supposed to feel like his head was splitting?

"Because of Marisol, we know it's Arden's men," Dade said.

"How did they link the women to the vulnerability patch?" Roarke asked.

Jock clicked some keys, pulling up phone records and text messages. "The man Wren kicked in the balls at the end of the night? He doesn't like rejection. Put a bug in Darren's ear about her after the events of the night before didn't add up. Then they dug into the catering company's employees. Swore Marisol's identity was airtight, but they must have found a weakness. At this point, they think she's just an ex-con causing trouble."

"That's not totally a lie," Marisol mumbled.

"Fuck," Roarke said. "So at this point, they think it's just Marisol and Wren causing problems?"

"Far as I know," Jock said, his fingers once again attacking the keyboard.

"They have no reason to kill her. Yet," Dade said. "They took her for a reason, probably to make us rescind the zero-day patch."

Roarke sucked in a breath. "So whoever bought it from him is pissed..."

"And is now holding it over his head." Dade shrugged. "Just a guess."

A million images of Wren raced through Roarke's mind. What were they doing to her? Was she okay? If they touched her...

He bent at the waist, gripping his head, wishing he'd made it to that gun faster, that he'd been more careful, that he hadn't gone to her apartment.

That he'd never let her get involved in the first place. His one worst nightmare was coming true, and he was powerless to stop it.

He slowly rose and when he stared at his crew, they were all watching him. He was the leader after all, the one who'd gotten them all involved in this. The pain was receding, or maybe his body didn't have the capacity to handle his all-consuming anger and rage at the same time as the pain. "I'll kill him."

Dade raised his eyebrows, and Erick stepped in front of him, blocking his vision. "Roarke. Stop. You always said—"

"I don't give a fuck what I always said." Roarke squared his shoulders. "Fuck the police, the law, whatever. Eye for an eye. I will take him apart."

Marisol was deathly silent, and Dade whistled long and low, leaning back in his desk chair.

Jock was watching Roarke, his normally impassive expression slightly pensive. "I got some leads on property Saltner owns, so—"

A phone rang, cutting through the large room. Everyone checked their pockets, but it was Jock who came up with a beeping phone. He frowned at the number and answered it. "Hello."

There was a pause, then a tinny voice filtered through the speakerphone. "It's me."

Roarke and Erick grabbed each other at the same time. Roarke leaned on his friend as they both shook with relief. Wren's voice. She was alive and could speak. There was hope yet. Roarke had always been logical, and he knew their odds were shit, but when it came to Wren, he didn't give a fuck if they had a one-in-a-hundred-million shot. It was better than nothing.

Marisol leaped off the desk and raced over to plaster herself to Jock's back. He immediately began to type, no doubt working to trace the call. He held up a hand, signaling them to be silent. "Are you okay?"

"I'm okay," Wren said. A male voice said something unintelligible in the background. "Um, Arden has me. Along with…some guards. I'm to tell you Arden has files on me and Marisol, and he's in the process of working on all your identities. If you don't drop this, he will ruin you. His words."

Roarke wanted to speak up, to let her know he was okay, but he didn't know who was listening to this phone call. She'd called Jock so he stayed silent, but he wished he could reach through the phone and hold her. He was dying inside listening to her speak and not knowing how she was being treated.

"Anything else?" Jock said.

"Arden said if the patch isn't removed, he'll kill me."

The deeper voice filtered in through the background again.

Wren sighed. "Okay, he wants me to tell you that he actually said he'd cut off all my fingers one by one, then kill me." She sounded irritated, and he would have smiled if it wasn't about violence. "So I'm going to remove it."

Jock frowned, and he opened his mouth like he planned to protest, but Dade smacked his hand against Jock's stomach. Jock clenched his jaw shut, glared at Dade, and said, "Okay. Do you need anything from me?"

"It'll take me about an hour and a half, and I need you to let it happen. My life is on the line here, okay?"

Erick left Roarke's side and shoved Dade out of the way, typing quickly on the computer as maps and lists flashed across the screen.

"I won't interfere," Jock said.

"Thank you." Her voice cracked on the last word. "I'll...see you soon."

The line went dead, and Jock slammed his fist down onto the table. "Fuck! She wasn't on long enough for me to trace."

"It's okay," Erick said. "There!" He pointed at a topographic map on his computer screen. "I ran every property the Saltners own in all of their names and LLCs, and this one in Maryland is within an hour and a half, and the closest to the tower that broadcast that cell phone signal." Erick turned to them with wide eyes as he pounded the computer screen with a shaking finger. "She's there. Looks like an abandoned warehouse. If she's got an hour and a half to pull the patch, then we've got less time than that to get there."

Roarke began walking to the exit. "Let's go."

"Whoa, whoa," Marisol said. "I don't think you're going anywhere."

He whirled around, ignoring the vertigo, and pointed one by one at every person in the room. "I am going. To rescue Wren, and to put Saltner in the ground. I don't give a fuck what any of you say because it's not up for debate. Dade, you stay here with Marisol. Jock, Erick, and I are about to take over a warehouse. Is everything understood?"

Four heads nodded. Not a word was spoken.

"Good," Roarke grumbled. "Jock, grab the weapons, and let's get the fuck out of here."

The man was on it, quickly pulling a black duffel holding their cache of guns out of a locker in the back. With the two men he trusted most at his back, Roarke strode out of HQ.

* * *

Wren would kill for an Advil or ten right about now. The pain in her jaw had spread to take over her entire face, and the force of the blow must have twisted something in her neck because pain jolted up her spine with every movement of her fingers on her keyboard.

It pissed her off. If she wasn't tied to this chair, she'd show him how much bodily injury she could do. The two men who had taken her from her apartment were watching her, one puffing steadily on a cigarette and the other dozing while she pretended to remove the patch. It wouldn't take an hour and a half to fix the patch—maybe thirty minutes, tops. She wasn't doing it though. She had other plans, which could maybe work if Jock understood all her clues.

She didn't know if she made sense on the phone. Arden had been watching her the whole time with his beady eyes, and it'd taken all of her energy to maintain a cool facade when inside she was screaming.

Arden and his two men were visible, talking at a table in another part of the warehouse. Smoker Man kicked Dozer—the one who shot Roarke—who jerked his head up with a glare. "What?"

"Don't fucking sleep, that's what."

"The girl is tied to a chair, she weighs like a buck ten, and Arden threatened her limbs. Chill the fuck out."

Smoker narrowed his eyes. "Don't underestimate anyone, asshole."

"That's what you said about the Brennan job, and you took him out easily."

She tried not to flinch at the careless way they talked about Flynn. If only she could get her hands on them…

"Hey, honey," Dozer said.

She didn't even lift her gaze away from the screen, where she was writing scripts of random code. "What?"

"Any chance you can finish this up early? I saw a burger place on the way near a hotel, just saying."

She turned her head slowly, first because she didn't want to show fear and second because it really fucking hurt. "No thanks. And no, I don't think I'll be finishing this up early."

Dozer crossed his arms over his chest and sighed. "Yeah, I figured."

She tuned them out as they talked in low tones about the next job they'd been hired to do. They weren't her problem. She had more issues to worry about than two hit men. She wondered when this mission went bad. Darren had seemed to accept her excuse, so did this have to do with Franklin cornering her at the party? She couldn't understand where the leak was, how they figured out she wasn't who she said she was. She hoped it didn't have to do with Darren, because if they found out her tie to Fiona…Wren squeezed her eyes shut. She didn't want to think about that. After this was over, if she made it out alive, she'd have to contact Fiona, install some sort of protection for her, especially if Darren was still around.

Minutes went by before Arden walked over to her, and she pulled up the patch correction and began to work on it. He watched her steadily, and she knew he didn't trust her. The feeling was mutual.

"So how did you figure out who I was?" she asked.

"That you weren't Lacy Kim? Well, we've been noticing some activity on our accounts for weeks—from our bank to our phones. You were someone new, someone who Darren had decided to let into our inner circle against my wishes."

"We only wanted to prevent the zero-day from being exploited," she said quickly. "Really, when this is all over, we'll never bother you again."

Arden sighed heavily and scraped a chair across the dirty floor to set it down beside her. He plopped his large body on it so the legs creaked. "Ah, Wren, do you think I believe that?"

Shit, the way he was looking at her, all sympathetic, like she was a moron, she knew whatever he told her next wasn't going to be good. "I know your brother is Erick Lee, I know Flynn Brennan was his lover, and I know Roarke Brennan was in your bed last night. I also know Marisol Rosa was in my home, and you have some other ex-military hacker working with you." He shook his head. "You almost got away with it, I'll give you that. But when you ran from my house, your Roarke forgot to cut the cameras like he did on the way in."

She swallowed, but her mouth was the Sahara. Fuck. He knew. "Does…does Maximus know who we are?"

He cocked his head a minute, like he hadn't realized she knew the hacker. "No, of course not. I want to continue to do business with him, and he'd disapprove of how messy this situation got. He thinks you're lone vigilantes and I plan for it to stay that way."

Why was he so calm? He knew what information they had on him. "So…"

"So, if I'm correct, then your crew, or part of it, is on its way here. You gave them clues on the phone, didn't you?"

She stayed silent as her heart beat against her rib cage like a trapped bird. He knew, he knew, and oh fuck, it was probably a trap, and this was going to end in tragedy.

He smiled sadly. "That's what I thought. Well, we're ready for them." He gestured to the computer. "You better get to work. I don't think you want to see what I'm capable of if it's not done by the time they get here."

She swallowed and focused back on the monitor. Her fingers hovered over the keyboard as she considered her next move. With her jaw on fire and her heart racing to an unknown finish line, she couldn't concentrate. Who'd show up to rescue her? Erick? Was the team in chaos without Roarke at the head?

Shit, she couldn't go there now, couldn't entertain the thought that Roarke's body was still lying in her apartment in a pool of blood. Whoever showed up to rescue her wouldn't be a match for whatever Arden had planned. Fuck, why hadn't she thought to warn them? She should have questioned him more, worked harder to read him. But his backhand to her face had thrown her off. She was wary now, worried he'd hit her again and do something permanent. Like cut off a finger.

She had about twenty minutes left in her hour-and-a-half time frame. Depending upon when her crew left, they would be arriving soon. She had to make her decision now. Her original intent was to fake it. Code a program that would make the patch undetectable so the zero-day would be usable, up until the hacker tried to download the supposedly mined data. Except it wasn't real, and anyone worth their salt would see that right away. It would buy her an hour or two though, and hopefully by then, she'd be far away from this place.

But now, with the knowledge that Saltner was prepared for her crew, that he knew this was personal, she wasn't sure that was the right decision. Maybe she should remove the patch. Do what Arden said, and hopefully a happy Maximus would make Arden feel merciful and release her and the crew from whatever hell he had planned.

Because if Maximus found out the patch hadn't been removed while she was still with Arden... Well, she didn't think that would go over well at all.

Her fingers tapped the keys, a clacking rhythm in the cavernous space of the warehouse. She glanced up at Smoker, who was still smoking, and at Dozer, who was still dozing. Arden stood at the front of the warehouse with his two men.

Outside, she heard doors open, and she froze, waiting to see if her friends were dragged inside in handcuffs. She imagined Erick, his face beaten and dirty, pleading with her to do something to get them out of this situation.

When the warehouse doors opened, five more men walked inside, all with rifles over their shoulders. They stood in a deadly circle with Arden like they weren't planning a trap for her crew and hadn't orchestrated stealing the personal data of millions of people. Like they hadn't murdered Flynn in cold blood or protected a son who did unspeakable things to women like Fiona.

Wren clenched her jaw, wincing at the pain, and focused again on her task. She wasn't the praying type, but she prayed to something, her eyes squeezed shut and her lips moving. She thought of the flowers in Seocheon between the earth and the afterlife—she wished she had the revival flower to bring back Roarke and the destruction flower to wipe out entire armies. If she had both, she'd make it through this.

When she opened her eyes, she knew the right decision. She wasn't sure if it was the one Roarke would have chosen, but it was the one she thought was right for her, for this mission.

Her fingers flew across the keyboard, and within five minutes, it was done. She blew out a breath, staring at the screen. Her hands lay clasped in her lap, trembling over what she'd just done and the potential consequences of her actions, and just when Arden and his group of men began to walk toward her with determination and she opened her mouth to tell him she'd done what he asked, the lights went out, and the warehouse was plunged into darkness.

CHAPTER EIGHTEEN

AS soon as the lights in the warehouse went dark, Roarke exhaled. Night would have been best, when they'd be under the cover of darkness. Instead, the afternoon sun slipped in and out of the clouds.

Erick had broken just about every traffic law to arrive at this warehouse in the middle of Nowhere Maryland. On the way, Roarke and Jock had worked together to hack into the electrical grid to control the power. They hoped there was no generator, and based on the still-dark warehouse, there didn't seem to be one.

Jock slipped his rifle under the rusty tractor that hid them from view. They'd parked a half mile away and walked after ensuring there was no security system around. Now they crouched behind antique farm equipment that hadn't been used since the seventies and waited.

Roarke had his Glock, and Erick had his handgun, too, but they were both poor shots. Jock, on the other hand, had many talents, and one of them was sharpshooting. The man kept mum about his training, and Roarke wasn't entirely sure of the guy's whole background. All he knew was that he trusted Jock, and Jock trusted him, and he was so damn glad Jock was on his crew.

The door at the front of the warehouse remained closed.

"Roof and sides," Jock muttered. "Aren't gonna walk out the front. Unless they're dumb fucks."

Roarke's head was still a mass of pain, but he managed to understand what Jock was telling him. "Erick, you watch each corner on the ground. I'll watch the roof."

"On it," Erick said. They both had binoculars, and Roarke adjusted the focus to scan the roof.

None of them trusted Arden, and if he knew who Wren was, then he probably knew she had a crew behind her. A crew who was capable of finding where she was and would attempt to rescue her. Jock had told them on the drive that assuming *they* had the element of surprise was a death knell.

So they'd come prepared.

Movement on the roof caught Roarke's attention. The top of a man's head and his large sunglasses peered over the top. Before Roarke could even open his mouth, a muted *zrip* sounded beside him, and the man's head kicked back with a spray of blood.

Roarke lowered his binoculars and stared at Jock. "I didn't even tell you yet."

"Too slow," Jock said, not taking his eyes away from the scope on his rifle.

"Christ," Roarke muttered. He went back to studying the roof, just in time to see a man crouched along the top, running to help his companion. "Movement—"

Another *zrip*, another spray of blood, and the man wasn't running anymore.

The front of the warehouse opened, and a third man walked out, assault rifle drawn. It was one of the men who'd broken into Wren's apartment, the one who *fucking shot him*. Jock took him out immediately. "There's always one dumb fuck," he muttered.

Roarke didn't feel much remorse. He held his breath as a breeze caught the front door of the warehouse, and it slammed against the side of the building with a loud clap. The sound was louder than Jock's rifle, and the bang sent a chill down Roarke's spine. They crouched in silence, all three. Roarke didn't breathe or blink, and forced himself to keep the panic down while he waited. How many more men?

A scream ripped out of the warehouse, a female shriek of terror that could be none other than Wren, followed by a crash.

His instinct, his heart that belonged to Wren, called to him to throw caution to the wind and barrel into the warehouse with gun drawn. But the firepower he'd already witnessed led him to believe they knew someone would be coming to rescue her. Still, he ground his teeth, the echoes of her screams in his head. They were like fuel to his analytical brain, as gears turned with every possible scenario to rescue her safely.

A handful of men poured out of the warehouse, and Jock's sniper rifle went off, followed by the staccato sounds of the men's rifles, as well as the piercing shots of Erick's handgun. This was Roarke's chance, the chaos he needed to get to Wren. He took off at a dead sprint and managed to duck to the right before the other men saw him, crouching behind barrels he hoped didn't hold something flammable.

Roarke's fists clenched as more screams carried on the breeze from the warehouse, with curses mixed in now. He squinted out of a small space between the barrels. If he ran like the wind, he could slip in behind the men, who now dwindled to three, while they were engaged in a firefight with Jock and Erick.

Roarke had to get inside.

He took a deep breath, prayed like hell he still had a sense of balance with his head fucked up, and took off toward the warehouse. A shout pierced the air that didn't sound like Jock or Erick. He'd been spotted. That eerie feeling of being chased and watched spurred him to move faster, so he ran harder, lungs burning and fists pumping. He dove inside of the warehouse door just as a bullet pinged off the metal latch near where his back had been. He didn't have time to think about how fucking close he'd come to getting shot a second time that day. He scrambled to his feet and plastered himself to the wall. He'd never felt this exposed in his life, and he was so fucking out of his element that he was just waiting for the bullet that wouldn't miss this time.

He followed the shouts and crashes to a loft on the left. Wren's lavender hair caught in a small patch of light as she struggled against a pole she was tied to. In front of her stood Arden and another man, and the insults she was hurling at them were quite clear over the sound of the gunshots outside.

Roarke ran behind a rusted car frame and crouched, even though he was sure he'd been spotted.

"So the brother lives?" Arden glanced at the man beside him—who Roarke recognized as one of the men who had broken into Wren's apartment.

The guy shrugged and took a puff of his cigarette, blowing out the smoke in rings. "That was Hank's shot. I had the girl."

Well, Hank was dead now, thanks to Jock.

Arden's voice traveled through the empty expanse of the warehouse. "This is all for nothing, really, this whole valiant rescue. The girl took off the patch like I asked her, and trust me when I say that you have no evidence on me that will stick. I have a good lawyer and bought out every judge in the district. Plus, once I leave here, you won't find me for a good, long while. You're not *that* good of a hacker, Brennan."

Fury and helplessness warred in Roarke's heart. All this time, he'd wondered if the law would be just, if he'd be able to get away with winning this mission with a clean conscience. There'd be no clean conscience now.

Wren had gone completely still, her gaze searching the warehouse. From here, he could see her trembling and the tear tracks down her face. The side of her jaw looked bruised, and some blood was on her T-shirt. Those fucking bastards. He wanted to tell her he was alive, that this would all be okay, that soon they'd be on the beach in the Caribbean with him slathering his tattoos in sunscreen and her running around in a bikini.

They'd be happy, so fucking happy. He wanted to believe that right now, more than anything.

His vision blurred as sweat dripped into his eyes. The saltiness stung the raw skin around his stitches. With a shaking hand, he reached into the holster at his belt and withdrew his handgun. He wiped quickly at his eyes and blinked to focus. Then he took aim, right at Arden's chest. He had maybe one shot, one chance.

"Do it," Arden said.

Roarke hesitated. Was Arden telling him to shoot?

Then the man beside him kicked over a barrel of slick liquid and, with a flick of his fingers, sent his cigarette soaring to the puddle.

The whoosh of the flames was deafening. From fifty feet away, Roarke had to cover his face at the sudden flash of heat and light. Gunshots rang out, pinging off the car frame he was hiding behind so he was forced to duck.

When the gunshots fell silent, he peered out. Arden and the man were running across the loft in the opposite direction, where steps would take them down and out of the warehouse out the back. Roarke raised his gun and took a shot, but the fumes from the fire distorted his view.

Wren's shouts carried over the crack of the flames. "Roarke! Go after them!"

Was she fucking crazy? She was tied to a pole on a loft surrounded by flames. If the fire didn't get to her first, she'd die once the loft crashed to the floor of the warehouse.

Roarke watched helplessly as Arden reached the bottom of the steps, moving fast. All this time, mostly all his life, Roarke had been fueled by revenge—for his parents and for his brother. If Arden got away, what was Roarke's purpose? What was this all for?

Wren's scream reached his ears again. "Roarke, fucking go! For Flynn!"

Roarke stood slowly as Arden reached the back of the warehouse door and flung it open. In the doorway, Roarke saw a helicopter touch down, the grass bowing with the force of its rotating blades.

Running after Arden—leaving Jock and Erick and Wren to fend for themselves—that wasn't for Flynn. Roarke knew his brother well enough, knew how hard he loved, how much he cared for Roarke, that the decision to chase Arden right now would never be what Flynn wanted.

It wasn't what Roarke wanted either. The icy fingers of revenge that held Roarke's heart hostage loosened their grip with every pump of his hot blood.

He chose Wren over hate. He chose Wren over revenge. She'd proved to him he was more than a mindless mission.

She'd been his mission all along; he'd just been too fucking stubborn to see it.

Shoving Arden out of his mind, he raced toward the stairs leading to the loft, taking them two at a time until he reached the top. A wall of fire raged in front of Wren, but he locked eyes with her through the flicker of the flames. She was struggling with the rope tied around her wrists, rotating her shoulders as she coughed and choked through the thick black smoke. The loft was creaking as the fire ate its way through the old, rotted wood. He was on borrowed time already, and the only way to get to Wren was right though the fire.

He walked back as far as he could, until the edge of his boot hit the edge of the loft. "I'm coming, okay?" he called to her. "Just hold tight. Try not to inhale too much."

"How the hell are you"—a cough interrupted her—"getting to me?"

He pointed in front of him. "Right. Through. There."

In a move he swore he *did* see John McClane make, he ran and leaped through the flames, holding his arms over his face. The burning heat licked at his back and his legs—thank fuck for rubber boots, thick denim, and his trusty leather jacket.

He landed on the other side of the flames and didn't roll because he didn't dare come into contact with the highly flammable oil coating the floor. He rushed to Wren's back and immediately began tugging on the thick rope. It wasn't tied well, but tight enough she couldn't wriggle out of it herself. Part of it was frayed, where it seemed she'd been sawing away at it with her nail.

He ripped out the knot and tossed the rope away, catching Wren as she nearly fell to her knees. "Are you okay? Can you walk?"

She nodded, but he could feel the wheezing in her chest as he clutched her to him. "S-smoke." She coughed and stared up at him with wide eyes and a face covered in soot. "Air."

It was getting to him, too, but she'd been up here longer. He threw her arm over his shoulders and wrapped his arm around her waist as they made their way to the back stairs of the loft, the same ones Arden had used to leave. As they tripped down with heaving breaths, Roarke focused on the fact that Wren was alive, and so was he, and they were so close to getting the fuck out of there. He had no idea where Erick and Jock were, and he could only hope they had taken care of the remaining men and were safe and sound.

As they burst through the doors, they were nearly blown back by a blast of air. Wren's hair whipped around them as Roarke glanced up to see Arden's helicopter only about fifty feet in the air, twisting wildly. He stood still, watching it and waiting for it to speed away. Except it wasn't leaving. It was descending to land.

Wait, no, it wasn't descending it was…

"Holy fuck, it's going to crash into the warehouse," Roarke said. "Run!"

With his heart in his throat, he grabbed Wren's hand and sprinted away from the building. The helicopter was heading right for it, and the mix of fire and gasoline was going to send a fireball to fucking Mars. There was no way Roarke was going to let anything happen to Wren now.

She kept up with him, surely in pure adrenaline survivor mode. Even so, he could see her gasping for air, stumbling as he tugged her along behind him. A crash sounded behind him, and he whirled around, scooping Wren into his arms and continuing to run in one smooth motion. The screech of metal and crack of wood was ear-splitting behind him.

He had one good thought, that maybe they were far enough away, that everything was okay, when an explosion at his back shoved him off of his feet, bowing his back as he clung to Wren.

She wrapped herself around him just as he hit the ground, and they tangled in a ball of limbs while debris fell all around them. He grunted at the pain and wondered if his head really was in two pieces this time. Even so, he had the last-minute strength to grab Wren and cover her with his body as best he could. He wrapped his jacket around them and hoped the leather did him one last solid in this life.

Beneath him, Wren was still fucking breathing, and he panted against her hair. When the deafening sounds of the crash quieted to the crackling of flames, Roarke peeked out from beneath his jacket. The warehouse was still burning, the barely visible helicopter blades twisted among the wreckage. He sat up and immediately checked on Wren, stretching her out beside him. She was unconscious, and her eyes were closed, but she was alive with a steady pulse. He took stock of all her limbs and they all seemed to be working normally, none bent at an odd angle.

He brushed her hair off her forehead, wishing he had some water. "Wren," he whispered. "Little bird. Wake up, baby."

He gripped her hand, pressed a kiss to her split lip, and ran his fingers over the bruise on her jaw. He was rubbing the soot off her face with his T-shirt when her eyes flickered open. Oh, thank Christ. She blinked at him a couple of times through bloodshot eyes. He had never been happier to look into those dark eyes. Her lips moved, but there was no sound.

She tried to sit up, but he placed a hand on her chest. "Hey, hold on. I'm not sure how badly you're hurt."

She rolled her eyes, a sass-monster even when she was barely conscious. "Everything hurts, but I can sit up, I promise." She did so with a wince, and he helped her the rest of the way.

She didn't take her eyes off his face, and she ran her fingers over his forehead, nose, cheekbones, and lips before finally moving to the gauze that covered his stitches. "I knew you weren't dead."

He pressed a kiss to the heel of her hand. "Yeah?"

"Yeah, you couldn't be. Because I hadn't told you I loved you yet, and there was no way in hell you were dying before I could say that to your face."

He squeezed his eyes shut and touched his forehead to hers, wondering what Flynn would say now, if he'd be proud of Roarke, if he'd be glad he finally had someone who made him feel something other than anger. If he'd be happy Roarke had finally convinced someone to love him back. "I love you, too."

Something crashed behind them, and he jerked away from her to see that a wall of the warehouse had caved in.

"So," Wren said, and he turned to watch the flames dance in her eyes, "Arden was in that helicopter, right?"

"I think so."

Her eyes shifted to him. "How do you feel?"

"I can't say I'm sad. But I can say, I think Flynn would be okay with this outcome. Arden's outcome, and ours."

She smiled at him. "He used to tell me when we were teenagers that he wished you'd let me in."

"So it took me a long time—a revenge mission, and a fiery rescue—but I did it."

Wren laughed but then broke off with a coughing fit. Roarke pulled her to her feet. "Your brother and Jock were with me, by the way. They should be around the front of the warehouse."

A throat cleared, and Roarke whipped around, drawing his gun and pointing it at the sound.

Erick stood at the edge of the trees with his hands up, with Jock next to him looking irritated. "Put the damn gun down," Jock growled.

Roarke did, just as Wren choked out a sob and flew into her brother's arms. He picked her up and spun her around.

Jock approached Roarke and nodded his chin at the destroyed warehouse. "Saw Arden get in the chopper. Took off and a few minutes later, seemed to lose control."

Roarke peered at him. "What do you think happened?"

"Hacked?" Jock shrugged. "But it wasn't me."

Wren and Erick had fallen silent, and Roarke glanced at Wren's face, which had now drained of color.

"Um"—her hands twisted in front of her—"I have a confession. A couple."

Roarke raised his eyebrows at her.

She spoke quickly, her words running together. "I didn't fix the patch. I made a fake program to make it look like I did, and it was Maximus who bought the zero-day, so if anyone brought that helicopter down it's him." She ended out of breath and bent over coughing. Erick pulled a water bottle out of his back pocket and shoved it in her face. She drank greedily while watching Roarke over the rim.

Maximus. Of all the goddamn hackers, he had to be involved. Dade had warned him when this all started that it could go higher than Arden Saltner. He just hadn't known it would go all the way to the very top.

He glanced behind him again at the fire. "So, Maximus knew you didn't really remove the patch?"

"Guess so," Wren said.

"Thinking Maximus doesn't take too kindly at paying three million for an unusable zero-day," Jock said.

Erick was looking up at the sky, like Maximus was going to drop in on them any minute.

Roarke sighed. "Let's get the fuck out of here. If Maximus doesn't know who we are yet, I'm not waiting around for anyone to figure it out."

Jock didn't look convinced they were in the clear. And if Roarke was being honest with himself, he didn't either.

Not at all.

CHAPTER NINETEEN

WREN and Roarke sat in the back of the car while he valiantly tried to keep his eyes open. They'd stopped at a McDonald's drive-thru and inhaled some burgers and fries. Wren wanted water. Bottles of water. She could still smell the soot in her nose, her mouth, her hair, and her clothes.

Roarke slumped against her shoulder, and she eased him down until his head landed in her lap. The side with his bandage faced her, and she winced at how filthy it was. She didn't remove it though, because nothing in this car was clean; better to wait until they were somewhere more sterile.

She surveyed his jacket, checking for any burn marks. Surprisingly, it was in decent shape. Despite all the time they'd spent together recently, she hadn't seen him sleep, not since they were teenagers. His face was less harsh, the tension lines smoothed, and it took her back all those years to when she'd peek in on him and Erick when Roarke slept over in Erick's room. It was the only time Roarke lost the scowl, the ever-present aura of distrust.

"Called in an anonymous report," Jock said. "Cops should be all over that warehouse in a minute. I'm not gonna trust what they tell the press, but I'll check the records. Make sure Saltner was in the chopper."

"We were watching it the whole time though," Erick said. "There's no way he could have gotten out."

Jock shrugged. "Still checking anyway." His phone rang, and Jock brought it to his ear. "Yeah."

The car fell silent while Jock listened to the caller. When he spoke, he used about three sentences to describe everything that had happened, including Saltner's death and the fact that they were on their way home. He fell silent again. Then without a word, he handed the phone to Wren. She frowned at it.

"Marisol," Jock said.

She grabbed the phone. "Marisol!"

"Fuck, it feels so good to hear your voice!"

"Good to hear yours, too," Wren said as Roarke stirred on her lap but stayed asleep.

"Everyone okay? Roarke was messed up when he left..."

"He needs his wound cleaned, and I could use an ice pack."

Marisol hesitated. "For what?"

"Saltner gave me a nice backhand. It's fine. I'll live, just hurts."

"I'm glad that fucker is dead, or I'd kill him."

"You and me both. Look, we'll be at HQ in about a half hour or so."

"Great, Dade and I are waiting. Well, I'm waiting, and he's sleeping."

Wren smiled. "Yeah, I can picture it. And I'm so glad I get to see your faces again."

"Yep, see your face soon."

Wren handed the phone back to Jock and stared out the window. The only thread left untied was Darren. She'd handed over his phone files to Jock, but they hadn't had time to go through them or match them up to any information they'd already gained.

With Arden Saltner dead, there was no way the crew would be able to stick around. And with Darren still blowing in the wind, Fiona was at risk.

"Jock," she called.

He twisted around in his seat and met her gaze with his deep brown eyes. "FBI has Darren under surveillance. It's only a matter of time."

She blinked at him. How did he— "Okay, one day we are going to discuss how you read minds. But that day is not today. How the hell did the FBI find out about Darren?"

"Dade sent evidence to the police last night. They got a warrant for a property he owns in Pennsylvania. Found loads of footage and paraphernalia. He crosses state lines with the girls, so it's a fed case."

"Do you think..." She swallowed. "Do you think Fiona is okay?"

"Got a friend watching her," he said. "Anything happens, he'll call me."

Wren relaxed a bit. "I'll call her as soon as I can."

Jock watched her for a minute before nodding and turning back around.

* * *

As the car rumbled to a stop at HQ, Roarke finally stirred. His eyes seemed unfocused, and Wren worried about a concussion. "How many fingers am I holding up?" she asked, throwing up a peace sign.

He shot her an irritated look as he sat up and stretched his arms over his head. "I don't have a concussion, just groggy as fuck and in need of some goddamn painkillers."

He glanced at her and did a double take. He turned her jaw with gentle fingers. "That fucking bastard."

She nodded. "I could use some painkillers, too."

He'd been shot and had stitches in his head, but he looked most in pain studying her face. He pressed a kiss to her jaw, right over the bruise. "Let's debrief with the crew. Then we go home, sleep for twenty-four hours, and get the fuck out of DC."

A small shot of exhilaration raced through her stomach. She'd always dreamed of jetting off with Roarke. The dream was slightly sexier than the reality, because the present held very real danger. Still, she couldn't imagine being anywhere else right now. "Yeah, that's a deal."

When they walked into the basement, Dade was awake, watching them under hooded eyes, his ever-present smirk on his face. Marisol threw herself at Erick and Jock but hugged Roarke and Wren much more gently. She immediately took Roarke away to clean his bandage while Dade handed Wren an ice pack.

He stood in front of her with his hands in his pockets, rocking on his heels, as she placed it on her face with a wince. "I saw what you did with the patch."

"How was my work?"

"Good." He scratched the corner of his mouth. "Maximus will dig. He took out Saltner, and he will come find us. You do know that, right?"

"How do you know about Maximus?"

Dade rolled his eyes and turned on a heel. At his desk, he began to put his laptop and supplies into his book bag. "I only agreed to this because I knew he would be involved in the end."

"What?" Wren followed him. "What's that mean?"

Before Dade could answer, Roarke spoke up from the

table he sat on while Marisol kneeled next to him, rebandaging his stitches. "So, I'll try to make this brief. As far as we know, Saltner is dead, and Wren tricked them into thinking the patch was removed. Bad news is that Saltner sold to Maximus—Ouch! Fuck, Marisol!"

"Sorry!" she wailed. "You said his name, and my hand slipped."

Wren shot Marisol a commiserating look. Girl looked terrified. Not of Roarke, but of Maximus.

Roarke heaved a sigh. "Best thing we can all do right now is split up. Get out of town for a bit, use cash, aliases, you know the drill." He pointed to a case along the far wall. "In there are burner phones, all programmed with the other numbers. We need to get a hold of one another, use those phones. No names. Just texts. Got it?"

Everyone nodded.

"Hopefully"—he paused—"we don't have to get in touch with one another. We can go back to what we were doing before I decided to crash into your lives with my agenda."

Wren's heart went out to Roarke. This hadn't ended the way he'd wanted. She wasn't sure he would have been happy with any outcome relating to Saltner. Nothing was bringing Flynn back, and she could see that knowledge sink further into Roarke's skin with every breath. She wanted him alone, to hold him, to show him there was still more to life than grief and revenge. There was love, too.

Roarke glanced at Marisol, who sat still beside him, watching his face, and he took in the crew in front of him. "Thank you, everyone. For all you did here for me underground. For all you did for Flynn. I'm in your debt. If you ever need anything, you can call me. And I'll be there."

Fuck, he looked tired, his head lolling on his shoulders.

Dade made the first move, striding across the floor toward the door. Wren took off after him, wanting to know where he was going next, even though he probably wouldn't tell her. When he reached the door, he looked over his shoulder. "Roarke, good to see you defeated your man and got the girl. What a lucky bastard you are."

His eyes went slightly dark a minute, before he glanced down at Wren. His lips tilted up, and he gripped her hand, lifting it to press a kiss to the back of it. "My dear, it's been my joy to see you work."

He dropped her hand and walked backward, hitching his book bag higher on his shoulder and boosting his voice. "It's been real, but this is the time I make my exit. Code to write, people to ruin, and all of that." He pointed at Roarke. "Don't forget I got one of your chips, and I'll be around sometime to cash it in." With a shrug of his shoulder, he was out the door.

Wren started to go after him, but a hand rested on her shoulder. "Let him go, Duck."

She turned around to face her brother, frustrated that Dade never asked for help from anyone and was such a secretive asshole. She'd help him if he ever let her. But he probably wouldn't, and he'd drawn the boundaries. She had to spend her emotional energy on the people who wanted her. Like those left in the room.

With her shoulders slumped, she fell into her brother's arms. "I'm so happy to see you."

He squeezed her. "I can't express how happy I was when we saw you and Roarke alive after running out of that warehouse. Pretty sure this entire mission has given me an ulcer."

She laughed but the sound broke off on a groan. "Don't make me laugh, hurts my jaw."

Erick just squeezed her tighter.

She leaned back so she could look into her brother's eyes. "You're coming with us wherever we're going."

He lifted his eyebrows. "That's not a question."

"Nope, you're coming."

"Okay, as long as we get a second room for Roarke." She stared at him, and his face cracked into a grin. "I'm kidding. Love birds stay together." He pointed at himself with a thumb. "Third wheel gets his own bed and hooks up with a hot local."

Roarke finally stood up from the table, where Marisol had been helping him. She reached for his face again, but he batted her away. "I'm fucking done. This is fine. It'll heal—"

"You're going to scar," Marisol said.

"Like I give a fuck," he grumbled back.

"Yikes," Erick said. "He's had enough."

Wren broke away from her brother to approach Jock, who was gathering up his things and looked to be going the way of Dade. "Jock?"

He glanced up at her wordlessly.

"Thanks," she said quietly, always feeling a little nervous under his gaze. "For all you did. And for watching Fiona."

He nodded. "I'll keep an eye on her until I feel it's safe. So I'll be in touch."

"Okay, so..." This felt weird, to just watch him go. "Maybe we can have dinner sometime. With Roarke. The three of us." Why was she so awkward?

Jock might have smiled, maybe—there might have been lip movement—but she couldn't be sure. He reached out like he planned to touch her before withdrawing his hand. "Maybe. Talk soon."

After a brief convo with Roarke and suffering through a

hug with Marisol, Jock walked out the door. She wondered if she'd ever see him again.

Marisol didn't seem to want to leave. Her eyes were a little wet, and she kept sniffing suspiciously. Wren walked up to her with her arms out, and Marisol fell into them, burying her face in Wren's sooty hair and squeezing her so tight that she had to gasp to catch her breath. Marisol pulled back, gripping Wren's face but taking care not to touch her jaw. "Loved working with you, princess," Marisol said. "Always wanted a good friend, but I'm too much for a lot of women, and for most men, too, so..." Her cheeks colored, and she shrugged. "Never mind, I'll shut up, probably making more out of it—"

"Love you, Marisol," Wren said, wanting her to know that she did mean a lot to Wren, that she'd been inspired by Marisol this whole mission. "You're brave and smart, and you have the best hair on the East Coast. We'll meet again soon, yeah?"

Marisol's smile lit up the room. "Yeah, you bet, princess."

Once Marisol was out the door with a blown kiss to everyone left in the room, Wren stood with Erick and a leaning Roarke. She stood next to him and wrapped her arm around his waist. Roarke let her take some of his weight, which was a small gesture of trust she never would have imagined weeks ago.

Erick took Roarke's other side. "I'll drive you guys to Roarke's place."

"I'd like that," Wren said.

By the time they reached their destination, the sun had set. Erick helped her bring Roarke inside and lay him on the bed. She followed Erick to the front door, where he placed a kiss on her cheek. "Call me when you wake up. I'll get new IDs and passports together for you. I think we should start from scratch again and not use any of our other aliases. We'll leave as soon as possible."

She nodded. "Erick?"

"Yeah?"

"We didn't get a chance to talk yet, about Flynn. I'm sorry, brother. I'm so very sorry."

Erick's face didn't cave like she expected it to. He blinked a couple of times and focused on a spot over her shoulder before meeting her gaze again. "I need some time. Time away from all of this, from the anger, pain, all of it. I'll heal. I have no other choice, but not an hour goes by that I don't think about him and miss him with every part of my soul."

Wren hugged him. "Drive safe."

"Don't worry about me," he said. "Take care of your man, and we'll talk soon."

She waved after him and shut and locked the front door.

Roarke hadn't moved from where they'd laid him on the bed, but his eyes were open, watching her. She walked past him, stripping her clothes as she went. "I'm going to take a quick shower. I have to get this smell out of my hair."

"What about me?" he said, and the slight pout in his voice made her laugh.

She paused in the doorway of the bathroom wearing a bra and her underwear. "You want to come with me?"

"Marisol said I can't get my stitches wet, and also I'm not sure I can get up."

She rolled her eyes and walked over toward him. After a short struggle, she managed to get him on his feet.

The next ten minutes were the unsexiest minutes of her life. Roarke was like putty, slipping through her fingers, his wet skin impossible to grip as she fought to keep him upright in the shower. They managed to clean their bodies.

Despite the ache in her jaw, she was feeling okay, but

Roarke's head wound and the force of the explosion on his body was nearly too much.

They fell into bed naked after she pried his mouth open to take some painkillers and downed some herself.

Roarke lay facedown and surprised her by nestling close, burying his face in her wet hair. He reached down and laced their fingers together, resting their hands beside her head.

She turned to face him, and he had one eye open, the other smashed into the pillow. "How do you feel?" she asked him.

He opened his mouth and stilled.

"What?"

"I was about to say fine."

"Is there something wrong with fine?"

He shrugged. "It's a pat answer. It's what I always say to avoid further dialogue with someone I have no desire to talk to."

She laughed. "Okay, and now?"

"Well, I want to talk to you. I want to…tell you things."

She squeezed his hand. "That's good."

"So, my answer is that I'm not sure. I have all these emotions I think I should be feeling, but instead I feel…okay."

"Well, you might need time to process. It's been only a couple of hours."

He rolled onto his side. "Yeah, but I'm not sure this'll change. I swore after this was over, I'd shrivel up inside. I didn't think revenge would make me happy, not at all. But it consumed me, like I couldn't do anything else until I avenged Flynn. That was it. Now that it's over, now that Saltner is gone…Flynn still isn't here."

"No," she said softly, "he's not."

"But you are." His voice dropped to barely above a whisper. "You let me back into your apartment after finding out

I'd spied on you for ten years, and you forced me to talk. And you're still here with me. You told me you loved me."

She'd never ever take for granted this honest, vulnerable Roarke. "I do. I meant it."

He blinked at her. "Why?"

"Why do I love you?"

"I know I love you because you make me happy. Because your heart is so big that you risked your life for Flynn and for your friend. That you're brave and charming and so beautiful, it hurts to look at you." He smiled. "I mean, I guess I'm an okay human generally speaking, but I'm not a prime specimen."

She rolled onto her side, bringing their hands with her and laying them between their bodies. "I don't need you to be a prime specimen. There's nothing wrong with you, remember?"

He laughed softly. "Right."

"There's nothing wrong with you," she repeated. "So we're two imperfect but not wrong misfits who deserve to travel the world and run from explosions together."

He surged forward with strength that surprised her. "Not wrong," he mumbled against her lips.

"Not wrong," she mumbled back.

She went to deepen the kiss, but when Roarke didn't respond, she pulled back. His eyes were closed, lips parted.

He'd fallen asleep.

She laughed, snuggling closer to him under the covers, slipping her legs between his and laying a kiss on his neck tattoo. "I'll be here when you wake up. And we start our adventures."

EPILOGUE

ROARKE adjusted his sunglasses as Wren emerged from the Atlantic Ocean and trotted toward him. Her newly dyed black hair barely grazed the top of her chest, and her silver string bikini sparkled on her tan skin.

He was still white as hell and hiding under an umbrella. He would have worn long pants and sleeves to the beach if Wren hadn't told him it would draw attention to them.

She came to a stop at the end of his beach chair and shook like a dog. He yelped as the water hit him. "Hey!"

He grabbed her around the waist and tugged her into his lap. She shrieked with laughter and wriggled around until she lay beside him on the chaise longue.

"You're making me wet," he grumbled.

"Are you complaining that I'm here? In this bikini? I can go cover up or go find someone else—"

He tickled her at her waist, and she dissolved into laughter. He wrapped his arms around her and dropped a kiss onto her wet head. "I'm not complaining. Wouldn't want to be anywhere else right now."

They'd been in Trinidad for two weeks, renting a guest house in Manzanilla with Erick. He didn't leave the house much, preferring to watch Netflix by himself. Roarke had been worried about him, but every day he seemed to be more like himself, lifting out of his grief. It could be the sunshine and leaving DC behind, but either way, it was great to see his friend again.

They'd received one message on their cells so far, and all it said was "Evelyn gone." Roarke knew it was from Jock, using Flynn's code word for Saltner to let them know he was dead.

They'd followed the news to learn Darren had been arrested on drug charges related to the club. Those were the only charges that could stick, which Wren seemed very upset by, but there was nothing they could do. She hadn't been able to get a hold of Fiona—who was a freelance writer in New York—but traveling back to the States now was too dangerous. Roarke knew Wren had wanted to do more for her friend, but Darren was behind bars because of her efforts.

He ran his hand up her back, swirling the water drops that clung to her spine. He knew they'd have to leave here eventually. Roarke had jobs waiting for him, and Wren would have to come with him. He wasn't quite sure what their lives would look like together, but he knew he couldn't imagine her not in his.

They lay there as the sun set, and Wren might have dozed off a little, drooling on his bare chest before jolting awake. She stretched, hair kinked where she'd been resting on him, and blinked with groggy eyes. "I'm hungry."

"Erick texted a bit ago, said he got mango curry takeout for us."

"Mmm," she said, sitting up beside him and poking him in the thigh. "Did you really stay under here all day?"

"Sun fades tattoos."

She rolled her eyes. "Weirdo."

He went to tickle her again, but she jumped off the chair with a giggle. He lunged to his feet and grabbed her wrist and planted a kiss on her lips when she crashed into him. "Maybe I just like the view," he said as he nuzzled into her neck. "Watching you run up and down the beach, in the water…better view than anything, better hobby than anything."

She pursed her lips. "Okay, fine, you are excused because of your bomb compliments." She ran her finger down the scar on the side of his face, like she always did, and grabbed their bags. "Come on, let's go before Erick eats it all."

They'd bought an old pickup so they threw the chairs, umbrellas, and their bags into the truck bed before climbing inside. Roarke left the windows down while Wren closed her eyes. As he drove, he admired the small freckles that had begun to pop up on her nose and shoulders from the sun. He'd told her they were cute the other day, and she'd wrinkled her nose at him. He'd never known her skin freckled. He treasured these days, when they had time to learn more about each other, like how Roarke hated the sun and Wren made coffee with a scoop of cinnamon.

The house they rented was a small, two-bedroom cottage with a full kitchen and one bathroom. It wasn't fancy, but it was theirs alone, and they didn't have to worry about a hotel front desk. When they got to the house, Erick wasn't in the kitchen. Roarke grabbed a Diet Coke out of the fridge. Wren flopped down on the sofa and raised her hand to turn on the TV when a beeping echoed throughout the house.

Roarke froze mid-sip as feet pounded down the stairs. Erick flew into the kitchen, sliding on his bare feet, while Wren scrambled over the back of the couch to join them.

The three of them stared at one another, and Roarke's heart sank to the floor at the incessant sound.

"That's . . . not a text," Erick said.

The beeping continued, which Roarke now recognized as the ringer from the burner phones, sounding where they kept them in a cabinet in the kitchen. He reached inside and withdrew them, seeing that the same number was calling all three.

He handed one to Wren, one to Erick, and kept one for himself. Then he answered the phone. "Hello."

"Ah, Roarke Brennan and his wired and dangerous crew." Maximus's alien voice weaseled into his ear like poison. Wren made a small gasping sound and clapped a hand over her mouth. Erick's eyes were bugged out of his head. "I see you've all picked up your phones now. On this line, I've got Marisol, Jamison, and even . . ." He hesitated. "Even Dade Kelly."

Roarke's heart pounded in his ears, and he grabbed the counter to stay upright. He didn't say a word and motioned for them all to stay silent.

"Great. So now that I have you all on the line, I want to commend you on bringing down Arden Saltner. I mean, you didn't actually bring him down—we all know who did *that*—but I appreciate you showing me what a sloppy individual he was. So, I guess I should be thanking you." There was a smile in his tone, heard even through the distorter. The man smiled? Well, Roarke wasn't even sure Maximus was a man.

"But I want to caution you from further meddling. Darren has been arrested on drug charges, and I suggest you don't try to delve more into his affairs. In fact, he won't even make it to trial alive, but don't tell anyone I told you that." Goddamn, the man planned to take down Darren just like he took down Arden. "Roarke, I know you've been on forums you weren't supposed to be on, checking out the…shopping list. I think it's best you forget about all of that. If you think Darren was in charge, then you'd be mistaken. If you need some incentive, then know that I'm aware there are people involved who can't protect themselves as well as you can. A certain young woman in New York, for example. You understand, right?"

Wren trembled, her eyes wide over her hand as she watched Roarke. So Darren might have preyed on young women, but he was taking orders from someone else—Maximus. And a threat from the infamous hacker shouldn't be taken lightly. He'd crashed a damn helicopter after all, and there were rumors he'd shut down an entire cruise ship in the middle of the Atlantic to gain access to a man on board. A man who was never seen again.

Roarke said the only thing he knew to say. "Yes."

"Great," Maximus answered. "Maybe one day, we'll meet. Although then I'd have to kill you." He laughed, and the line went dead.

Roarke hung up and tossed the phone onto the counter. Their formerly secure phones were compromised now.

Erick and Wren repeated his movements, and Wren ran into his arms. "Fiona!" she said. "I don't trust him not to use her against us. We have to—"

Roarke's other cell buzzed in his pocket. He had a text from an unknown number, and all it said was "I'll take care of her -J." Roarke showed Wren his phone. "Jock's protecting her. You know he's the most qualified."

"Where will he take her?" she asked.

"Knowing Jock, probably a safe house," Erick said. "No one's getting past him."

Wren relaxed a bit in Roarke's arms. "I'm not going to relax until I know she's safe."

Roarke rubbed her arms, thinking that this two weeks of peace had been too good to be true. "I'll ask him to keep us updated."

Wren shivered. "We knew Maximus was involved in the zero-day, but I didn't think the assaults went higher than Darren…"

"I've learned it always goes higher," Roarke said. "Always."

He gripped her face and pressed a kiss to her forehead. "It's all right, little bird. Let's enjoy our last couple of days here. Then we'll check in with Jock and head out to start our next job."

He held out his arm for Erick. "Come on, give me a hug, guys. It'll be okay. We stay out of his business, and he stays out of ours."

Erick shuffled toward him, and the three of them snuggled into a three-person hug. "I'm thinking…this might not be the end of our crew."

As if in answer, his personal cell beeped.

You got me if you need me (Marisol)
I'm happy for you to be more indebted to me (Dade)

Roarke laughed. "Good to know. We've already worked out the kinks in the first mission, right? I'm sure the next one will be smooth sailing."

Erick gave him a suffering look, and Wren raised a suspicious eyebrow.

"Herding cats," Wren muttered.

In the future, the driving force behind any mission would be protection—of Roarke's new life, which he cherished. He'd choose defending something over wanting revenge any day. Apparently being in love suited him well. Flynn would be so proud.

ACKNOWLEDGMENTS

This series is a long time coming, and to finally see it in book form on a bookshelf takes my breath away. Thank you so much to my agent, Marisa Corvisiero, who never gave up on this book and worked tirelessly to find it a perfect home.

Thank you to Alex Logan, who saw something special in this ragtag team of keyboard warriors and was willing to give them (and me!) a shot. Your edits were spot-on and I feel so lucky to work with you, as well as the entire Forever team.

Thank you to my writer friends, who helped me on perfecting the plot, pitch, and first couple of chapters—AJ Pine, Natalie Blitt, and Lia Riley. I couldn't do this without you ladies. AJ, you are the blurb whisperer! Santino Hassell, thank you for always being there for me and for helping me to "grit up" this manuscript! (Take a shot, haha.) Thank you to Keyanna Butler. You did so much for me with this book, and your encouragement, friendship, and assistant tasks are essential to me.

Thank you to all the members of Meg's Mob—I love you all. So much. You make me so happy every day, and you are the corner of the Internet where I go to smile. I hope

I return the favor. And thank you to all my readers, who follow me no matter what I write. I don't deserve you!

I have to thank my husband, Neal, for being an inspiration to me to write this book. You and I met online fifteen years ago, and the first time I ever saw you in person, you were typing on a keyboard. Four years of college with you were full of me delivering you food and coffee while you pulled all-nighters to work on programming projects. I am always amazed at how freaking brilliant you are. Thank you for sitting with me and pouring over the details of the book, especially when I was so tired, I couldn't even remember what a USB port was called (that plug thingy?).

Thank you to my family, who supports me 100 percent in all I do. Thanks to my parents, and my kids, for putting up with my scattered brain, and when I stare off into the distance because I'm working out a plot problem in my head.

And last, but not least, Andi—you'll never be one of the little people. I love you.

DURING COLLEGE, FIONA WAS DRUGGED AND KIDNAPPED BY MEN WHO DID UNSPEAKABLE THINGS. SHE'S TRIED TO PUT THE PAST BEHIND HER BUT SHE'S STARTED TO WONDER IF SOMEONE IS WATCHING HER...

JAMISON "JOCK" BOSH HAS BEEN SENT TO PROTECT FIONA—BECAUSE HE KNOWS THE THREAT IS REAL.

A PREVIEW OF DARKEST NIGHT*—THE NEXT BOOK IN THE WIRED & DANGEROUS SERIES—FOLLOWS.*

THE humidity was so thick that Fiona could barely breathe. Add to that the ever-present Brooklyn smell of meat and spices, plus the exhaust from way too many vehicles, and she was about done.

As she ducked her head and speed-walked up the street to her apartment, she felt naked without her constant canine companion. She hadn't brought Cas, which was stupid, but the grocery order she'd placed had come in, and her usual delivery person wasn't available. She hadn't wanted a stranger at the door so she'd gone to pick it up. Juggling groceries and her dog sounded difficult at the time. Now she wished she'd brought him. At least she had protection in her purse.

She thanked her workout routine for her arm strength, but even this far of a walk was taxing as she regripped her bag and continued on. Despite the low crime rate of the neighborhood, she didn't feel safe. She hadn't felt safe for over ten years. She'd probably never feel safe again.

"Calm your shit, Fi," she whispered to herself as she blinked sweat out of her eyes and squinted at the glare of the evening sun. She'd give just about anything to head to the park down the street, to read her book there on a bench without a care in the world, but she didn't know what that was like. Maybe she'd try with Cas by her side.

She passed an alley, and a chain-link fence rattled. Her steps faltered and her stomach cramped with nerves. No no no. No way would she be caught out here like this, on a hot night with a clear sky, carrying produce. Had she really needed fresh vegetables that bad? She couldn't have lived on canned goods for a while?

She picked up the pace, and by the time she turned the corner two blocks away, she was winded and all her senses were on alert. She hadn't had this instinct ten years ago, but now it was in full-alarm mode, blaring in her brain, coursing through her blood stream like a shot of adrenaline.

She tried to calm herself by thinking about the book she'd just read, but even an eighteenth-century widow and cowboy finding love wasn't enough to take her mind off whatever the hell was moving in the corner of her vision.

Something was there—alive. And that something could range from a rat to a kid to an adult intent on doing her harm.

Another block. Close to home. People here kept to themselves, and the last thing she needed was attention or someone calling the cops. A cat screeched and sprinted out of an alley, just as a human-shaped shadow melted back into the darkness.

Nope, that was enough.

She drew her gun, silencer attached, and pointed it at the dark alley. "Who's there?" No answer, not even a breeze. But something had scared the cat, and she'd seen the shadow. "I have a gun. Tell me who you are before I start shooting."

A rustle followed her words, the sound of shoes scuffing

on macadam and stepping on trash, and then a figure emerged from the alley. Her eyes adjusted to take in a massive man—tall, broad-shouldered, and scowling, and that was all she fucking needed to know.

She pulled the trigger.

The bullet whizzed by the man's head, and he jerked to the side, his hand coming up quickly to cup his ear. "Fuck, woman!"

He pulled his lips back in a grimace, and she should have felt bad, but it'd been only a warning shot. She hadn't hit him.

He dropped his hand, and dark red blood dripped from his earlobe. Okay, whoops? She'd tried to miss.

Still, she didn't drop the gun. What normal person skulked around in an alley? None. "What do you want?" she asked, trying to control the shaking in her voice. "Next time I won't miss."

He held his hands out to his sides, palms facing her, and his expression looked bored. "Put the gun away."

"You're not in a position to make demands."

"You just shot me in broad daylight."

"I'd call this dusk, to be honest."

His eyes narrowed slightly, and she wondered why he didn't look more scared. Oh shit, were there more of him? More big-ass dudes lurking in the shadows? She took her eyes off him for a minute and glanced around.

Big mistake. Huge.

For such a large man, he moved with a quickness that caught her off guard. He had the gun out of her hands and his beefy arms wrapped around her body within seconds, incapacitating her.

Her heart beat against her rib cage like it was prison bars, which only made her feel more trapped, as she was pressed against the man's body, her back to his front and well within the shadows of the alley.

She had a Taser and pepper spray in her purse, but she couldn't get to it, not with the man squeezing her. She couldn't cry. Not now. Tears would get her nowhere. Hell, they'd never even got her out of a speeding ticket.

"Fiona." His voice was deep, and the rumble in his chest vibrated her back. He knew her name, and the only answer that gave her was that she was fucked. She closed her eyes and swallowed, taking the time to gather some strength before she went full on wildcat to get out of his grip. He took a deep breath. "I'm friends with Wren."

Her eyes flew open, and she stared out into the street. Those were not the four words she'd thought he'd say. She tried not to react, not to show that she knew Wren, in case he was feeling her out. "What?"

"Wren Lee, Korean American. Parents live in Erie. Brother's name is Erick. You and her went to school together."

She wasn't prepared for this kind of conversation. She assumed, if they ever found her, they'd kill her on the spot. "I'm sorry, what?"

Another sigh. "Not going to hurt you. Will you promise to stay put if I let you go?"

She snorted. "No." Then she clacked her jaw shut. Shit, she was stupid. She couldn't have just said yes?

He paused for a minute and made a huffing sound that might have been a laugh. "You shot my ear. Think you owe me five minutes without running. Not. Going. To. Hurt. You. Okay?"

His arms loosened and blood rushed back into her hands. She curled her fingers into fists and waited until the heat of his body left her back. Then she whirled around and clutched her purse to her body. She had her pepper spray pulled out and pointed at him just as he pulled a cell phone from his pocket.

He arched a blond eyebrow at her but didn't make a big deal about the pepper spray canister in his face.

He pressed a button and waited, never taking his eyes off her. "Put Wren on" were the first words he said into the receiver. Then after ten seconds, all he said was "Made contact." Then handed the phone to her.

She looked at it, then at him, and then back to the phone.

"Probably have to put the pepper spray away to talk in the phone," he said slowly, like she was a scared deer.

She shoved it back into her purse and snatched the phone from him. "Hello?" she said into the receiver.

"Fiona."

The word was a gasp, and Fiona blinked at the brick wall, processing the fact that she hadn't heard her friend's voice in nearly a decade. "Wren?"

"I don't even know what to say right now. I wasn't prepared...what happened? Did someone try to hurt you?"

"Uh, I shot some guy." That was all she managed to be able to say as she stared at the man in front of her, standing with his hands on his hips, blood dripping from his ear.

"You shot someone?" Wren asked.

"The guy who handed me the phone?"

"You shot Jock?"

"I don't know. He didn't introduce himself! He was hiding in an alley like a creepy person, and I freaked out and shot him."

"Is he okay?" Wren's voice was reaching screech decibels.

"Fine," the man, who Fiona assumed was Jock, muttered loud enough for the phone to pick up.

"It's like...his ear, I think. I meant to miss, honestly."

"Kinda proud of you. I like knowing you're up there capable of defending yourself." There was a smile in Wren's voice, and Fiona's heart ached. She missed girls' nights out. All the things that came from talking woman-to-woman with someone who knew you better than anyone else. She'd had that one time with Wren.

But that was before...before everything.

"So can you tell me..."

"Oh, right," Wren cleared her throat. "So that's Jock, and you can trust him. He's been there for about a week watching out for you..." Her voice changed, and Fiona braced herself. "I can explain, or Jock can, but we have reason to believe they are looking for you."

Fiona's throat constricted, and a panic attack, which she hadn't had in years, which Cas could placate if he were there, threatened to drown her. She flared her nostrils, seeking more oxygen just as the edges of her vision began to blur. Fuck, fuck, all of this just for some fucking kale...

Arms were around her again, but this time they weren't contracting. There was something else about them, something that didn't elevate the panic attack but certainly didn't make it better. Wren was still talking, her voice sounding more frantic. Then the phone was out of her hand, and a deep voice murmured some words.

Fiona's legs buckled, and she wanted to cry for being this weak, for being unable to handle this news. She'd feared this for so long and knew it could happen but the actual truth was too much.

She never hit the ground though, despite her body giving out. She was airborne, and although that deep voice was no longer in her ear, a warm body was cradling hers. Her fingers slipped into coarse hair, and she held on, not sure where she was being taken, but Wren's words telling her she could trust this giant of a man were repeated in her mind.

Trust him. When was the last time she'd trusted anyone but herself?

ABOUT THE AUTHOR

Megan Erickson is a *USA Today* bestselling author of romance that sizzles. Her books have a touch of nerd, a dash of humor, and always have a happily ever after. A former journalist, she switched to fiction when she decided she likes writing her own endings better.

She lives in Pennsylvania with her very own nerdy husband and two kids. Although rather fun-sized, she's been told she has a full-sized personality. When Megan isn't writing, she's either lounging with her two cats named after John Hughes characters or...thinking about writing.

Learn more at:
meganerickson.org
Twitter @MeganErickson_
Facebook.com/meganjerickson

FALL IN LOVE WITH FOREVER ROMANCE

LUCKIEST COWBOY OF ALL
By Carolyn Brown

This special 2-in-1 edition features an all-new book from *USA Today* bestseller Carolyn Brown plus *Hometown Cowboy* by Sara Richardson! Carlene Varner's homecoming isn't going to plan. Within days of her arrival, her house burns down and she and her daughter have no choice but to move in with Jace Dawson, the father Tilly has never known. Jace is so not ready to be a dad... Yet the more time he spends with Carlene and little Tilly, the harder it is to imagine life without them...

FALL IN LOVE WITH FOREVER ROMANCE

ZERO HOUR
By Megan Erickson

The Fast and the Furious meets *Mr. Robot* in *USA Today* bestselling author Megan Erickson's thrilling new romantic suspense series! Hacker extraordinaire Roarke Brennan *will* avenge his brother's murder. His first move: put together a team of the best coders he knows. Only Wren Lee wants in, too. The girl Roarke once knew is all grown-up with a sexy confidence and a dark past…and, when years of longing and chemistry collide, they discover that revenge may be a dish best served blazing hot.